I0719548

THE MISADVENTURES

OF

CALLIE COMPTON

Alyson Root

J&M Books

©2025 Alyson Root

All rights reserved. No part of this publication may be reproduced, distributed, or

transmitted in any form or by any means, including photocopying, recording, or other

electronic or mechanical methods, without the prior written permission of the publisher,

except in the case of brief quotations embodied in critical reviews and certain other

noncommercial uses permitted by copyright law.

NO AI TRAINING: Without in any way limiting the author's [and publisher's] exclusive rights under copyright, any use of this publication to "train" generative artificial intelligence (AI) technologies to generate text is expressly prohibited. The author reserves all rights to license uses of this work for generative AI training and development of machine learning language models.

Human Authored™, Reg #: 4135472, https://authorsguild.org/human

For permission requests, write to a.rootauthor@alysonroot.com

Published by J&M Books

483 Green Lanes, London, N13 4BS

Print ISBN: 978-1-917785-02-0

Ebook ISBN: 978-1-917785-14-3

Developmental Edit by:

Tara Sullivan, The Write Gal Co.

www.thewritegal.com

Line & Copy Edit by:

Linda Slate

Cover Design by:

Angelique Breton

For my grandma Shirley, who was a formidable woman.
(not a crime boss)

The Misadventures of Callie Compton is written in British English.

One

Callie

It's **definitely going to** sound like I'm trying to rap the theme song from *The Fresh Prince of Bel Air*. The song kind of fits, though, so... This is the story all about how my life got flipped and turned upside down. I'd like to take a minute, so just sit right there (or, you know, stand) and I'll tell you how I became a twenty-eight-year-old woman on the run from her seventy-two-year-old crime boss nan.

Okay, not the same as Mr Will Smith, but infinitely more interesting!

The reason I have decided to start a written record of what has happened, and what is happening, is because I'm pretty sure I'm going to die soon.

Dramatic, I hear you say. Maybe. Maybe not, but I have been on the run long enough to know, when my Spidey sense is tingling, I should listen. Right now, my

Spidey sense is doing a flamenco dance through my body, complete with castanets. The hairs on the back of my neck are at attention and that, my friends, is worrying. I haven't felt that in the whole six years I've been running.

I should probably back up a bit first. *Why are you on the run, Callie?* I hear you call. Good question, and thanks for asking.

Cast your mind back to the days of headbands, scrunchies, tube tops, and chained wallets. That's right; I'm referring to the '90s, actually '98 to be precise. Now, picture an eight-year-old Callie: red pigtails and mucky dungarees, drawing unintelligible pictures—because I have zero artistic ability—in the dining room of a typical English cottage. Can you see me? Good.

Okay, now the story starts to head down a dark path...*sorry*. There I am, happy as a pig in shit and giving Van Gogh—on his craziest day—a run for his money, when in pops good old Nan aka Betty Compton, of Crosby Ravensworth in Yorkshire. Fifty-two, hair styled like Queen Elizabeth II, sporting comfy old lady slacks and a nice fitted blouse. Church attendee, avid knitter, and host of several village clubs and committees—the woman has been the quintessential old lady since her forties.

Anyway, Nan wastes no time dropping into the chair next to me and telling me my mum—who works for the family business—is dead. Just like that. "Callie, love, your mum is dead."

What the hell do you say to that? *"Oh, cheers, Nan. Thanks for letting me know!"*

She gave no more explanation. She just dropped the bomb and left me to it. I mean, what the fuck, right?

My mum was often away, constantly travelling for work. Even so, her usual prolonged absence didn't stop my world from crumbling when I found out she was gone for good. Nan gave me two whole days to grieve before she swooped in and began her work training me.

Obviously, as an eight-year-old, I didn't know she was grooming me for a life of crime. The days playing dress up were the best days of my life. Every day, without fail, Nan would set up imaginary scenarios and have me play a multitude of different characters. It was awesome.

At the age of sixteen, I grew a tad suspicious. Playing make-believe as a teen didn't feel normal. At first, I thought Nan was just super supportive, pushing me into the performing arts. Then I wondered if she was getting early-onset dementia. Then, I was sent on my first job, and it all clicked.

Now let's fast forward to 2008: I'd just turned eighteen when Nan decided to fully bring me into the fold. My "jobs" up to that point had all been observational, gathering information on people. Nan told me the people I was spying on were competitors and my listening to their conversation was helping her keep the family business in the black. I earned the name "Callie the Chameleon" because I was so good at blending in. I could perfectly play any character Nan needed.

Two days after my eighteenth birthday Nan sits me down in the kitchen, pours me a cup of tea, and then proceeds to tell me she is the head of the biggest crime family in the UK. I'm talking drugs, weapons, extortion—you name it; she did it. After laughing at what I thought was unbelievable crazy talk, I nearly choked on my own spit when I saw her face crease with anger.

My disbelief earned me my first slap to the face. Shit really changed after that. Gone was my sweet Nan; the woman who played with me and settled my tummy when I was ill. The woman I knew and loved died that day, and from the ashes rose Betty Compton, or as she was known by everyone in "The Family"—the self-ordained "Queen B."

A little too Godfather-y, I know, but that's how she described the business, all the people under her employ, and herself. Can you believe the ego?

I quickly learned to toe the line, but Nan didn't raise an idiot. I played the game. I did the jobs. For nearly four years, the assignments ranged from observation to theft. Meanwhile, I put every penny I earned into a secure account out of Nan's reach. I prepared myself, mentally and physically, for the biggest job of all: my disappearance.

No one knew my plan. I kept the only two friends I had in the dark. I couldn't risk Nan extracting information from them—because she would have. One thing was certain. My nan was—and still is—a sociopath. I would never have been allowed to leave; not alive, anyway.

It was June 12, 2012. I worked my magic, completing my orders for the last time. I played the part of the dutiful and loyal granddaughter beautifully. Nan was ecstatic to see me so enthusiastic about my position in the business. She was so happy she didn't think twice about letting me take a holiday for a week in Devon. Trips abroad were forbidden and, for once, that rule played in my favour. I kissed her goodbye, jumped in my Ford Focus, and set off. That was the last time I saw Betty Compton.

I dumped the car when I was far enough away from Yorkshire, swapping it out for a motorcycle registered under one of my aliases. As well as stashing money, I also built a cache of fake identities—none of which were known to my nan or any of her cronies. With my duffle bag strapped to the bike, I headed in the opposite direction to Devon.

I have fond memories of the Outer Hebrides. Those cold-as-fuck islands were my first stop. I spent a lovely time tucked away in a shack with Shelly the Sheep as my only companion for three months. God, those were the days. Ha! I'm pulling your leg...it was bullshit!

As much as I'd planned the perfect getaway, it was still rough making it on my own. Knowing I had the full weight of Betty's crew hunting me didn't help with my Zen, but after a couple of weeks, I learned to tune out the fear.

Number one rule of being on the lam: Don't stay in one place too long. Callie Compton was gone; buried in the back garden of that picturesque English cottage in the Yorkshire dales. Long live Sarah Hay, Becky Smith, Holly Pace, and Jane White. Those are just a few of the names I've used over the years. My identities were—and are—airtight. I could travel without the authorities being any the wiser, which should really beg the question: How was I—and still am—able to fool the world's authorities so easily? It's a scary thought, right?

Anyway, after my delightful time in the Scottish Isles, I moved around Europe: Norway to Spain, Italy to The Netherlands. You name a place in Europe, and I've probably been there.

A massive downside to that way of life is the loneliness. Hey, listen, I was never the most social of kids, but I was always surrounded by people. Even the ones I didn't want to be around gave me some level of comfort. Travelling left me alone with no backup. I found solace in one-night stands, but that's as far as I could ever take a relationship. I made acquaintances in each country I visited, but they never got close enough to know my situation.

My *current* situation is this: me, in Sweden, sitting in a café I have frequented a handful of times. The hairs on the back of my neck are still pinging with anxiety. Someone has caught my trail; I can feel it. Now I need to decide how to handle it. I thought if Betty's moronic henchmen ever found me, they wouldn't be subtle. I envisioned getting jumped and then dragged into the back of one of those sketchy-ass Ford vans that scream serial killer to everyone in the world. It makes me wonder if Betty has trained her guys a little better than I'd anticipated.

Oh, one thing I forgot to mention: when I scarpered that day, I took something as a kind of insurance—Betty's little black book. She actually *kept* a physical copy of all her operations and employees. Fuck me, the UK's lawmen would cream their pants if they ever got hold of it. Betty knows that, too.

By taking it, I was telling her she had to think very carefully about her next move. Rashness could be her undoing. Making her stop and think gave me some extra breathing room to escape. She taught me to always have a back-up plan, and that book was mine. But now, after six years, maybe my time is up. Maybe Betty has finally come up with a plan to get her book and me!

My coffee is cold. I'm purposefully taking my time, pretending to read a book as my eyes scan my surroundings, looking for anything out of the ordinary. Nothing. It doesn't matter; Sweden is burned. I have to move on. I can't risk staying. Pity...I really like it here.

Oh well. I pull out my little pocket map of Europe. I pause... Maybe it's time to fly farther afield? America, Mexico, Australia, or New Zealand? Even though I detest Betty Compton and everything she is, she's still my family. Leaving Europe feels so final. Fucked up, right?

I shake my head. I need to get moving. With my eyes squeezed shut, I jab my finger at the map. Southern Spain. Peering a little closer, I pick a small town outside of Malaga. It's go-time.

The hard part is yet to come, though. I need to evade my hunter, get to my get-away car, and then drive the hell out of here, all without being caught by someone I haven't spotted yet! It would be easier to flag a cab and go to the closest airport or train station, but that would be stupid. I have no control over planes and trains. There's no telling if they'd stick to schedule, or end up getting cancelled. Plus, it would make tracking my movements too easy.

My adrenaline spikes, sending a thrill coursing through my body. God, it's been years since I felt this kind of rush. Is it wrong that I kind of like it? Don't answer that.

With money left on the table for the pretty waitress I was hoping to bed at some point this week, I head for the toilets. I already know there is a window in the bathroom I can fit through. Bag first, then me. I could have probably stuck the landing better if I'm honest. But I didn't land on my face, so...win!

Another great thing about Sweden; they're really clean people! I didn't land in garbage or piss, which is nice.

From my bag I pull a blonde wig. For the first time in two years, my hair is its natural colour. I now see I made a mistake. Bright red hair isn't exactly subtle. It is, however, longer than when I first ran away. I grew up a bit of a tomboy. My nan kept my hair shortish to make sure I could wear wigs easily. I didn't mind because I had no time to fuck about with my hair as a kid. I was too busy playing to bother with that kind of thing. Now I'm pretty adept at whipping my bushy mane into a knot and quickly donning a wig. It only takes me seconds to transform myself. Whoever is watching won't recognise me if they catch up enough to spot me.

I edge my way to the front of the building and peer around the corner. I still can't spot anything out of the ordinary, but that doesn't mean my intuition is wrong. I trust my Spidey sense. Lesson two of being on the lam: Make sure you can leave in a hurry. No matter where I am, I always carry my possessions with me.

Karl the Kia is waiting for me. Yes, I name inanimate objects. I stop twenty metres away. Something is wrong. What is *that*? A smudge on the rear driver's side... Someone has touched Karl! Fuck, *no one* touches Karl but me. Okay, that sounds a bit weird, but you know what I mean.

Shit. I can't enter him now.

Okay, that phrasing was on purpose; no need to lose my sense of humour.

Plan B. I backtrack two streets. Cilla the Scooter is tucked behind a disused building. She looks intact—no one has touched her. Cilla won't get me to Spain; she's a city bike. But she *will* get me to my second get-away car thirty minutes away.

Goodbye, Sweden. You've been wonderful. I hope I can visit again someday. It won't be for a while, though. I let myself wallow for a few seconds. I was really looking forward to getting to know that cute waitress a little better. I'll just have to rely on Daisy a little longer. Daisy is my dil...never mind...you don't need to know that. Jesus, I need to find someone to have a sane conversation with.

The roads are empty when I emerge from the back of the building. One last scan... Nope, nothing.

Am I letting this life get to me? Paranoia is a genuine issue. How could it not be?

No, I'm right. Someone *has* found me, and it's now my job now to blend and vanish. Nice try Betty!!

Let's go, Cilla. It's just you and me now.

Two
Daisy

Day one of Operation Find Callie Compton; therefore saving my dipshit brother from getting a bullet in the head. His employer is Betty-Fucking-Compton. So far, I have nothing. There is no trace of that beautiful woman anywhere. I should know, because despite what Betty thinks, I've been searching for her granddaughter since the day she disappeared.

I grew up with Callie. My dad, or "Waste of Fucking Space," as he is better known, moved us to that godforsaken Yorkshire hellhole when I was three and my brother Daniel was one. Obviously, at the time, I had no idea the little village I called home was the HQ of Queen B's criminal kingdom. I learned that later.

Growing up in that environment was different for me than it was for Callie. Being Betty's granddaughter wasn't something she could walk away from. As far as Betty was concerned, Callie was born into the "family business" whether or not she wanted it. Fortunately for me, I was born deaf, so I was never considered an option for "The Family." Deafness didn't equate to usefulness; thus, I was left to my own devices, even by my own dad.

What those arseholes never figured out was I could've been more useful to them than they ever imagined. I am ridiculously good at lip-reading and quite formidable with puzzles and codes. Clearly, I never told them about all that. I was quite happy being left alone. It meant they weren't paying attention to me. Big mistake, Betty!

From the age of sixteen, when I figured out who Betty was—I began collecting evidence against her. I told no one, not even Callie. She wasn't ready to hear it and I didn't want to put her in an impossible position. I was confident, one day, she would realise what was happening around her, and when that day came, I would share what I'd collected.

Unfortunately for me, I was away at university when Callie disappeared without a trace. Daniel—the aforementioned dipshit brother—told me a week after she'd left for a supposed "holiday," she'd never shown up in Devon. From my dorm room, I spent every spare minute looking for her. But Callie was called "The Chameleon" for a reason.

Let's zip to six years later, when the Wicked Witch summoned me. A bold, beefy "nephew" of Betty's escorted me from my flat in Edinburgh to her country cottage in Hellsville, UK. In reality, she has no nephews, but calls all of her henchman by that moniker just to make them feel truly part of a family.

I hadn't been in the cottage for over ten years. I knew she meant business when I saw an interpreter standing next to her. The poor guy was visibly shaking, clearly not there by his own design. I sat down, keeping my nerves in check. Callie could be the only reason she wanted to see me. As far as Betty knew, I had no knowledge of anyone or anything connected to her business.

So this is how the meeting went:

The interpreter tried to sign, "Good to see you, Daisy." His hands were shaking so violently, that if I wasn't so good at reading lips, I would have struggled to understand his signing. Jesus...that poor guy. To save him from pissing himself, I leaned forward and put my hands on his. My eyes locked with Betty.

"I don't need him to sign. I will understand."

It's possible that was the first time Betty had ever heard my voice. I worked hard while growing up to speak like a hearing person, because people expected—and still expect—*me* to adapt to them to make their lives more comfortable. I succeeded, but my voice still holds a nasal sound.

"Fine." Betty snapped, dismissing the quaking man. Hopefully, he wasn't going to be dispatched. "Daniel tells me you're rather good at solving things." Ah, my dear brother, the useless prick. "Is that true?" I nodded. "Good. Find Callie, and find her fast. She has something of mine...and I want it back."

"Mrs. Compton, how do you suggest I do that? Callie has been gone for years. I wouldn't even know where to start!" Not true. I'd started six years ago, but she didn't need to know that.

"Figure it out, and before you speak again, know that I have an incentive for you."

The door behind me opened. I felt it scuff on the carpet. I turned around and, of course, my brother was there with a gun to his head. Who could've predicted how this was going to turn out? Oh, right...me. Years ago. Hence why I will always call my brother a dipshit for not listening to my warnings. Oh, and fun add-on, it was my dad holding the weapon.

I probably should've feigned shock at sweet old Betty threatening me. As far as she knew, I had no reason to think she was the type of person to pull such a thing. I couldn't summon the energy to pretend. I turned back to Betty and nodded. There was no reason for her to explain her threat to me. Daniel would get a bullet if I declined.

Honestly, the meeting could have been done over email. What a waste of time dragging me to Yorkshire for that.

"Bold and Beefy" escorted me back to Edinburgh. That was a fun train ride! With a knowing grin on his smug face, he left me at my flat door. Prick. When I was sure "Bold and Beefy" was gone, I opened my laptop and stared at it. There were no new clues to Callie's whereabouts. I closed my eyes and pictured eighteen-year-old Callie. I pictured the day before I left for university, wishing with my whole heart she had been going with me. That would've been impossible, though. Betty would never have let her go.

Regrets are stupid, in my opinion, but leaving Callie without telling her how I felt about her is a regret I will carry with me forever. It's super fucking cliché to fall in love with your straight best friend, although some would say it's a rite of passage for all baby gays. Either way, I know she didn't feel the same, but nonetheless, I should have been honest. Maybe she would have been honest with me about leaving. I'll never know. Well, actually I might, if I can ever track her down.

How do you find someone who doesn't want to be found? Social Media. I should have thought of it sooner; like six years sooner!

The revelation was like being struck by a bolt of lightning. Yes, it was a long shot, but I had nothing else. I spammed every social media platform with Callie's picture, begging the internet population for help. I spun a heart-wrenching story about her being my sister who had disappeared. Once it was posted, I sat back and waited.

The internet is full of useful people...and crazy ones. It hadn't even been a week before I started getting legitimate messages from people all over Europe, claiming to have seen Callie. By the end of the month, I was up to my eyeballs with supposed sightings. My living room resembled a war room. I had a map of Europe pinned to the wall where my flat screen once hung. It took me weeks to sift through all the data.

Finally, I started to see a pattern. It was a surprising pattern, to be honest; one that made me rethink Callie's assumed heterosexuality. There was a woman who looked like Callie, travelling around Europe, bedding women along the way. I'd received no less than thirty messages from women claiming to have had sexual relations with Callie, or with a woman who looked like her.

Little red pins dotted my map: Norway, Italy, Spain, Germany, and many more. Nearly every country in Europe had a sighting. I spent my evenings after work chatting with women, gathering more information. I couldn't just assume they were telling the truth or that it really was Callie they'd seen.

I won't lie. My heart jumped at the thought of Callie being with women. It was both irritating and exciting. I wasn't surprised in the least when each woman I contacted gave me a different name they'd known Callie by.

She wouldn't be stupid enough to use her real name, nor would she keep her appearance the same. The one thing she couldn't change, though, was her freckles. Callie has beautiful hair; it's like looking at fire. Along with her red hair, she has distinctive freckles on her face. A couple of the women I spoke to described her freckles perfectly. That's when I knew I was on to something tangible.

The real breakthrough came yesterday morning. I got a DM from a waitress in Sweden. She claimed Callie was in the village where she worked. The only way to know for sure was to go and verify the information myself.

Less than twenty hours later, I was checking into a quaint little B&B in Malmö, Sweden. I updated Betty with vague messages. They seemed to work for now.

Thank God I work remotely and that my supervisor has been trying to get in my knickers for the past year, therefore giving me what I want without much protest. Gary is a thirty-five-year-old man-child who doesn't take no for an answer. I should tell him I like ladies, but why should I have to explain the reason I don't want to go out with him? Oh—and he thinks shout-talking at me is okay, as though I'll suddenly hear him if he gets louder. The only thing I get is a disgusting view of his tonsils. Anyway, enough about that tool.

Google Maps tells me the café is only thirty metres away. I hadn't planned to be that close, but it worked out well. I could stand by the window in my room and watch for any sign of Callie, but first, I needed to make sure the person the waitress saw *was* Callie.

Thirty minutes later, I confirmed with Freja, the waitress, that she had indeed served Callie a few times over the past couple of weeks. Finally, I was getting somewhere. My next steps were crucial. Callie has been on the run for a long time, and I had no idea how she would react to seeing me. The last time we saw each other, I was still pretending I had no idea Betty was a sociopathic crime boss, and that I liked boys.

After talking to Freja, I headed back to my room and parked myself at the window. I had to get eyes on Callie myself. Freja told me Callie usually took a coffee around 11:30 a.m. It was 11:45 a.m when I caught a glimpse of her beautiful flaming hair. It was her; I was sure of it. All I wanted to do was run into the café and take her in my arms. I hadn't realised what seeing her again would do to me.

I resisted, but did get a little closer. There was a boutique across the street that gave me a decent view of Callie sipping her coffee. She was definitely checking out Freja too, which pissed me off. As my irritation spiked, Callie paid for her coffee and left.

Now, as I've said before, Callie was, and probably still is, a great chameleon, but I'm no slouch myself, and I can easily disappear into a crowd. It comes from years of being ignored. I learned quickly I could use the skill to my advantage, and I taught myself to blend into the background. Honestly, that's how I was able to get so much information on Queen B without anyone becoming the wiser.

I followed her through some back streets. Curiously, I saw her flick her head in the direction of a little Kia. She didn't stop, only looked. I dropped back. The look might have been nothing, but I had a feeling the Kia was one of her getaway cars. I went over to check it out. Nothing obvious. I could have been wrong. It was a gamble to stop following Callie and check out the car. Sure enough, when I turned around, she was nowhere to be seen. I would have to wait until tomorrow and pray she returned to ogle Freja.

It's now 11:27 a.m., one day after seeing Callie Compton for the first time in ten years. I'm standing in the boutique window again watching. There she is, her hair flowing freely, with the sunlight illuminating its fierce colour. I'm surprised she's kept her hair natural. It's not very subtle.

She takes her seat and pulls out a book. Her demeanour is off, though. She looks edgy. Shit, I think she knows someone is following her.

Ten minutes later, she heads into the toilet with her bag. I wait nervously for her to return. A minute passes, and I know she's decided to run.

I take off towards the café. Instead of going in, I head to the alley at the side of the building. Fuck, she's gone.

There's an open window, which I presume she crawled out of. Sneaky.

I pick up my pace, hoping I can catch up. As quickly as I can, I head towards the Kia. As I turn the corner, I stop and back up. There she is, walking cautiously to the car. The blonde wig is a nice touch. What is she looking at? Shit, shit, double shit. I accidentally left a smudge on the back of the car, and she's seen it. Backing away, she hotfoots it in my direction.

I should just step out and let her see me, but I think that might be a big mistake. Betty's reach is immense, and Callie hasn't seen me for *so* long. It's reasonable to think she will believe I'm under Betty's thumb. Which I am, kind of.

I can't feel the vibrations from her footsteps anymore. I need to see where she's going. I take off in the direction I saw her last. The street leads to an abandoned building. Another vibration pulls my attention, and a scooter whips around the corner at the far side of the property. Bollocks, it's Callie, and she's going to get away again.

There's nothing I can do right now to catch her, so I take down the licence plate. Now that I have the information from a vehicle I'm positive she's using, I can implement my other talent to help her. My job is... Let's just say it revolves around technology and I am stupidly talented. That's not me being egotistical, it's just a fact. I can't describe my actual job in detail because I would get sent to prison, so I'll stick with the umbrella term of "technology" as my occupation.

Taking out my laptop from the built in safe in my room, I open a programme I should *not* be using for personal tasks, but I don't care. I came within touching distance of my best friend and the love of my life. I have been with plenty of women, but, as Sinead O'Connor correctly sang, nothing compares. No one else comes close to owning my heart; not whilst Callie is on the earth.

Concentrate, Daisy. I have work to do. I enter the licence plate of the scooter and find out it's registered to a Cilla Black. I can't help but laugh. For whatever weird reason, growing up, Callie had a thing for Cilla Black. I would put money on her naming the scooter Cilla. She used to name everything. Her favourite chair in the kitchen was called Chelsea. She was too adorable sometimes.

Callie was the only person in my life when we were kids, who saw me for me. I fell in love with her at first sight. I didn't know what it was, though, because I was too young then. I just knew I wanted to be with her all the time. I was eleven when I fully understood what I was feeling.

I should have told her.

Three
Callie

Cilla did me proud. It sucks having to leave another vehicle behind, especially her. She was a zippy little thing. But I have no choice. Now that I know I've been found, I have to be extra careful.

Shit, how was I found? I have no online presence, change my name and appearance regularly, and I never stick around one place too long.

Those questions will have to wait. There are three thousand kilometres between myself and my next destination. After dumping Cilla, I made it to my next car within the hour. I implemented some evasive manoeuvres just in case I still had a tail.

Tanya the Toyota iQ, is patiently waiting for me. Almost a year has passed since I parked her up and covered her. She might be small, but she packs a punch. I paid for every upgrade possible. I can't have many material things, so the ones I do have are top-of-the-line.

With my map unfolded on the steering wheel, I take some time planning the route. Ideally, I want to stay off the motorways, even if they are the quickest route. They're fast, but they're also jam-packed with surveillance equipment. It's going to take me over thirty-two hours to get to my destination. A ball ache, but a necessary one. I have to put as much distance between myself and Malmö as possible.

Just south of Frankfurt, I sense a problem with Tanya. I then *see* a problem with Tanya as smoke starts pouring out of her bonnet. Fuck my life with a spoon. I can't call a pickup service because that attracts too much attention, and I'd be leaving an identifiable trail. That only leaves one option: hitchhiking.

Let me tell you that hitchhiking is shit! I did it for a few months in the beginning, and to be fair, I did meet plenty of cool people, but also some crazies. My favourite was Enid Pit. She was in her late sixties, with purple hair, and had a penchant for taxidermy, as evidenced by the full menagerie in her car. Have you ever driven one hundred miles with a stuffed parrot staring at you? No? You should try it. I guarantee you won't sleep for a week. Fun times.

Well, I have fuck all choice now. I grab my bag and stick out my thumb. The sun is shining, which is a small mercy. I once had to wait three hours in a storm before someone took pity on me and gave me a ride. It's only forty minutes this time. An original Split Screen VW Camper Van pulls up. Hippies…I adore them.

My German is good enough I can tell them where I'm heading. They tell me they can take me as far as Lyon, in France. Perfect. Is my luck changing? I certainly hope so.

Wolfgang—what a friggin' awesome name—and Heidi are delightful. The air in the van is thick with incense; something sage-y I'm guessing. I spot a bong in the back and wonder if they're game enough to share. I could use something to take the edge off. Although I'd probably end up paranoid.

Vicky the V'Dub, as I have affectionately named her, is not the fastest of vans. Wolf—he insisted I call him that, before doing a marvellous howl—and Heidi don't seem to be in any rush either, considering we've stopped seven times to "feel nature's warm embrace." Of course they're vegan, so dinner is a bowl of green. I shouldn't complain, though. They've happily shared everything they have with me.

One hundred kilometres from Lyon, I allow myself to analyse what happened in Malmö. Betty is an astute businesswoman and scary-as-hell crime boss, but I don't think she has the skill—nor do her goons—to track me. Who could possibly have found me? I can't think of anything I've done that could alert anyone to my presence.

I have no answers. Sleep might help clear my mind. Running myself into the ground isn't going to help. I still have a long way to go, and I'll need my wits about me. Vicky has a super comfy bench seat, perfect for a nap. Heidi shakes me awake when we reach Lyon.

Relying on the kindness of strangers is too unreliable. I have to hire a vehicle. It's not a problem; I have all the right ID, in many names.

Considering someone got close, I can't re-use any of the aliases I've used in the past year. In fact, I'll use my emergency persona that has never seen the light of day. That way, no one can make a link. Rose Pickford here. Nice to meet you.

My French is much better than my German, so getting a car takes me no time at all. I want to drive to the nearest hotel and sleep for a week, but I can't. I have to keep moving.

Lyon to Barcelona takes me just under fourteen hours. I treat myself to an Ibis Budget hotel room. I lost count of the times I slept in my car, too worried about getting caught on a hotel's camera system. I know underestimating Betty would be a mistake. She might not have the skills to track me, but by recent events, she's finally found someone who can. I should lie low in my car, but I need a bed and a shower.

The hairs on the back of my neck are at half-mast. I can feel the immediate danger has passed, but it's not completely gone. A burning hot shower helps release some of the tension from my shoulders. Masturbating helps relieve the tension built up by missing my roll in the hay with the cute waitress. I'm only human, for God's sake.

After a relatively decent meal from the restaurant next to the hotel, I'm back in my room, tucked up in bed. Questions and panic surge through me. Life on the run is getting harder.

I have all the tricks needed to evade Betty forever—I know that—but my mind is struggling. It's hard having no lasting relationships, no friends to call. I close my eyes and think of Daisy. My sweet Daisy.

Daisy was my best friend in the whole world. She was beautiful, with raven hair and eyes that were nearly black. When she looked at you, it felt as if she were seeing through to your soul. Everyone around us passed her off as unimportant. I never understood why until I was older. To

Betty and her "Family", Daisy had no value because she had no usefulness. Apparently, being born deaf was enough of a reason to be cast out, even by her own dad. He's such a twat.

Their loss was my gain, though. I studied sign language for months because I wanted Daisy to have someone who saw her as the perfect person she was. Everyone expected *her* to adapt to *them*. That's why she tried so hard on her speech. I didn't want that for me. I wanted to adapt to her. I remember the first time I signed to her, she almost cried. We had a great conversation, and she didn't mock me once when I buggered up a word or sentence. Every time we saw each other after that, we signed.

Why am I thinking of Daisy? Because I'm lonely, obviously. But it has been a while since she invaded my thoughts. When I left, I had to put her in a box in the back of my head. It was just too painful to think of her. It surely hurt her to find out I'd left without saying a word, but I couldn't risk Daisy's safety. What I would give to have five glorious minutes with her right now.

I wake to my phone beeping. Alarms are the Devil's work. I hate them with a vengeance. There is nothing more disturbing than being jolted from your dreams by an incessant beeping. Unfortunately, they are sometimes necessary. I need to be up and away early and I know myself too well. I'd still be snoring if it wasn't for that godforsaken alarm.

A breakfast of hot chocolate and churros from the café close to the hotel turns my mood around. Only a thousand kilometres to go. No sweat.

My road trip supplies look like a ten-year-old was let loose with money in a sweet shop and my teeth already hurt at the thought of eating all that sugar.

There is a young guy close to my rental car when I return from the café. I don't have the heart to name this one. I know I will be giving it up soon.

Who is he? My hackles raise. Is this the person who has been tracking me?

Ducking behind a close-by vehicle, I watch him. After several minutes, I see he isn't my hunter. He looks lost—not physically, but emotionally. I can see it in his face.

"You okay?" I speak in English because he doesn't look Spanish.

"Oh, shit, sorry. Am I blocking your car?"

He's been crying. I can see the streaks on his cheeks and his eyes are red.

"No, it's fine. Are you okay?"

I watch his shoulders round, more tears spilling from his eyes. I look at him closer. He has a backpack and nothing else. His clothes are well kept, so I don't think he's homeless, but he's definitely a stranger to this city.

"What's your name?" Why the fuck am I asking? I need to leave.

"C-Chris."

He's a spluttering mess. Whatever is going on with the kid is serious to him.

"Well hi, Chris, I'm Rose."

"Hey," he replies weakly.

His eyes are downcast. I should just smile and walk away, but there's something about him that's keeping me rooted to the spot.

"Okay, Chris, you look super upset, and I don't feel right leaving you like that. Fancy telling me what's up?"

I see him take a deep breath, like he's steeling himself to face whatever has him so upset.

"I ran away from home last week. I told my dad I was gay, and he went nuts. He started screaming at me. He said he was going to send me somewhere to get better, and that he hadn't raised a faggot."

My heart hurts when I hear his words. What the fuck is wrong with people?

"How old are you?"

I have no idea what my next step is if he is a minor.

"I'm nineteen, twenty next month."

Oh, thank the universe. He's an adult—a lost one—but still, a legal adult.

"Well, the way I see it, you didn't run away. You left a toxic environment."

"I don't know what to do. I took everything I had in my bank account and hopped on a plane. I was so scared he would follow me and make me go to one of those places."

"How much have you got left? Is there anyone you know you can visit for a while?"

"No, it was always just me and my dad. I have about fifty euros left."

Well, shit! He won't get very far with that. Chris might be approaching twenty, but right now, he looks like a scared little boy.

"Listen, I'm travelling down south. You're welcome to come along if you want."

Callie, you fucking moron, what are you doing?

Maybe my loneliness has finally become too much. Chris doesn't know me. He thinks I'm Rose, and, as long as it stays that way, I should be fine to have a little company for a while.

"But why? You don't know me?"

He's right, of course. I don't know him, but I understand how he's feeling.

"I'm no stranger to running away. Plus, I'm a lesbian. Wouldn't it be nice to form a queer car share?"

Chris laughs, which is good. "Where in the south are you going?"

"Just south, I haven't figured it all out just yet."

He spends a few seconds looking at me. I can see the cogs in his head going round. Suddenly, his face erupts into a gigantic smile.

"Thank you, Rose. I would be really happy to travel with you. I was starting to panic."

His mood is significantly better than five minutes ago. I also feel better. After years of having only fleeting hookups, I'm finally going to have someone to talk to. Chris might only be around for a few hours—I have no idea—but it's the most personal interaction I've had in months. Let's just say the women I meet aren't up for long stints of conversation.

"Come on then, let's go."

We haul our bags in the back of the car. I pile my sweets onto the backseat. Chris is impressed with my mountain of goodies. His eyes light up when I say, "Good job you're here, really. I'd probably end up in a sugar coma if I ate all this by myself."

We set off. In all honesty, I'm happy I ended up pointing to Spain in that little café the other day. It's one of my favourite countries. I've visited many of the large cities and a lot of the small villages. The country has always felt as close to home as possible. There is nowhere in the world that truly feels like home to me now, though.

I've been laughing my ass off for the past ten minutes. Chris is a sarcastic little shit and I love it. We didn't take long to warm to each other. He feels like a kid brother, the one I always wanted. We haven't spoken about his dad since we left Barcelona. I don't see the point of bringing that cunt nugget up again. If I ever saw him, I would happily share my opinion on his parenting skills, ideally with a knee to his junk.

The sign for Granada sails by. I've been driving for thirteen hours, and my eyeballs are drier than a nun's... Er, never mind, they're just dry. It's only another two-and-a-half hours to Torreguadiaro. I've never been there before. It's a little town between Málaga and Gibraltar, right on the coast. I need some sea air. To be fair, Malmö was by the sea, but the North Sea is a far cry from the warmth of the Med.

"I've only ever been to Barcelona. This is awesome," Chris says as he scans the passing scenery.

He's pressing his face against the window like an excitable puppy and it warms me to see him so giddy. I love discovering new places. It's thrilling. Watching him light up at the unknown land around him makes me feel like I'm discovering it again for the first time.

The anxiety and worries which have flooded my body since Sweden are gone. I know it's only temporary, but I'll take it. I will be ready for whoever is after me, I can guarantee that, but in this moment, I'm going to enjoy my time with my new travel companion, in this magnificent country.

Four
Daisy

Penny's face lights up my phone. We haven't spoken in a couple of weeks due to my schedule and her upcoming wedding, which has turned into a battle of the in-laws. Penny was assigned as my interpreter at university. I'd never had one before and my first instinct was to rebuff her help. Thankfully, she persevered, and we became close friends. It was the first time in my life—except for Callie—that I had someone there just for me.

She gives me a broad smile. "Hey there, lovely lady."

Penny always signs to me, regardless of the fact I can converse with her perfectly well through lip reading. She helped me accept my difference and be proud of it. All my father and his fucked up adopted family ever did was make me feel less than. Penny made me feel worthy, and I will be forever thankful for her friendship.

"Pen, my love, how are you?"

She looks like she's not slept in a week. The war of the wedding planning must be bad.

"Oh, you know, psychotic mums waging war over flower arrangements. My soon-to-be husband showing how much of a yellowbelly he really is by leaving me alone to deal with them both. The usual. How are you? Better yet, where are you?"

Oh, right, I didn't let anyone know that I was leaving the country on a woman hunt.

Penny knows the bare minimum about my life before university. She knows my mum was absent, and my dad was a loser scumbag who had no interest in raising a "deaf kid." Parent of the year right there! Seriously, that's how I was introduced. Not by name, but by the thing that made my dad so disappointed to have me as his child.

"I'm in Sweden."

Penny's eyebrows rising into her hairline make me grin.

She leans closer to the screen and narrows her eyes at me. "Pray tell, why are you in Sweden?"

"I finally have a lead!"

An explanation isn't necessary. Most of the information Penny knows about my life in the Dales is based around Callie. She was the one who comforted me when I found out Callie had vanished.

"And it took you to Sweden? Wow, Daisy, you're sure it's valid?"

"Yes, I saw her."

I'm regretting holding back. I could kick myself now. I should have just gone to her and talked. If I had, I wouldn't be grasping at straws trying to locate her again.

"Oh, Daisy, that's excellent. Did you talk to her?"

I shake my head. Penny creases her eyebrows in confusion. Great, now I'm going to have to explain how I panicked and followed her instead of talking to her. She beats me to it.

"You didn't approach her, did you?"

My face burns with embarrassment. I shake my head again.

"Is she still in Sweden?"

Jesus, can Penny read my mind, or has she bugged the room?

"No, she fled. Clearly she knew someone was following her, and she spooked."

"Daisy!"

Then she signs a bunch of things which I won't repeat. Penny isn't a shy person, and she never holds back telling me what she thinks, even if it's a string of expletives.

"I know, I know. I still have some info to follow, though. It's not all lost."

"And what does pervy Gary say about your little excursion to the land of IKEA?"

"I'm pretty sure the population of this wonderful country would like to be known for something more than their flat-pack furniture. What else is Sweden famous for?"

"Clogs?"

"Isn't that the Netherlands?"

"I don't have the fucking foggiest. Why are we talking about clogs?"

"You started it with IKEA!"

"Bloody hell. Can we get back to the question of Gary?"

"Right. So I explained I needed to take some personal time. He wasn't going to say no, was he? Not when he thinks I'll end up owing him for it. I guarantee he'll use it against me when I get back. I bet fifty pounds he uses it as a thinly veiled threat to get me to go for a drink with him."

I've told Gary numerous times I'm not interested in him in the slightest, but being rebuffed only seems to spur him on, which is unfortunate. If he doesn't get the message soon, I'm going to have to report him. Joy! Even if Gary is in the wrong, I'll still be seen as the uptight bitch who dobbed him in. I roll my eyes at the thought.

Penny waves her hands, refocusing my attention. "If he continues harassing you, Daisy, you don't have a choice. Report that sleazy fucker."

"There is a silver lining to him being gross, in that he lets me do what I want."

"Daisy, you can do what you want, anyway. You're the fucking brainchild in that place. Gary has a title, and that's it. I'd bet my firstborn that if the higher ups had to choose between you and Gary, you would come out on top every time."

Penny is right. The company needs me.

"I'll deal with him when I get back. Right now, I need to focus on Callie. I'm so close, Pen, after all this time."

"And I am shitting rainbows for you, sweetie." Penny is a real wordsmith. "Just be careful, okay? Will you let me log into your phone finder? I would feel better knowing where you are."

I should have thought of that. Penny doesn't need to know about Betty. That would put her in the crosshairs, but it would be a comfort knowing there is someone in the world looking out for me.

"Yeah, go for it. You know the password." My laptop flashes and vibrates, scaring the living shit out of me. I almost launch my phone and Penny across the room. "Pen, I have to go. I have something."

"Okay, I love you."

"Love you, too."

The phone screen turns black as Penny ends the call. I barely said goodbye before I dropped the handset and replaced it with my laptop. Bingo, I have a lead. The scooter Callie escaped on was found just outside of Malmö. I need to get to that dumpsite. There could be cameras in the area. Surely Callie would have chosen the dumpsite carefully, but she couldn't anticipate *all* the cameras. Our world is monitored 24/7; no one can hide forever.

Putting the coordinates in my phone, I go to the local taxi rank. Swedish people are like the friendliest fucking people in the world. Hell, maybe after all this is over—and if I'm still alive—I might just move here. The taxi man speaks fluent English. He actually apologised for not knowing how to sign! There *is* still decency in the world.

Not that I expect everyone to be able to sign—although it's my strong belief sign language should be taught to everyone in school—it's nice to have someone think about making my life easier rather than me just being expected to adapt to the hearing world.

It takes half an hour to reach the place where the scooter was recovered. The driver, Lars, as I now know him, looks a little disturbed leaving me in the area alone. I assure him I will be fine. I've had years of martial arts training and I will fuck a person up if they put their hands on me—something Gary should be made aware of.

Lars leaves and I scan the area looking for cameras. It's not surprising to see there are none in the immediate vicinity, but all's not lost. There is a main road fifty metres to my left. Callie would've had to take it, and I'm certain there will be something that can help me find her again. Et Voilà! I find what I'm looking for as soon as I round the corner to the main road.

What I have to do next is super illegal. Well, doing it for personal reasons is, but no one will ever know. I'm the best at what I do for a reason. I just need a comfy place to set up. The coffee shop across the street will do nicely.

The smell of sweet pastries nearly knocks me over. I'm suddenly ravenous. One or two little treats can't hurt while I'm working. Four pastries, that's how many I end up shoving in my gullet. Oh well, I'll do some yoga or something later. Ha, I won't.

I sit so no one is able to see my screen. It takes me nearly three hours and a ridiculous amount of coffee to find what I need. There she is, jumping into a little Toyota iQ. Now the hard work begins.

Following her using the cameras around her sounds simple, but it really isn't, especially when you don't have explicit permission to access said cameras. Oops. I'll send a fruit basket to the right people once I'm done.

The cafe is about to shut and I'm still following her on the cameras. So far, she's reached Frankfurt. The waiter is looking at me impatiently. I just need a little longer. I look at him pleadingly. Hell, I have bought more coffee than a seasoned bean addict. He could cut me some slack. My powers of pleading are obviously excellent because he starts cleaning the counter he's already cleaned twice. My eyes bore into the screen, hoping something will happen in the limited time I have left in the café. Hallelujah, there it is. Callie's little Toyota breaks down.

I head to the local hotel. It's basic, but it will do. My nerves are sizzling. I'm excited. I will find her again. After a mildly warm shower, I settle on the bed. It's getting late, but I just can't stop. I have to know what she does next. When she left the car, she walked a little further down the road. Did she hitchhike? Yes, that's confirmed when she gets into a VW van with two hippies.

My eyes are closing against my will. It's been a long day and I need to be fully on it tomorrow, so I give in to sleep. Hopefully, the enthusiastic lovemaking next door will stop soon. I can feel the headboard banging rhythmically on the wall.

My phone tells me it's later than I thought. Travelling took it out of me, as did the hours of screen time. But now I have to get up. There is work to do!

The little coffee machine in my room splutters and gargles. It's a pod machine, so hopefully, I will get a decent cup out of it. My laptop boots up while I wait for my java. Thankfully, I still have one more night booked in the hotel. I don't want to leave until I have a solid idea where Callie is heading.

I was wrong about the coffee; it sucks! I dread to think how long it's been since the machine was cleaned. No matter, I still drink it. Breakfast is equally disappointing.

Who the hell invented granola bars? They are the worst. Honey and chocolate, my sweet arse. Cardboard and disappointment are much better descriptors for that garbage. I don't have time to go out though, so it will have to suffice.

Tracking the VW is mind-numbing. It goes at the speed of an electric wheelchair. Why did they pull over so much? Never mind—they finally drop Callie off in Lyon. Now it's getting interesting. Will she try to grab a lift off another stranger? My job just got infinitely harder. Following a vehicle is one thing. Trying to follow one person, in a city, is quite another.

I crack my knuckles and smile. Callie used to playfully slap my arm when I did that and would always tell me I'd get early arthritis. I scour the cameras around where she was dropped off. My heart sinks. I can't see her. My breathing is coming faster. The idea that I've failed to find her makes my stomach drop. I can't lose her...not again.

Several minutes later, my persistence pays off. The logo on the building she enters tells me she's hired a car. Excellent. The camera outside the rental place gives me a licence plate. Game on! My guess is she's going to head south. Spain, maybe. Possibly Portugal.

Hmm, I see she's chosen Barcelona, nice. I always wanted to go to Sitges, which is located a few kilometres west. I manage to track her to the city. She parks the car and leaves, but not for long. When she returns there's, someone by her vehicle. What will she do?

Very interesting, she's picked up a passenger, a young man. Who the hell is he? Are they friends? No, they can't be. Callie has been alone. The guy must be hitchhiking or something.

My questions are left unanswered as I go in the search of food. The wanky Granola bar did nothing to satiate my hunger. McDonalds it is. I'm not making the best choices, nutritionally, right now. I can only blame it on nerves.

My phone vibrating distracts me from my Big Tasty with Bacon. It's a text message from Betty. She wants an update. More questions arise in my mind as I stare at the message. Callie has been gone for six years. Why is Betty so insistent she's found now? Something must have happened to set her off. Callie must have something on her—something that Betty can't afford to get out.

The reply I send back is vague, at best. I need her to think I'm on to something without giving her anything substantial. The message works, but she sends me a reminder of her power in the form of a photo. It's Daniel.

He has a black eye and has been crying. I want to scream. I thought I'd left this world behind. Daniel is a grown man. He made his choice and I should let him deal with the consequences. He's still my brother, though. Goddamn idiot.

Betty is getting sloppy. In the rush to show her dominance, she has given me more proof of her malevolence and criminal ways. I save the picture in my virtual vault. That's where all my evidence against her is kept. Maybe with whatever Callie has, we can finally bring Queen B down.

Fuck, Callie has disappeared again. She's gone off-road—not literally—she's no longer using the highway. What do I do now?

I have another hunch. I think she is going to the south of Spain. I don't know why I think that, but my gut tells me I'm right. I book a flight to Málaga and cross my fingers.

The temperature in Málaga is very different from Sweden. I'm not dressed for the heat and I have no other clothes. The hot air slaps me across the face as soon as I land in Spain. My armpits start to eject water at an alarming rate. I'm a sweaty, gross mess. There has to be a shop at the hotel. I just need some shorts and a tank top. Flip-flops, too.

I'm laden down with clothes I intend to purchase when my phone vibrates again. Gary. Oh joy.

"Daisy, where are you? I thought you'd be back by now."

His weasel face makes me want to visibly cringe. There is no reason he should be calling to check up. I work remotely and only go to the office once a month. I visited last week.

"Can I do something for you, Gary? I'm rather busy."

"Just wanted to make sure you were on top of the High Tree file."

I grimace. He knows better than to speak of any files over an open line. He is a moron of the highest class. I glare at him without responding. If he wants to shoot himself in the foot with the bosses, he can. I'm not going to do the same.

"Shit, sorry, shouldn't have said that. Anyway, now I have you on the phone. The annual gala is approaching. I thought it would be good for us to go together. Show a united front to the bigwigs."

I can't stand it anymore. I have tried to be nice, but enough is enough. "Gary, I will not be going to the gala with you. I will be taking a date, a female date, because I am very,

very gay. Your mother has more chance of going out with me than you. Do you understand?"

Puce: that's the colour his face is turning. Did I go too far with the mother thing? Probably, but I'm tired and he needs to step the fuck back. I have more pressing things to concern myself with than his fragile masculinity.

Five
Callie

Torreguadiaro is absolutely beautiful. It really is a Mediterranean paradise. I've booked the only hotel in the town. It's a seafront property with its own private section of the beach. The room is a twin bed, with a balcony looking out over the water. I could easily forget my worries here.

Chris is a cool guy. He offered his last fifty euros to pay towards the room bill. I didn't take it; he needs it more than me. The amount of money I stashed away before running was significant. Even after six years, I still have the majority left. I enjoy picking up off-the-books, cash-in-hand jobs as I travel. Bar work is low key, and it's my preferred choice.

Speaking of work, I noticed the local beach bar is looking for someone part time. I'll speak to the manager later today. For now, I need a stiff drink and some food.

Chris was careful not to ask too many questions as we drove down here, but I can see his curiosity is piqued. He wears his emotions on his face. Should I tell him? I think I can trust him, and he has a right to know why being near me could pose a threat to his wellbeing.

The wig I have been wearing since Sweden is irritating me. Chris blinks rapidly when I whip off the offending item and release my red locks.

"I think we need to have a conversation," I say, hoping I haven't just scared the living shit out of the lad. His face tells me he's a little nervous, but not scared.

"Are you in some sort of trouble?" He has kind eyes as he asks.

"Yes and no...mainly yes. It's complicated, but if you want to stay with me, you should know it might not be completely safe for you."

"Why not?"

Okay, here goes. I take a big swig of the cerveza we picked up in the local market. I love Spanish beer, especially when it's ice cold like this one is. I swallow and launch into my story. He doesn't need every last detail, just enough for him to make an informed decision. I won't blame him if he wants to leave. I'll miss the contact, though. We had a blast in the car.

"Wow, that's a lot. So, your real name isn't Rose, I take it?"

"No, it's not. I won't tell you my real name, for your own protection."

"Fair enough. I want to stay though, if that's okay. We're both on the run from assholes. We might as well do it together, right?"

A weight I didn't realise I was carrying, lifts. My life is scary, but a little less so with Chris by my side.

"Chris, are you sure? I don't know how they found me in Sweden, and I don't know if I lost them again."

"That makes it all the more important you're not alone. We can deal with it together. I can be an extra pair of eyes and ears. Rose, for the first time in a really long time, I feel like I belong somewhere, and that's because of you and your kindness."

Fuck, this kid is going to make me cry. I simply nod. I don't trust my voice not to break. We sip our beers, watching the water.

"Have you any ideas about how they found you?" he asks after several silent minutes.

I have no clue. I have been wracking my brain. I've done nothing different, and that has kept me safe for years, but I obviously fucked up somewhere along the way.

I find it strange after all this time, someone is pursuing me. I knew Betty would search for me in the first few months. I believed once she realised I had no intention of releasing her little black book to the authorities or competition for pure shits and giggles, she would let me go. Is she that hell-bent on revenge that I'll never be safe? Or has something happened that's forced her to resume her search for me?

"How long do you stay in a place? Like two weeks...a month?"

"The longest I stayed somewhere was six months, and that was only because I got in an accident and had to recover. Every time I move, I use a different alias, I change my appearance, and sometimes my accent. I was in Sweden for two weeks before I realised someone was watching me."

"Okay, what about friends you've made along the way?"

"Chris, you're the first, mate. I keep my distance, even from the people I temporarily worked with."

"Girlfriends? Don't tell me you've spent the past six years being a nun!"

"No, I haven't, but they were all one-night stands. None of them knew my real name, and like I said, I changed my appearance regularly."

Chris rubs his chin in thought. "Yeah, I get that, but you have distinct freckles. You can't change *them*."

I crease my forehead in thought. Shit, have my bloody freckles given me away? No, surely not. I mean, how the hell would anyone even know the women I slept with?

Chris is tapping furiously on his phone. His face pales and then he looks between his screen and me. "I think I know how they found you."

He turns the screen towards me. He's found a post on Facebook requesting anyone who may have seen me to contact the Facebook account directly. The name on the account is false—I can tell that much. It was a public post, meaning that even if they *did* have people messaging, that could be thousands of false sightings. Sure, there could be a few true ones, but how the hell could they whittle it down enough to pinpoint my location in Sweden?

Chris seemingly reads my mind. "I think someone very smart picked up a pattern. Have you hooked up with a woman in every place you've travelled to?"

I can see where he's heading. Whoever sent out that post somehow caught on to my sexcapades. It's true I found a girl in every port, so to speak. Had some of those women seen the post and messaged the unknown user?

"You think they made a link between me and the women I slept with?"

I know that's what he thinks. I just need a little extra time to compute what I'm hearing.

"That's exactly what I think. Whoever is after you knows how to think outside the box. They probably didn't know for sure they were right until they saw you in person. I bet that's why they were in Malmö but didn't approach. They needed visual confirmation."

Chris is one smart cookie. I'm glad I have him on my side. He reminds me of Daisy in a way.

"So, what do you suggest? I become celibate for the rest of my life?"

"No," he laughs, "you gotta find out who it is that tracked you. If they found you once, they'll find you again."

Wow, that's reassuring. Thanks Chris. The sun is setting and I'm emotionally drained. I have no clue what to do next. Should I run again? Go to America maybe? I don't know.

My brain needs a distraction, and for whatever reason, Daisy is on my mind. "Do you want to learn some sign language?" I ask him.

It's been way too long since I got to sign and I think everyone, hearing or not, should learn the language.

"Sure," he replies.

Chris is indulging me. He can see I need time to process. He grabs another beer for us both and we begin. I show him the basics: how to say hello and introduce himself. We go through the alphabet, and because I'm a child at heart, I teach him as many swear words as I can. We end up laughing and relaxing. Chris is a quick study. I wish Daisy was here. He would love her and she would adore him.

The night sky is stunning this evening. I need to get out of the room for a little while. Chris did a great job of distracting me for a bit, but now I need a little time to think.

"Chris, I'm going to see the manager at the beach bar about some work. Do you want to come?"

"I'm going to grab a shower and then head to bed if that's cool. It's been a long-ass day."

He isn't wrong. Today has stretched on for an age, and I don't blame him for wanting to crash. If my mind could settle, I would be doing the same thing.

"No worries. I have a key, so I'll see you later. You know where I am if you need me, okay?"

"Sure, Rose. No worries."

For the first time in six years, it bothers me I'm not able to use my real name. When I first learned about Betty,

I was so angry, that everything linked to her pissed me off, including my own name. Betty was the one to give it to me when I was born. So when I went on the run, it was an added bonus to be able to shed Callie and become someone else entirely.

I make my way to the bar. It's not packed, but there are enough customers to warrant the job advertisement that's placed in the door. My Spanish is decent enough to take a few drink orders. I head for the last stool by the wooden bar. Spanish music is softly playing in the background. There is one barman serving and one waitress delivering cold glasses of cervesa to the tables. My eyes roam up and down her very pleasing form. I wish I could keep my libido in check. Isn't that the whole reason I'm doubling down on hiding again?

I order a sangria because I've had enough beer tonight. The cute waitress stops behind the bar to drop off some empty glasses. Her black hair is in a high ponytail. God, Spanish women are gorgeous. She's wearing a simple V-neck T-shirt and shorts that only just cover her arse. She looks at me and I know I could have her tonight if I want, and I do. I haven't been able to dispel the sexual frustration that built up in Sweden.

The barman sweeps over to refill my glass I emptied too quickly. My pulse is racing at the thought of having sex again. Being able to feel another woman's skin against my own is intoxicating. *This is why I was caught*, I remind myself. The concern is less potent than earlier. My body is overriding my mind and all reasons why it's a bad idea to hook up with this woman are going out the window.

To take my mind off my throbbing clit, I talk to the barman. He's the owner's son, and the waitress is the owner's daughter. I need to tread lightly because I do not need the locals chasing me with pitchforks because I've debauched their beloved Rosa. I know that's her name because the barman spoke to her briefly before talking to me.

Rosa. It rolls right off the tongue. Sublime.

Pedro, the barman, agrees to give me a shot at bartending. According to him, he's only filling in. Their father is sick and can't work for several weeks. It's perfect for what I need and it's cash in hand. Pedro continues to work down at the other end of the bar, leaving me with Rosa.

"Can I buy you a drink?" Not the most original of pick-up lines, but I'm tired.

She bites her lip and gives me a cute smile before answering. "I have an hour left on my shift and then I would like that."

Her English is excellent. It's likely she has spent time in the UK. She winks and sets off to collect more glasses. I'm more than happy to wait. I watch her as she works. Her hair is a tad lighter than Daisy's and her eyes are more hazel. Daisy has chocolate-brown eyes; they look almost black sometimes. Why is Daisy in my head so much?

Rosa slides on to the stool next to me. She already has a drink. I don't care; I just want her attention.

"So, what's your name?" she asks me with her delicious accent.

"Rose," I say. She grins.

"Hmm, Rose and Rosa. They sound good together."

The look in her eyes tells me everything I need to know. Rosa doesn't need or want me to wine and dine her. She wants what I want. Sex.

"I think there is a lot about the two of us that will be good together."

Her smile widens, and she sinks her drink. "Follow me."

She hops off the stool and heads outside. The moon is full and lights up the sand outside the bar. Rosa walks closer to the shoreline. I'm following a few paces behind, ogling her arse. I hope she doesn't want to get it on outside. The thought of sex on the beach is not as appealing as it sounds. Sand in your arse or vag is not fun. Trust me on that. I continue to follow her until she starts heading up the grassy dune.

We've walked a couple of hundred metres. There is a small house silhouetted in the moon's glow…Rosa's place, I'm guessing. It's small and cute—very Spanish—which I adore. Maybe if I weren't so horny I would spend some time taking in the decor, but right now, my mind is solely focused on getting Rosa naked. A thought flashes through my mind. I didn't put my wig back on. Rosa has seen my natural hair. If she comes across that social post, she could point whoever is looking for me straight to my temporary doorstep.

I shake my head. If I lose sex, lose this part of my life, I'm not really sure what I'm living for. Fuck it, I need this.

We haven't uttered a word since leaving the bar. We're standing in her living/dining room. I close the distance between us in two steps. My 5'9" height comes in handy when I need to close a space quickly. If she's surprised, she doesn't show it. I rip off her T-shirt, then her shorts. She isn't wearing underwear. I am going to devour Rosa.

I love it when I find a woman who reflects my predilections in the sack. Rosa wants it hot and fast, and that's what she's going to get. I don't even bother looking for her bed. The table is right there. I slam my lips on hers. The kiss is frantic and wild.

Before she can relax into it, I spin her. Her hands land on the table. Instinctively she bends over, thrusting her perfect arse and pussy into me. I kick her legs apart. Her slit is glistening with her excitement. I brush two fingers through it, coating them before thrusting into her. Her deep moan soaks my knickers. Once I'm done with her, she will tend to me, on her knees.

It takes Rosa several minutes to come. I like building a woman up, getting her to the edge, and then easing off. I've done that several times with Rosa. When she growls at me to let her come, I laugh and then thrust harder. Her scream echoes around the room until I withdraw my hand. My breath is just as rapid as hers. She spins and drops to her knees. Rosa is the perfect playmate. At least for tonight, I can forget what's coming for me. Rosa will help me with that.

Six

Daisy

I'M SURPRISED CALLIE HAD been so careless. She rented a car from Lyon under the name Rose Pickford. It was child's play finding her again after that. Callie has made a mistake. I now know she's in a small town between Gibraltar and Málaga. There is only one hotel there and the car she rented is parked out front.

I'm grateful to be the one tracking her. If she'd made that mistake with one of B's men after her, she would be in real danger. This time when I see her, I will not hide. Together we can make it so she can come home.

I snag a room at the same hotel. Now I just have to get there from Málaga. My bank account isn't going to like me very much after this is all over. It's a good job I'm paid an exorbitant amount of money for my skills. A few taps on my phone and I have a car. The day is sailing by. I need to get on the road.

Just under an hour and twenty minutes later, I pull in front of the hotel. The sun has long set, but I feel completely wired. For the past few days, all I've done is sit on my arse, waiting for my laptop to give me good news. I'm restless. Usually I hit the gym every other day to work off my excess energy, but for obvious reasons, I've had to skip leg day.

The woman at the desk is nice. She speaks a little English. I make it easier on us both by showing her the reservation on my phone and handing over my ID. A few clicks and I'm all checked in. The room is nice. It has a sea view, which is welcomed. I can't sit in my room, though. I need to walk. Finding Callie will have to wait until the morning. It's likely she's already holed up in her room, anyway.

The access to the beach from the hotel is mighty handy. The sand is so soft, and it's still warm from the day's sun. I slip off my flip-flops and push my toes deeper into the sand. The last time I felt sand like this was... Jesus...I can't remember. My life revolves around work. I love my job and I lose myself in projects far too easily. I need to put a reminder in my calendar to actually take a break.

The thing is, when you've been told you are—and made to feel—useless your entire life, it has a knock-on effect. I know full well why I'm a workaholic. I don't need a shrink to figure that out. For the first time in forever, I'm useful. My bosses need me. The company needs me. What I do is specialised, to the point that I'm one of only a handful of people in the country that can... Nope, still a no-no on the job description.

The moon is so bright the entire beach is lit up. It's just me, myself and I.

I'm alone.

As usual.

I huff out a breath. As fulfilling as my job is, I want someone to go home to. Dating has always come second, by design. Once Callie was gone, I had no interest in anything deeper than a good shag. Penny tells me I'm ridiculous. She has several friends who have asked her to set me up with them. My answer is always a resounding "No!"

Anyway, enough of my depressing love life.

The air is delightfully warm. I have no idea how long I've been walking. I should probably turn back and go to bed. My footsteps are lazy and my mind is unfocused. It could just be fatigue, but it's more likely my brain simply can't process the fact I will see Callie tomorrow.

There's a small house just up the bank to my left. I'm almost level with the door when it opens, and two women stumble out, laughing and kissing. My heart clenches. How I wish that were me and... Hang on a minute. No, it can't be. Even in the glow of moonlight, Callie's hair is unmistakable. Well, fuck. My. Life.

I am frozen to the spot. I watch as Callie leans in and kisses the Spanish beauty again before turning towards me. Her steps falter and the laughter that was etched across her skin melts away. Her eyes open comically wide, and her mouth forms an "O." Her hand is still laced with the mystery woman's, who is also staring at me. I'm sure she's wondering what the hell I'm looking at. Maybe she thinks I'm being homophobic.

I see her mouth move but can't understand what she is saying. I think she's speaking Spanish. Callie's eyes momentarily leave mine. She's replying to the woman. In a flash, her attention is back on me. I still haven't moved. I know I was going to see her tomorrow, but bumping into her like this has me spinning out. She signs to me, "Daisy?" Senorita Big Tits—seriously, you should see them—catches Callie's hand movements and looks between us before speaking again. Callie doesn't look at her this time, she just repeats my name.

I have to snap out of it. Callie, *my* Callie, is right there, and she's talking to me. I shake my head to physically dislodge my thoughts before nodding at her. I sign back, "Hi, Callie."

The Spanish lady doesn't look impressed Callie has just dropped her hand and is taking steps towards me. Personally, I'm over the bastard moon.

My whole body comes alive when Callie scoops me into her arms and holds me tight. I breathe her in. Her smell hasn't changed in ten years. She smells of cherries. I used to take the piss out of her for buying L'Oréal for Kids Cherry Shampoo. She would laugh and tell me she never had to suffer from stinging eyes because her shampoo was tear-free. Clearly, she still stands by that.

I could bask in that smell forever. My arms hold her just as tight. We stay wrapped in each other for what feels like hours. I feel her press her nose to my neck and inhale. She's reacquainting herself with me. Hopefully, I haven't changed from what she remembers.

Her arms unfurl, and I want to weep. She takes a step back and her eyes search my face. I have to say something. Now I'm quite glad that not everyone in the world can understand sign language because I don't want the other woman getting involved in our conversation.

"Callie, you look good."

I get the obvious out of the way. She may have been running for her life, but she looks fucking fine doing it. At eighteen, Callie was fit. At twenty-eight, she looks phenomenal. I would guess weights and yoga.

"What... How are you here?" Callie's hands are trembling as she signs.

"I never stopped looking for you! Why didn't you tell me you were going?"

Alright, so my twenty-two-year-old self is still pretty upset she left without a word. I should be delving into the "Betty has my brother at gunpoint" spiel, but my heart has other ideas. I need to understand why she left me.

"I couldn't put you in danger. Betty would have hurt you. You don't know her like I do!"

Oh, Callie. "I know exactly who she is. I've known since I was sixteen."

Her hands drop to her sides, and she stares at me. I can see the expression on her face turn from joy to suspicion in an instance. Her eyes start darting about. She's looking for something or more like someone. Callie thinks I'm here to take her to Betty.

I roll my eyes, just like I would when we were kids, and she'd do something ridiculous. "Callie, relax. I'm not with Betty, for fuck's sake."

"You're not?"

"Of course I'm not. We need to talk properly!" I glance towards Titty McTitterson, who is watching us intensely. Callie whirls round to face her bedmate. It was obvious what they'd been up to when they fell out of the door. My jealousy spikes and I want to punch the woman in the throat. Yes, I know she didn't do anything wrong, but my irrational anger is just that—irrational.

Callie squeezes her hand and speaks, then she leans in and kisses her on the cheek. I have to look away before I commit murder. I could get away with it too, I'm sure of it.

Alright, psycho, rein it in.

I step back and wait until Callie walks over to me. The woman is still watching us. I clearly interrupted their goodbye, and she's pissed. Tough shit, lady.

We walk towards the hotel. There is still a way to go—plenty of time to chat. Callie puts her hand on my arm and stops us. The waves lap gently on our feet. How I wish we were here under different circumstances.

"It was you in Sweden?" Her eyes are shining in the light as she looks at me.

"Yes, I found you."

Her hands move furiously. She's getting worked up. "Why the hell didn't you show yourself? I thought one of the nephews had found me."

"I panicked. I thought you would think I was with B! Then I realised I made a mistake, and by that time you'd figured out someone was following you and left on that scooter."

"Cilla."

I laugh out loud. I knew it! She grins at me because she knows I figured it out.

"After that, I was able to track you."

She's staring again. I feel her eyes roaming every part of me. She draws me into another hug. This is why no other woman has ever compared. Being with Callie feels like I'm coming home. The moment she touches me, I'm hers, unequivocally.

She points to the hotel. "I'm booked in there."

"I know, I have a room, too. There is a lot we need to talk about."

I should go back to my own room, get some sleep and then meet up with her again in the morning once we're both rested. I can't do it, though. Now she's here, in front of me, I can't let her out of my sight.

"Uh, I have a guest staying with me."

She looks nervous, telling me. The rational part of my brain concludes it must be the young man she met in Barcelona. The other, uglier part of me is grimacing at the idea she has another woman waiting in the room, in her bed.

I nod. If it's a woman, I will force myself to leave her again. I cannot stomach watching someone else kiss her. I'm being ridiculous. Callie literally just left a woman she'd clearly fucked. There's no way she would have done that with a woman waiting for her in her room, right?

Honestly, I don't know. The Callie of today is very different from the Callie of ten years ago. It's as if she can read my mind, because she quickly tells me it isn't a woman.

The light in her room is on. Callie steps aside to let me in. The young man she met in Barcelona jumps to his feet. His laid-back chill has been replaced with panic. I can see it in his eyes. I wonder if Callie has told him about me?

Callie places a hand on his shoulder. "Chris, this is Daisy."

She turns to me and smiles. There is nothing more beautiful on this planet than Callie Compton's smile. It only takes him a second before his panic is replaced with a warm smile of his own. He's looking at me now as if we are old friends. To my utter astonishment, he slowly signs his name. He looks from me to Callie, checking that he did it right. She is beaming at him, and I am beaming at her. After all this time, I've still been on her mind. Enough so that she told a stranger about me and taught him sign language.

I reciprocate. "Hello, Chris, it's nice to meet you." I smile as he scratches his head. He didn't catch everything I said and doesn't want to say. This time I use my voice. "It's a pleasure to meet you, Chris."

His smile becomes wide again. I can see why Callie has taken a shine to him. He has this little brother vibe going on.

"I'm sorry, that's all the sign I know," he replies with a shy grin.

My heart is melting and thudding at the same time. I need to keep myself under control. There is a right time to be mushy and sentimental, and this isn't it. Callie needs to know what's going on.

"Do you want a drink?" Callie has already opened a bottle of beer for herself. I nod. I could do with several drinks to be honest. Chris settles back on his bed. I settle on the little couch with Callie.

Half the bottle of beer is gone in the first swig. I don't want Callie to panic when I tell her that, technically, Betty did send me. I take a deep breath and brace myself.

"As I said, I never stopped looking for you. But Betty does have something to do with why I'm here now. Before you get the wrong end of the stick, hear me out."

I glare at her with one of my most penetrating stares. Something else I used to do when we were younger, to make sure Callie knew I was being dead serious.

"Okay, I'm listening."

"Betty called me in a few weeks ago. I haven't laid eyes on her since I left for university. She told me I was to find you. Daniel, the absolute douche canoe, informed her I'm good at solving things. She's obviously desperate to find you and the thing you took. She wants it back, Callie. To make sure I do what she wants, she has dear old dad holding Daniel hostage, gun included."

Callie's face pales. "Shit, shit, shit. Is that why you're here then, to take me back?"

Her eyes have gone cold. I'm more than a little hurt. She thinks I would trade her in. Daniel is my brother, but he knew what he was signing up for. I tried so many times to get him to leave that village. Fucking moron.

"Callie, do you honestly think that's why I'm here?" I need to know that there is still some of the Callie I know left in her. I understand her life has been hard, probably very lonely, and that can have a lasting effect, but I hope to God she knows deep down I would never betray her like that. She studies me and then her shoulders slump. Her hand lands on my knee and I inhale sharply. I've made an involuntary noise because her eyes snap up to mine.

"Sorry," she says, moving her hand. Her eyes go from my face to her lap. Bugger, I made her retreat when all I want is her hand touching me, but not on my knee. "I'm sorry, Daisy. I..."

Catching her under the chin, I gently tug her head up so her eyes are on me again. "It's okay. I'm here to warn you and hopefully work with you."

My hand lands on her knee this time, and I give it a little squeeze. Chris is adorable, but I wish to high heaven he wasn't here right now. I want to tell Callie how I feel...how I've missed her. Then it dawns on me... Less than an hour ago she was probably face deep in another woman.

Yes, Callie Compton has thought of me over the years—that's evident in her talking to Chris about me—but that doesn't mean she likes me in that way. She never has, otherwise she would have told me all those years ago, right? I need to get that through my thick skull once and for all.

Seven
Callie

HOLY SHIT! DAISY SIMPSON is here, in my room, in front of me, looking like a goddess and she has her hand on my knee! She also caught me coming out of the house of that lovely Spanish woman I'd just fucked for a couple of hours.

I'm trying with all my might to keep my head on straight, so to speak. My brain is screaming at me to be cautious. I haven't seen Daisy in a decade and all of a sudden, she's here with a story about her brother and Betty. I want to believe her completely, but surely that would be idiotic. I know how much Betty wants that book and I know the lengths she would go to. Queen B would absolutely use someone's family to get what she wants.

Would Daisy sell me out, though? Ten years ago, the answer would have been no. I wouldn't have ever questioned her. But now? How can I really know? I have no idea what she's been doing with herself for all this time. It's unlikely, yet possible, Daisy has been working for "The Family."

My gut is twisting, because even as I think it, I know it can't be true. Fuck, my brain is scrambled. And what does she mean "she's here to work with me?"

I feel like my body is on overload. I can't process anything. I stand up and start pacing. Daisy's eyes track me, as do Chris's. I need some time alone. I think better alone.

"Can we pick this up in the morning? I need to sleep."

I can see Daisy is reluctant to leave, but once again, I can't decide if that's because she's worried I'll run and she will have to tell Betty, or because she is genuinely happy to see me after so long and doesn't want our time together to be cut short.

"I'll go to my room. Can we have breakfast together, just the two of us?"

Why doesn't she want Chris there? Is breakfast a way to get me alone before Betty's goons pounce? My ears are buzzing and it's driving me insane. I will meet her in the morning, though. I have to know what she has in store for me.

I nod. "Okay, breakfast it is—8 a.m. in the hotel's dining room."

I will explain to Chris later. There's no way he understood any of that. Daisy's hands are too fast. She nods and stands. I see her hesitation. She wants to stay. Instead, she steps towards me and hugs me tightly. This is the third time we've hugged in an hour. Tears pool in my eyes because she feels so damn good. Like home.

The door clicks behind her as she leaves. My breathing stutters. Chris squeezes my shoulder. He doesn't know the full extent of my past, but he knows Daisy was one of the most important people in my life.

"Hey, you okay?" Chris asks.

Laughable question, really. Physically I'm fine, but mentally, emotionally, I'm a wreck. I just smile and slump back on the sofa. I feel a cold bottle pushed into my hands. Alcohol probably isn't the sensible option, but damn, I need something to take the edge off.

"I can't believe she's here."

Finally, I've voiced the phrase that's been circling the fringe of my mind ever since seeing her staring at me outside of Rosa's house. Fucking hell, she saw me with Rosa. It shouldn't be a problem, but it is. I don't like the thought of Daisy seeing me with another woman. Double fuck. That's how she found me, isn't it? Not because of Rosa, but because of the women I banged. Daisy knows

I like women, and she knows I've been wandering around Europe, sleeping with as many as possible.

Never, in all the time I've been running, have I felt bad for my sexual exploits, but now, knowing Daisy made the connection? I feel...guilt? Shame? I don't even know.

Jesus, Callie, get some perspective!

Now is not the time to worry about feeling guilty. Daisy is here. I have to figure out why. "Chris, I'm going to have breakfast with her tomorrow. I need you to have everything packed and ready to go."

"Do you think she's working for your Nan?"

I haven't referred to that woman as my nan in a very long time, so when Chris says it, I feel a sliver of anger roll over me. It's not his fault. He doesn't know what that word does to me now.

"I hope not, but I can't take any chances? If it goes tits up tomorrow, you need to be ready to run."

I take a breath because the reality of our situation is startling. Startling because it's a "we" situation instead of just an "I" situation. Chris is now smack-bang in the middle of my shit.

"We can't take the car again. Not now. She knows about it." The young man is a quick study. Maybe he just watches too many crime programs. Whatever. I'm grateful he has common sense.

"No, the car stays here. I'll report it to the rental agency. I'll tell them it broke down, but we couldn't wait around until they arrived."

The survivalist in me is taking over. I hope with every part of me that Daisy isn't a threat, but I can't just take her at face value.

Chris nods. "Okay, so I'll be ready to go. How do we get out of here?"

"Listen, Chris, you don't have to stay with me. In fact, it's probably better if you go. Getting caught up with Betty is not something I want for you—"

"Don't make me leave. Please, Callie."

I stare at him. I forgot he shouldn't know my real name. He must have picked it up from my conversation with Daisy. His face reflects the scared boy he was when I first met him.

"Please, Callie."

Jesus, I can't watch the poor lad beg. "You don't have to leave, but think about what you're getting into."

Honestly, the thought of Chris leaving hurts my heart. We hardly know each other, but I have this overwhelming need to protect him. It's weird.

"I know exactly what I'm in for, Callie. I feel safe with you and, for the first time, accepted. I don't want to give that up. I know we're not exactly best friends, but..."

"I know..." And I do. He is feeling the same as me. We need each other.

"Good, that's settled then. Where do we go if we have to run?"

"Anywhere. We can make a plan when we're out of immediate danger. You just be ready to go, and I'll do the rest."

Chris goes to bed and starts snoring. I'm wiped but I can't sleep yet. I need a plan for tomorrow, but there isn't one forming yet. Usually, I'm excellent at planning ahead. Seeing dangers beforehand is my specialty, but Daisy has me all turned around. That's why Betty sent her to fuck with my head. I've almost convinced myself breakfast is an ambush, and I'm devastated.

I wake up to sunlight piercing my eyelids. I fell asleep on the balcony. No matter how hard I tried to plan, I have nothing. If it all goes to shit this morning, we won't have a way out, and that really pisses me off. My phone tells me I have half an hour before meeting Daisy. The shower allows fifteen minutes for me to calm my mind. I *must* get into the right headspace.

Daisy is already sitting at one of the dining tables when I enter the room. She's looking out of the window, unaware I'm watching her. My God, she's a sight for sore eyes. Her long black locks are in a high ponytail, accentuating her high cheekbones. She's a magnificent-looking woman. Well, she always was.

I'm guessing she bought her clothes at a local tourist shop. The "I Love Málaga" T-shirt doesn't seem to be something she would keep in her wardrobe. That makes me smile. With my spine straight and my head on a swivel, I sit down opposite her. There is already a coffee waiting. Black, no sugar. She remembered.

"Hi," she signs.

Her smile is so bright and infectious, I can't help but mirror it. This hotel, this part of Spain, would be perfect for a holiday with a loved one. It would be perfect with Daisy. The dining room is bright and open. We're sitting at this little table, overlooking the bluest of seas, with the sun shining down. I have to remind myself I am definitely *not* here on holiday with Daisy. I am running for my life.

I take a sip of coffee. It's liquid energy I need. A caffeine boost will help if I have to make a quick escape. Daisy is watching me. A small grin forms on her beautiful face.

"What?" I ask.

"There is no one else here. I did not bring a gang of Betty's nephews to kidnap you. I swear on my life, Callie, I'm not here to hurt you."

Her eyes are so sincere I'm finding it hard not to give in. The survivalist in me is still fighting, and she's not ready to let go just yet.

"I want to believe you, Daisy, so much, but..."

"I knew about Betty before you did, Cal. I figured it out when we were sixteen."

The confession stuns me. She's known all this time, even before me. How is that possible? Daisy can still read me like a book. She understands what I'm thinking before I do. Well, that's how it seems.

"We were kids. I didn't know how to tell you what I'd found out. I just hoped you would see it sooner rather than later. Then I left for uni and well..."

The day she left was one of the hardest days of my life. My mum dying was the only thing that topped it as the world's shittiest day in the life of Callie Compton. I wanted more than anything to go with her, but Betty made it clear I wasn't going to be leaving any time soon.

"You should have told me—"

"And you should have told me you were leaving," she shoots back. Pain flashes through her eyes.

I hate that I'm the cause of it. How do I explain to her I loved her too much to put her in harm's way? How could she possibly understand? Hell, she's probably got a fella waiting for her at home. I think finding out her best friend was secretly in love with her for the entirety of the friendship might be too much, especially in these circumstances. It's a complicated, shitty mess, as is.

"Betty would have come for you sooner. You know that." I hope she can see the pleading in my eyes. I need her to understand it was for her own good.

Daisy sighs. "I would have gone with you."

Oh, God, my heart is clenching so hard. I can only imagine how different the last six years would have been if I'd had Daisy with me. I shake my head rapidly.

"No way. You had your life. You'd escaped and were free to live the life you wanted. I could never have dragged you into this."

I see her open her mouth and clench her fist. She looks like she wants to strangle me. I've never seen her look so frustrated. Finally, she snaps her mouth shut and breathes heavily out of her nose.

After a few silent moments, she speaks again. "It doesn't matter now. We have to work together."

I scrunch my forehead in confusion. For the life of me, I can't see what we could do to stop Betty. Her reach is far too long. Even if I did leak the black book, there are too many ways for her to discredit it.

"How?" I ask, hoping Daisy has a plan, because I have zilch.

"I have all the evidence we need. That, along with whatever it is you took, should be enough. We have to try, Cal. You deserve to come home and have a life."

My throat seizes. I haven't entertained the idea of going home in years. It always hurt too much to think about it. "What evidence?"

"Their ignorance is going to be their downfall."

When Daisy says "their" I know she's talking about her dad and Betty. Watching the dismissal of someone you love, purely because they're different, is awful. Growing up, I wanted to weep on a daily basis for her. Her dad—or sperm donor would be more accurate—treated her like she was nothing, all because she is deaf.

"What do you mean?"

"Treating me the way they did was cruel. Ignoring me was a mistake. It's amazing what I was able to pick up from them. They thought, because I couldn't hear their conversations, I didn't understand. Oh how very wrong they were. Callie, I collected as much shit about Betty and her entire operation as I could. For two years, I smuggled information into my own virtual vault."

My mouth is hanging open; I can feel it. I'm shocked, and surprisingly turned on, by what Daisy has just said. I always knew she was a formidable person, but this... Daisy Simpson is a fucking ninja spy.

"How... What... How?"

She laughs at me. Her eyes light up and I want to take her face in my hands and kiss her. It's ridiculous how those feelings I so carefully tucked away are now spilling out.

"What did you take from her?" She asks me.

"Her little black book."

"Are you kidding me?"

I shake my head. "No. I found it seven months before I left. I was already planning on running, but I held on until I knew I could secure it as insurance."

"Callie, we can do this. We can take her down."

I love her enthusiasm, but it isn't as easy as she's making it sound. Betty's empire stretches across all of

England. I read some of her book; I know the names of her colleagues, and they are not to be trifled with. Presenting the police with a book, and whatever Daisy has, isn't going to suffice. We need to cut off several heads—metaphorically speaking—before her reign will end, permanently.

"Daisy, we are three people. She has an army. Her goons might be meatheads, but they will fuck us up if they find us. What about Daniel? She won't hesitate to kill him."

"Daniel made his bed. He chose that life. Callie, she has to be stopped. You will never be safe...and...I need you safe. I need you *home*."

One good thing out of this conversation is I am now, one hundred percent sure Daisy is not a threat. As for everything else that may happen, I don't even know where to begin. I drink some more coffee and gaze out the window. Daisy doesn't interrupt me. She knows I'm processing.

Okay, together we have enough ammunition to dismantle the biggest crime family in English history. That being said, we need to do it right. The information needs to get into the right hands. There's no point handing our treasure trove over to some Beat Bobby.

Bloody hell, am I actually entertaining the idea we form a team and attempt this?

Fuck, I could never say no to Daisy.

Eight

Daisy

Her mind is busy working, I can see it. She used to gaze off into the distance whenever she was thinking through a problem. I don't mind; it allows me time to sit and drink her in.

I wish I could caress her hair. It's so vibrant and soft. I remember once, when we were seventeen, we were chilling in one of the many fields that surround the village. I was leaning against a big oak tree and Callie had her head in my lap. I had absentmindedly started stroking her hair, and it was the best sensation in the world. At the time, I panicked, because I was sure Callie would pick up on my attraction. She didn't.

How I wish we could go back. I would've told her everything that I knew and then I would have run away with her. I understand she didn't tell me because she was worried, but if she knew how much I loved her, maybe she would understand her leaving me behind was a kind of torture even Betty couldn't upstage.

Why would she believe me, though? I left her behind first. Callie would love Edinburgh. Maybe once this is over, she will come back with me. I'm getting ahead of myself, I know, but I can't help it. I know we can do this. If we are together, we can bring that old witch to her knees. I must be patient though, because if I push too hard, Callie will retreat. A small smile blooms on my face. Even after all this time, I still know her. She's still *my Callie.*

I said I would tell her how I feel about her, but I'm putting that on the back burner. I'm not sure it's the best idea to add more complication to an already fraught situation, and I'm a complete and utter chicken shit. If she rejected me, I think I would die—not literally, I'm not that dramatic. I think the part of me that still believes in *happily ever after* would die. Callie has always been the end game for me. So, for a little while longer, I will keep my fairy tale as is: unmarred and safe in my heart.

Shit, in all my daydreaming, I've missed her talking to me. "Sorry, what did you say?"

"I asked if you really think we can pull this off. Daisy, we could end up dead. I think we need to be realistic here. Plus, I have Chris to think of."

"How did Chris end up with you after you met him in Barcelona?"

She is clearly taken aback that I know exactly where she met him.

"Look, I can't explain fully how I found you. If you knew I would have to kill you!" I say with a wicked grin.

She laughs. It's the best thing ever to watch her beautiful face bloom. I've missed it so much.

"Daisy Simpson, I think there's a lot more going on with you than you're letting on. What exactly did you study in university?"

Oh, if only she knew the truth, which she never can, not without the risk of me getting banged up.

"All you need to know, Callie Compton, is that I'm good at what I do, and with my considerable skill, I can help get you home, and clear of danger."

"Well, how the hell can I say no after that empowered speech?"

"You can't, so shall we get to it?"

Her perfect eyebrow arches. If only she knew how much I would love to get to it with her.

"We need to bring Chris into this. And to answer your earlier question, I brought him along because he needed someone, and frankly, so did I. His dad threatened to send him to a conversion camp, so he ran. Don't worry, he's nineteen. I checked his passport."

"Motherfucker." My hatred towards those camps is unwavering, as is my contempt for any parent who would ever consider sending their child to one.

"Whoa there, Daisy, that's some strong language," Callie laughs.

As younger kids, I didn't like swearing. I encountered it too often from my dad, and it was usually directed towards me. Now, well...I swear like a sailor.

"I'm not the sweet Daisy you remember, Callie. I'm all grown up." I arch my eyebrow back at her. We stay locked in a stare until we're interrupted by Chris. He's freshly showered and in a pair of cargo shorts with way too many pockets, paired with a loose tank.

"I take it we don't need to make a mad dash for the border, then?" He grins at Callie. They've formed a bond. It's plain to see.

"No, we're good. Grab some breakfast and join us. We have a lot to discuss."

He gives a mock salute, then disappears. Callie watches him for a few seconds before turning back to me. "So, how did you find me?"

"I followed the trail of women's panties you were dropping all across Europe." I almost laugh out loud when her eyes bug at my forthrightness. "I hope you get tested regularly."

At that, she almost chokes on her coffee, and I can't hide my grin.

"Jesus, warn a girl would you..." She's mopping up coffee that's dribbled down her chin. Chris sits down with coffee and a plate, full to the brim with pastries.

"What did I miss?"

I only just read his lips before a croissant is unceremoniously shoved in his mouth.

"Daisy was just telling me how she found me."

"It was the women, wasn't it?" he grins.

I'm impressed. I can tell he was the one to figure it out. Maybe when this is done, I could introduce him to my boss. The company is always interested in people with minds like mine. Someone like Chris if I'm not mistaken.

"Yeah," Callie mumbles, but she's still signing so I can understand. Her face has gone a delightful shade of red.

"You don't have to sign, Cal. I can lip-read."

As much as I appreciate her signing, it's a lot for her to do when I'm guessing she hasn't had to interpret for some time. I don't mind lip-reading for a while.

"No. Wet fish," Callie says seriously with a scowl.

I throw back my head and laugh. Chris is looking at us like we've lost the plot. Callie is grinning at the reminder. Back in the day, no matter who we were with, Callie would always sign. I knew she got the piss taken out of her for it. I'm deaf, not blind. I would see the other kids ask her why she bothered. As you can imagine, the children we grew up with were products of their parents, through and through: aka...arseholes.

Callie would never listen, though. She would always include me, and a lot of the time I felt bad I was causing her problems. I told her she didn't have to sign, and that I was okay to lip-read. Her response was to tell me, that if I said that to her one more time, she would slap me with a wet fish.

I have tears coming down my face, and my stomach is aching. I nod my head. "Okay, not the wet fish, I swear I won't say that again."

"Good," Callie mock huffs and then laughs.

"I've clearly missed something. Is it a lesbian thing?" Chris asks seriously, causing both me and Callie to stare at him.

"Is what a lesbian thing?" Callie chokes.

"The wet fish reference."

Chris is absolutely serious. I look at Callie and burst out laughing again.

"No, it bloody well isn't. Get your mind out of the gutter, young man," Callie laughs.

"Aren't lady bits..."

"Stop!" I shout. I can't take it anymore. The conversation has veered *way* off course, and I'm not talking lady bits with this guy. He smiles sheepishly, and then chuckles.

"Anyway, there's only one lesbian here, Chris, you..."

"Two," I interrupt. Callie snaps her eyes to me. "I came out the first week of university!" I add, just so there is no mistaking what I'm saying.

"Oh, I didn't know that."

"Why would you?" It sounds harsh, but we rarely kept in touch once I left. It was too hard.

"Yeah, I suppose I wouldn't," she says with a sad smile.

"Well, it goes both ways. When did you come out?"

She licks her lips, and my eyes trace every second of it.

"I was nineteen," she says, jolting me from my ogling. We sit and look at each other. These bouts of eye contact need to stop.

Chris clears his throat. I see his Adam's apple bob up and down. "Now that we've established our group is flying the rainbow flag all around, do you want to tell me what we're doing next? I presume you have a plan?"

Callie breaks eye contact first. "Not really, but yes, there are some things we need to fill you in on."

I let Callie tell Chris about our conversation. She fills him in on the rest of our history, too. I understand why she didn't want to tell him everything to begin with, but that's not an option anymore.

"I suggest we take a couple of days to regroup here before moving on. Betty only has a general idea of my location. I haven't told her I made contact with you."

"Are you sure you weren't followed?" Chris asks.

"Completely sure. My phone and laptop are encrypted, so even if Betty got adventurous and tried to track me that way, she'd hit a brick wall.

Chris raises both eyebrows. "Why do you have an encrypted phone?"

"She would have to kill you if she told you, buddy," Callie supplies before I can answer. I laugh.

"You two are weird. I love it," he smirks. Now all three of us are laughing.

"We are safe here for a little while," I add. I don't want Chris to worry.

"We have to figure out who to give the information to once we have it." Callie says, her eyes darting around. As funny as the conversation has been this morning, we need to remember that what we're doing is stupidly dangerous, and we must be careful who hears what.

"What do you mean once we have it? I told you my evidence is in my online vault. I can access that anytime and you have the book, so..."

"Yeah, about the book..."

"What about the book, Callie?" I can already tell our job is about to get a lot harder.

"It's in four separate pieces spread across Europe."

Well, fuck. I wasn't expecting that.

"Why?" I almost screech.

"For the simple reason, that if I ever got caught, they couldn't take the book and shoot me in the face." Can't argue with that logic. "All we have to do is go to my hiding spots and pick them up."

"We can do that!" Chris says, nodding. My phone vibrates. It's already laying on the table. We can all see it's

Gary calling. His name scrawls across the screen along with *Gross Pig* in brackets and an emoji. Callie raises both perfect eyebrows at that.

I pick up the phone and tell them both to be silent. "Gary."

By the expression on Callie's face, I can tell that Gary is practically shouting at me. She hates it as much as I do when people do that.

"Where are you?" He's a little sweaty.

"Why? Is there a problem?"

There isn't, because I have been communicating with the higher ups all through my travels. After talking to Penny, I finally decided to report Gary. My bosses informed me I no longer had to communicate with him in any way. I'm surprised he hasn't gotten the memo.

"I'm worried, that's all. You don't usually go running off."

"Gary, you have no idea what I do with my time. I see you once a month, at best. Why are you calling? You must have received the memo?"

I have to be cryptic when talking to him. Callie and Chris can't know any details about my work. I just hope Gary isn't stupid enough to mention anything. Again.

"Yes, I did. I thought we were friends. Can't friends check up on each other? Especially when one of them is travelling alone."

My bullshit-o-meter is pinging. It usually does when Gary opens his mouth, but it's going off for a different reason now. He knew I needed to do something personal. I never at any point told him I was travelling, though. Did he guess? Maybe. But why is he calling so often? That's unusual. Yes, he's creepy and sleazy, but not stalker-y. Something isn't right.

"Gary do not call again unless it is work related. In fact, even if it is, email me. I'm busy." I slide my finger across the screen to end the call. I need to get back to my room now.

Callie is glaring at my phone. "Everything okay? He sounds fun."

I'm already halfway out of my seat before answering. "I need to check something. Let's go to my room."

If I'm right, we need to move, and fast. Chris and Callie pick up on my increasing discomfort. They grab their things and we head to my room.

Once inside, I direct them to the balcony. "Look, I can't have you seeing what I'm about to do. Can you sit here until I call you in?"

They nod.

I set up my laptop on my bed and connect my phone. It takes me all of twenty seconds to confirm my fear. Gary, the slimy little bastard, has hacked my phone. I feel the heat of anger rush up my throat. I want to scream. I am religious when it comes to screening my tech. The company gives us new phones and laptops every month. They are untraceable, but the company can gain access in case an agen—I mean, colleague—needs a helping hand for any reason.

I last checked the phone in Sweden. He must have waited before hacking it. But why? Is it all about him being a Grade A creep or is he in Betty's pocket? I know it sounds like a leap, but it's more than possible. If he *is* in her employ, then I have a massive fucking problem. The higher ups have to know. It's vital, but that means I would have to explain what I'm doing here with Callie and Chris. Shit, shit, shit.

Okay, breathe. You can figure this out, Daisy.

First thing, I need to scrub my phone. No, wait, if I do that, he will know I've found his hack. Okay, I need a new phone. I run a check on my laptop to make sure it's clean. It is. I would have been surprised if he'd managed to hack that. His skills are basic, which makes it worse I got hacked by him in the first place.

I turn my phone off for now and pack away my laptop. Callie and Chris enter the room mere seconds after I call them.

"Okay, we have a slight issue," I say.

"What?" they reply in unison.

"Gary hacked my phone. He's been tracing me ever since Sweden."

Nine

Callie

For the love of beans. Could this get any more fucked up? It's bad enough we have to deal with Betty. Now we have some random guy called Gary getting involved. I mean, really. If I get thwarted after six years by someone called *Gary*, I'm going to lose my shit.

"Does he work for B?"

"I don't know. I'm so sorry." Daisy looks upset, but also seriously pissed. If I were Gary, I would run away. I've seen Daisy lose it twice in our lifetimes, and both were terrifying. The first time was when her little brother Daniel stole her diary and began reading it in front of everyone on the playground. He couldn't walk straight for a week. I'm pretty sure his ability to have children was significantly reduced that day. The second was when we were fifteen. A guy grabbed her ass in the street and Daisy punched him in the throat. It was the single best thing I've ever witnessed.

"No apologies, Daisy, we just need to know if he is a real threat." I don't want her feeling bad.

We have to get proactive now. My days of running are over and I'm ready to take the fight to Betty. My blood is boiling at the thought of someone following Daisy. If anything ever happened to her... I can't even vocalise what that would do to me.

"Give me some time. I'll find out if Gary is on her payroll. If he is, that changes everything."

She shoos us out of her room. It doesn't take a genius to know whatever Daisy's profession is, it's not working for the local council. If I had to guess, I'd bet she works for the government. But I'm not going to pressure her into revealing something that would get her into trouble.

Chris flops onto his bed. We haven't had a chance to speak alone since last night. I want to make sure he's doing okay. This shit is a lot to cope with.

"Chris, you alright?"

"Shouldn't I be asking you that?" he laughs. We sit in silence for a few moments. "Callie, you have to end all this. From what you've told me, Betty will never stop."

Of course he's right. I was naïve to think she would let me disappear. Even if I hadn't taken the book, she would have come for me, eventually. Queen B doesn't like to lose, and she doesn't like to be made a fool of, either.

In her eyes, I humiliated her in front of "The Family." Betty spent so long grooming me and showing me off to everyone around her, proud that I was her heir. I demolished that little fantasy when I left and she will want me to suffer for it. Maybe it's because of Chris or Daisy. I'm not sure, but I know that continuing to run isn't an option. People who I care about are in the firing line now.

"Should we start planning while we wait for Daisy?" He's as keen as I am to get this done.

"Yes. As I said earlier, the book is in four pieces. We can get the first one relatively quickly. It's here in Spain."

"Okay, so let's think about transport. We should play it safe. Let's use my name to hire a car. If this Gary twat has been tracking Daisy, he might know the aliases you were using."

"I doubt it. Daisy is pretty adamant that her laptop wasn't compromised. There's no way she would keep any information about me on her phone."

"But we can't be sure, Callie. It doesn't seem smart to use any of your names right now. We can't use Daisy's either. Mine, well, no one knows me from Adam!"

He does have a point. We really have no idea who is involved and what they know. "Okay, you arrange a car."

Chris sets about making arrangements. I sit on the balcony trying to gather my thoughts, which are all over the place. So much is happening. I just want it all to stop. I want to be able to do all the things regular people do. You know, like... Go to a job I hate. Spend eight hours bitching with my colleagues before going home to my house, where my wife is waiting for me. Eat dinner together and then veg out on the sofa. Watch a Netflix series we're excited about because the story line hints at a lesbian relationship, only to be disappointed when said relationship is just a kiss and the show gets cancelled. Things like that. Is that so much to ask for?

Daisy interrupts my daydream. She has a big smile on her face. "Gary is just a creep. He isn't working for B."

Her body language is relaxed. I drop my head to my chest and start laughing. Why I'm laughing is as much a mystery to me as anybody else. I have no idea what's happening. I think my body is finally reacting to all the stressful crazy shit that is going on. Once I've calmed down,

I look at Daisy. She's smiling and her eyes are sparkling. She's who I want to come home to after a long day at my shitty job. It's always been Daisy.

I need to avoid that minefield for now. "How can you be sure?"

"I have my ways. All you need to know is he was just stalking me, so it's fine."

My heart rate picks up speed, and the white-hot anger I feel towards that little maggot of a man takes me by surprise. Who the fuck does he think he is?

Daisy places a hand on my shoulder. "Calm down, Rambo. I can see you getting all bent out of shape from here. I've dealt with it."

"Daisy, he was..."

"And now he isn't, and he won't, ever again. I dealt with it. I forgot how protective you get." Her skin blushes slightly at her comment.

If only she knew how protective I was of her.

"We have a car... Oh, sorry, did I interrupt?" Chris is looking between Daisy and me.

"Nope, not at all. Daisy was just telling me Gary isn't an issue."

"Really? That's a relief."

"We should get going, though," I say. I want to get on the road as soon as possible.

"Where are we going?" Daisy asks.

"A tiny village east of Málaga. It's the closest of my hiding spots."

"Will it be easy to get to?" Chris enquires.

"Um, mostly. The piece of the book is hidden beneath a mango tree—"

"A mango tree? Really?"

"Or was it an avocado tree?" I didn't mean to say that out loud. I'm ninety percent sure it's a mango tree... Okay, seventy-five percent.

"When you say it's 'mostly' easy to get to, what does that mean, exactly?" Daisy asks. Her face is the picture of concern.

Alright, folks, here's the skinny: I hid that part of the book on a mango—or avocado—farm five years ago. I was banging the daughter of the farmer, and it felt—at the time—like a good place to stash the pages.

There is a strong chance Lucia—said farmer's daughter—won't be jumping with joy to see me again. I parted without a word. Douche move, I know, but I didn't see the point in saying goodbye. I told her it was a sex-only situation. Plus, I didn't think I would need to come back for the book part, like, at all. I had resigned myself to a life on the run.

Also, the particular tree is halfway up a mountain, only accessible by donkey. Four-by-fours haven't reached that part of Spain yet. Daisy and Chris don't need to know all that yet, though, so I fob them off. "Don't worry about it. Come on, let's get packed."

Three hours later and we are ready to roll. The Hyundai Kona Chris has hired is nice. It has all the gizmos, including SatNav, and a heated steering wheel and seats. Although the weather in southern Spain doesn't call for it, I press all the buttons. It's only when Chris declares his arse is on fire, and Daisy glares at me, I stop playing around. Jeez, people are way too serious.

"The farm provides tours every day at ten and two. After that, all of Spain goes on a siesta." I laugh at my own joke. I really have been alone for too long. "We've missed today's tours, so we'll have to wait until tomorrow."

"Why can't we just sneak in later?" Chris mumbles through a mouthful of Cheetos. *My* Cheetos, the cheeky little fucker!

"Because the farm is guarded by dogs. They roam the entire property and let me tell you something, kiddo, you *do not* want to fuck with them." His face pales and I laugh.

"There is no point drawing attention to ourselves by doing something risky. If we can go on the tour, nip off when no one is looking, get the book, and return to the tour before anyone notices, it's all good."

"And what if someone notices?" Chris again, this time with a red liquorice hanging out of his mouth. The kid is taking the challenge of eating my road trip food to heart.

"Then we are just dumb tourists who got distracted and wandered off. There's an abandoned farmhouse about two kilometres away from where we need to be. We can rough it for one night. I don't want to keep booking hotel rooms, not when everything is so up in the air."

"I don't mind a night in the open. I used to go camping all the time," Chris says with a wistful look in his eye. I wonder if he's thinking back to his dad and the life he left behind. It can't have been all bad. Well, I hope not. Poor lad.

"Fine with me, too. How do you know about the vacant house?" Daisy asks.

"I stayed there for a while."

Daisy doesn't need to know that was where Lucia and I would meet up. My explanation seems to satisfy her. We spend the rest of the trip in silence. It's probable the weight of our task is starting to sink in. My eyes wander from the road to Daisy, who is tapping her foot to the music. Her hand is resting on the speaker, feeling the vibrations.

The sun is still high in the sky when we reach the dirt track that leads to the abandoned house. I don't want to park our car out front because there are too many locals who would notice it and come snooping. Thankfully, the overgrown bush I used to hide my vehicle the last time I was here still remains, wild as ever. The bush won't cover the car entirely, but it will do the job for tonight.

We had the foresight to stock up on food, none of which needs cooking. I also picked up some flashlights, knowing we would have to do without electricity. It's a short hike up to the house. Nothing has changed. The front door is unlocked, as I knew it would be.

Inside is a bit dusty, but it's clear someone has been in here recently; probably Lucia with another woman. It's her spot, after all. There is only one bedroom, something I didn't think about when I made the plan to stay here.

"I'll take the couch, if you can call it that." Chris has already thrown his bag down and is settled on the old, beat-up two-seater. I wince, knowing how many times I made Lucia come on that thing.

"You good to share?" I ask Daisy. It shouldn't be awkward. After all, we had plenty of sleepovers back then.

But now? Well, I can't speak for her, but I'm feeling awkward as fuck. Daisy isn't my friend from ten years ago, she's the woman I've been lusting over for far too long and she's into women. My body is screaming at me to do something about how I'm feeling.

She interrupts my roaming thoughts. "No problem. Do you still starfish?"

"Yup, I'm probably worse now. I don't usually share a bed."

One of her lovely eyebrow rises. "You're telling me you don't even allow your conquests to stay the night?"

I know she's mocking me, but it kind of stings. I hate she thinks I'm some sort of Lothario. It's not by choice. I can't have normal relationships. If things were different, I'm sure I would have tried dating a couple of the women I met along the way. I shrug my shoulders, hoping to look unbothered by her remark. I see a flash of something in her eyes and I think she knows she hurt me a little with that comment.

"I'll put our bags away." I could do with a few minutes on my own. Just as I put the bags by the old bed, I feel Daisy's hand on my shoulder.

"I'm sorry, Cal, I was only joking."

"I know."

"I can't imagine what your life has been like these past years. I shouldn't mock or judge you for seeking comfort."

"It's okay, I know what it looks like. You picked up a bloody pattern of women, for Christ's sake. It doesn't make me feel good knowing you see me like that."

She cocks her head. "Why does it matter how I see you?"

She's stepped closer to me. Her eyes are boring into me. This is my chance. I should tell her she is, and has been, the only woman for me. I should tell her all the women I slept with never stood a chance, no matter what the circumstances, because none of them ever came close to her. I open my mouth to tell her.

"Cal, get out here, please!" Chris' voice is saturated with anxiety. Shit, what's happened? I race past Daisy and into the living room. Oh, for the love of... Lucia is here, and she looks pissed.

In a too lofty tone, I face her and wave. "Lucia, hi."

What follows is a torrent of Spanish swear words that would make even the most seasoned curser blush. I hear Daisy step behind me. Could this get any worse?

In broken English, Lucia starts another rant. "Don't hi. You give me all the orgasms, make me scream, and then boom, Monica is gone."

Wow, it definitely just got worse. I did give her all the orgasms, and then I did disappear. How the hell am I going to get out of this?

"I cry for a week, Monica," she rambles.

Oh, for fuck's sake. Okay, I'm an arsehole. There I said it.

"Lucia, I am so sorry. It wasn't you. I enjoyed giving you the orgasms. I had to leave, though. It was an emergency." That seems to calm her down a little. "I came back to apologise."

Not strictly true, although there was always the possibility that I would see Lucia, and I would have apologised.

Her face brightens, and she takes a step forward. "Okay, you give me the orgasms again?"

Dear Lord.

Ten
Daisy

I FEEL LIKE I'M in a comedy sketch. Here we are, in a rundown farmhouse in the Spanish mountains, with no hot water, electricity, or heat. We have basic food and only one bed. Add the very irate Spanish woman screaming at Callie, and we've got TV gold.

I have no idea what she said when she first started shouting, but when she slipped into broken English, I fully understood Callie/Monica "gave her all the orgasms." That explains why Callie was acting weird earlier. I'm curious to see how she digs herself out of this very angry Spanish hole.

Placation, that's how. A little I'm sorry, it was me, not you, and all is forgiven. I almost wet myself when Lucia—angry Spanish lady—asks if Callie/Monica will give her "the orgasms" again. I wasn't sure it was possible for

Callie to go as red as her hair, but here we are. Her face is on fire.

Chris is doing a very admirable job of keeping it together, although I can see his shoulders shaking with silent laughter.

"Yeah, Monica, are you going to give her the orgasms again?" he splutters, before losing it completely.

Ah, Chris, you were doing so well.

"Lucia, I am very sorry how I treated you, but I can't give you all the... I can't be with you again. I...I took a vow of celibacy last year."

Is she for fucking real right now? A vow of celibacy! What woman in their right mind would believe that horseshit?

"You really took vows?" Lucia asks. Her rage has vanished from the face of the planet, and I am actually stunned.

"I did. I needed to change my ways, Lucia. I'm just sorry that you got caught up in my selfish ways." Callie is laying it on thick.

"You changed your hair," Lucia states. Lucia is looking at Callie like she hung the fucking moon.

Callie moves a little closer to Lucia. "I went back to my natural hair."

I have to give her credit. She is masterful at what she does. *This* is why Betty had such high hopes for her. Callie could slip into any character she needed to.

"I like it." Lucia takes Callie's hand and squeezes. "How long are you staying for?"

"Just until tomorrow evening. I had planned to come and find you in the morning. I thought my friends would appreciate a tour of the farm whilst I spoke to you."

At the mention of her friends, Lucia finally seems to realise there are other people in the room. She looks at Chris, who has had to turn his back because he can't control himself, and then to me. Her eyes squint at me a little. If I didn't know any better, I would think she is trying to be intimidating. Lucia sees me as a threat to Callie's/Monica's celibacy. I step forward with my hand held out.

"I'm Norma, Monica's aide. I am travelling with her to make sure she stays on the path of righteousness."

Callie's eyes go wide and her nose flares. She does that when she's trying not to laugh. Hell, if she gets to be someone else, why can't I? Lucia nods along like this is the most normal thing in the world.

"Dick is my brother," I say pointing to Chris. He's now got himself under control and shoots me daggers because he now has to go along with the name Dick. I grin at him when Lucia isn't looking.

"Well, thank you for apologising, Monica. I'm proud of you. I would love for you to come along on a tour tomorrow. We can have lunch first."

"That's so kind, Lucia, thank you. Are we okay to stay here for the night?" Callie is back on full charm offensive.

"Of course. I will see you in the morning."

We manage to wait a full minute after Lucia left before bursting into laughter.

"What the hell was that?" Chris blurts. He's clutching his stomach with laughter.

"That was you witnessing 'The Chameleon' in action," I state. "I have to hand it to you, Cal, that was impressive."

Callie's laughter dies down. "I don't enjoy it, you know...fooling people. I never did." Her eyes are so sad my heart aches.

"I know." Jesus, she thinks I'm judging her again. Am I? "I know you, Callie. I know who you are."

"Do you? It's been a long time, Daisy. I wonder if you believe I'm like her."

I know who she's referring to. Callie is worried I think she's turned out to be like Betty. I see Chris out of the corner of my eye. He looks concerned. Mine and Callie's conversation has been completely in sign. He doesn't know what's happening, but I'm sure he knows something is wrong by the looks on our faces.

"You could never be like her, Cal. You are still the Callie I... My best friend."

Well done, Daisy, you nearly bloody told her.

Callie searches my face, then turns to Chris. "Let's sleep. We need to be focused on tomorrow."

She leaves and heads to the bedroom. I smile at Chris and turn to follow her. We lay on the bed fully clothed. It's a warm night, the sun hasn't fully set, and here we are trying to get to sleep. My body has never felt more awake, if I'm truthful. Callie's hurt face is swimming in my mind. I hate I was the one to make her feel that way.

"Callie?" Her back is turned, so I pull at her shoulder. She rolls over and my breath catches. My beautiful Callie has tears streaming down her face. I pull her into me and hold her. "Oh, please don't cry. I'm sorry."

She sniffs and wipes her face. "It's been so hard, Daisy. I never wanted to live like this. I never wanted to hurt anyone, and I hate lying."

"I know, sweetie, I know. I'm sorry if you thought I was judging you, Callie. You are the bravest, sweetest person I have ever known."

She pulls me even closer, and I tighten my grip around her. Callie needs this. She needs to feel the warmth of another person; someone she can be herself with, someone who won't leave.

"I'm here now, Cal. I'm not leaving you again."

The truth in my words hits me hard. I will never leave this woman again. Even if I can only have her as a friend, that will be enough. Callie deserves to have love and safety, and I will give her both of those things. I loosen my grip and she pulls away slightly. I look down at her. In our current positions I am lying slightly on top of her and, boy, does my clit know it.

"Daisy..."

I lose my marbles completely and kiss her. Yep, that's right, after all my bloody gabbing about keeping my feelings to myself, I kiss her, because the way she was looking at me was too much.

Fireworks erupt on my lips the moment they clash with hers. My body surges forward and now I'm fully on top of her. My leg slips in between hers and I'm gone. There is no coming back for me now. I have tasted her, I have felt her velvety lips, and it's game over for me. I fully expect her to push me away at any minute, maybe start shouting at me, but no... She's kissing me back? Hell, she's pushing her tongue against my lips seeking entrance. Come on in, Callie, and welcome to the inside of my mouth. Enjoy!

My hands rake through her gorgeous mane. It's exhilarating, and I scrape my fingers gently across her scalp. I feel the vibration of the moan she just made. She likes it, so I do it again. Her hands grab my arse and squeeze. If neither of us stops this, soon, we will be getting naked.

Neither of us stops it. Her hands have made it to the front of my shorts. She's fiddling with the button and zip. My hands are now heading south for her magnificent breasts. The pressure in my pants is starting to get uncomfortable. I need to climax, and soon.

I pull my head away and look into her eyes. I have to be certain she wants this. The lust radiating from her is palpable, and I don't need any other confirmation than that. I sit up and pull off my top. She does the same. Our bras are next to go, and I'm stunned at her naked chest. She has tiny freckles dotted across her breasts. Her nipples are dark pink and small, just as I imagined them. She is perfection.

My mouth instinctively seeks out her rosy buds. Taking her nipple in my mouth is pure joy. I suck and nibble. Her heart rate has picked up, and she's squirming beneath me. Our hips have started to rock. The friction isn't enough to get me off, but it's doing a great job of building me up. I'm suddenly flipped on to my back. Callie is taking charge.

Her lips and teeth nip and bite my neck. Her hands roam my body, caressing and stroking every bit of skin she can find. I groan when she pinches my nipple. Her mouth is back on mine. Our tongues swirl and fight. This is the hottest thing I have ever experienced, and then it ends. I feel her hesitation before she pulls back. Blue eyes penetrate me, but the lust I saw before is gone. Her breaths are ragged, just like mine. I want to say something, but what?

As quickly as it started, it's over. Callie rolls off of me and grabs her bra and top. She redresses, not once looking at me. My stomach is churning to the point where I might vomit. It's clear to me now I was foolish to kiss her. She doesn't want it, she just got caught up in the moment. Then a surge of embarrassment hits me. What if my moaning turned her off? I know I don't sound like "regular" women. This is probably the first time Callie has been with a deaf woman in that way.

Callie turns to me as she reaches the bedroom door. I'm still laid out with my tits on show, wondering what the hell just happened. She signs "I'm sorry," before leaving the room.

I slept like crap! Callie didn't return to the room. I presume she slept in the car because there wasn't anywhere else she could have gone. Well, she could have sought out Lucia, I guess. Maybe a good shag with someone who doesn't sound weird in bed is what she needed? Can you tell I'm angry and hurt?

There is no time to wallow. We have a job to do. The sun is already blazing down, and I am already sweating. Just a meal to get through and a farm tour, and we can grab the book piece and be on our way. Chris eyes me warily when I come out of the bedroom. He probably heard us last night. The door to the bedroom is made up of four slats with a couple of cross braces—not exactly conducive to privacy.

Callie is nowhere to be seen and I'm not about to ask Chris where she is. There is a granola bar on the table and a bottle of water. Not exactly the breakfast of champions.

I force the birdseed bar down my throat. Drinking half the bottle of water helps it go down easier. God, I fucking *hate* granola!

I take some time to check my laptop in the bedroom. If I really wanted to, I could tell Callie and Chris to retrieve the pages alone. Work would be a better distraction than sitting with Callie and Lucia. I can't, though. I need to be there in case something goes wrong, although what I would do to help is a mystery.

I sigh for the millionth time. My body is restless, and my mind is unsettled. Callie must be back because I can feel two sets of feet padding around in the other room. Well, it's time to face the music. I've decided to act as if last night never happened. I'll be keeping a distance from Callie, though. It's only right. My heart can't stand any more rejection.

Callie and Chris are huddled on the couch when I enter the room. I'm ready to go to lunch. I don't want to hang about. Callie gives me a tentative smile, which I return, but I know it doesn't reach my eyes. I'm trying.

"Ready to go?" I ask them both. Two heads nod. God, this is awkward.

We take the car to the farm. It would have been easy to walk, but the heat is already climbing to an uncomfortable level. Plus, if we need to make a quick run for it, we need the car close by.

Lucia is waiting for us by the door to a lovely farmhouse. She greets us with a warm smile and a hug. There doesn't seem to be anything between Callie and Lucia that indicates they shared a bed last night. I'm sure Lucia would be thanking Callie for "all the orgasms" if that had been the case.

The food is delicious. Fresh, authentic tapas are one of my ultimate favourite foods. I temporarily forget my worries as I stuff croquetas in my mouth. Callie and Lucia talk politely, catching up. Of course, every word that comes out of Callie's/Monica's mouth is pure fabrication. Finally, the time comes to go on the tour. How much is there to see, really? It's a field of trees, for God's sake.

Callie forgot to mention we would be taking donkeys up a sodding mountain. There are eight of them lined up outside the house. Normally, I would steadfastly refuse to use one of these poor creatures. I find it appalling that animals are still used for this kind of thing. In this heat, no animal should be made to carry our fat arses around. We should walk, but I can't voice all that today. Our mission has to take priority. I do, however, ask that water is made readily available. Lucia looks at me like I'm an alien. I don't care. Eeyore isn't going to collapse on my watch.

My donkey, who I have called Enrico, is a very chill guy. He's happy to plod along, following the lead donkey, Maria. I also named her. Callie doesn't get a monopoly on naming things. At least I name living creatures, not just cars and kitchen furniture. Okay, that's bitchy, but I'm pissed. She's acting like nothing is wrong—which I know I said I was going to do too, but that's not the point.

I subtly look over my shoulder. Coincidentally, Lucia's ride is linked to Callie's via a tack. Not in a line, but side by side. How the hell are we supposed to slip away now?

Eleven

Callie

WHAT A HEAP OF steaming shit! I want to punch myself in the face repeatedly. How could I have been so selfish? My go-to method when I'm feeling vulnerable is to fuck my way back to some feeling of normalcy. That's what I've been doing all these years, but I never thought I would do that with Daisy.

Yes, she kissed me, and that will need some processing, but I took it further. My libido and default method took over, and I almost ruined something special. Daisy is not a woman you shag because you're feeling a bit down and need a pick-me-up. Daisy Simpson deserves to be cherished and shown love.

It took everything in my power to pull away from her. I always assumed if I ever got to kiss her, it would be wonderful. Wow! I underestimated what kissing her would feel like. Think of every overused cliché to describe a kiss, and that's what it was! But I had to stop it. I didn't want my first time with Daisy to be in a run-down farmhouse, whilst on the run, and with Chris just an earshot away. Let's not forget the fact, that just a few minutes before, I had to deal with Lucia.

She was the reason I felt so shitty in the first place. Well, my deceit and behaviour towards Lucia were the reasons, but that's just semantics. I was mortified having to lie my way out of the situation with Lucia. I can't even imagine what Daisy thinks. She said she would never judge me, but shit, how could she not?

When I left her half naked on that bed, I wanted to break down in tears. Chris had shot me a bemused look when I came out of the room. He'd obviously heard us, but his smirk soon fell when he saw my expression, which must have shown a mix of pain and frustration. I couldn't stick around and talk to him. I wanted to run as far, and as fast, as I could, but I only ended up a few metres away in the back seat of the car for the night.

My poor bloody back protested wildly the next morning. My head felt heavy, like I'd been out on the lash, when really, I was just feeling the weight of my shame. It was an effort to walk back to the house. For all I knew, Daisy was going to slap me as soon as she saw me. Looking back at it now, I can't believe I left with only an "I'm sorry."

I mean, what the fuck, Callie.

I offered her no explanation at all. God knows what she was thinking. Daisy acted like her usual self... Well, to everyone who doesn't know her as well as I do, she was normal. I knew I'd hurt her. She wasn't cold, but there was a definite edge to her body language. I would have to sit her down and talk to her properly, but couldn't right then. We needed to meet Lucia, and grab the book pages.

My perfect, simple plan is already going down the shitter! Here I am, straddling a donkey, which is literally attached to Lucia. There is no possible way I can sneak off. Daisy is at the head of the group, so she's out. Our only hope is Chris, who seems to be having an issue with his steed. I notify Lucia that our young companion is falling behind.

Lucia gives Chris a cursory glance before snapping her attention back to me. "Don't worry, he is on Teddy. That donkey never keeps up. He will arrive okay, just a little late."

I look back at Chris and give him a salute, which is our signal. Before meeting Lucia, the three of us came up with the salute as a way to indicate that the person receiving it had to take the lead on retrieving the book piece. I told both

Daisy and Chris where the tree was and specifically, where the pages were hidden. The success of the plan is down to Chris now. I encourage Lucia to talk. Engaging her is the best way for Chris to be left unnoticed. Thank Christ for the slow donkey, Teddy.

The trek around the orchard seems to be a hell of a lot longer than I remembered it being. Daisy hasn't looked back once, and it's kind of screwing with me. I just want to know what's going on in that wonderful mind of hers.

Sweat is pouring out of every part of my body. The sun is relentless and after a few grumbles from the group, we stop under a large tree to hydrate. Lucia leaves me and goes to speak to some of the other members of the party. This is my chance to talk to Daisy, who has dismounted her steed and is leaning up against the trunk of the tree, wiping sweat from her brow. She looks like a model from a Coke advert.

"Hey."

She watches me with a look I can't decipher. There is a chance she will still deck me.

"Hi," she replies.

Okay, still a little stiff, but I'll persevere. "Can we talk about last night?"

"No, it's fine, I get it."

That confuses the hell out of me. What does she get?

"What do you get?" I need to make sure she hasn't come to a wrong conclusion. My gut feeling is she has.

"Callie, can we not? I'm embarrassed enough as it is."

"Why are you embarrassed? It was me who was in the wrong."

She looks away from me, eyes shimmering. Oh shit, she's going to cry, and it's all my fault. We're interrupted by Lucia before we can continue.

"I think we have to go back for your friend. He is still not here, and we need to continue the tour."

Right, Chris. I look at my watch. He's had twenty minutes to get the pages. I hope he has them. I really don't want to spend any more time here.

I mount Daryl. He's my donkey. When I'm about to turn back to look for Chris, we hear a donkey bray and Chris shouting expletives. Around the corner trots Teddy, followed by a dusty and red Chris.

"Mate, ride the donkey, don't walk it." He doesn't appreciate my attempt at humour.

"Teddy is an arsehole!" he shouts. I laugh, because Teddy clearly looks amused with himself, so yeah, he's an arsehole. Wouldn't you be, though, if you had to spend your day in the heat, ferrying people around? "He wouldn't walk, then as soon as I got off, he bolted. Every time I got close, he buggered off."

Daisy is beside herself laughing. Teddy is braying like he's the funniest thing on four legs. Lucia is rolling her eyes, and all I want to know, is if he did what needed to be done. His salute back confirms he did. Now I can laugh, and mock him endlessly.

We are all grateful when we arrive back at Lucia's. I spend ten minutes saying goodbye, apologising again for how things were left between us. Now, it's just the three of us again in the car, heading north.

"I put the pages in my backpack. Do you want them?" Chris says. He's talking to me. I shake my head. "Okay cool. Where to next?" I think the tension between Daisy and me is getting to him.

"Italy," I say, but don't elaborate. It's going to take us a full twenty-four hours to get there, and that's if we continually drive. I need to pick somewhere for us to stop and I need to get Daisy alone so we can talk. "We'll need to stop for the night. It's too far to drive in one go. Chris, can you check for a place to stay as we cross the border into France?"

"On it."

That will keep him busy for a moment. The problem with me driving, is that I can't sign to Daisy. I can't turn to face her either, so lip-reading for her is harder, right now. Did she catch what I said to Chris? Does she understand we're going to Italy? I keep sneaking looks at her, hoping she is looking back. She isn't. Her gaze hasn't left the passenger side window. This is going to be a long trip.

Five hours in, and I am seriously flagging. The morning, and lunch with Lucia, have taken their toll. Right now, all I want, is to hide away on my own for a little while. But that's not a possibility. I check the GPS. We are a couple of hours away from Valencia. We'll stop there for the night. I wanted to make it over the border, hence asking Chris to sort out a place to stay, but I can't. I need to be alone.

There is a petrol station just ahead. I swing the car into the parking space and let my head fall back. Daisy and Chris have both been asleep for the past hour and a half, which helped my mental state. I stretch my arms and exit the car. We don't need gas, but I need to pee and work out the kinks in my legs.

No line to the loo is my first bit of luck today. I relieve myself and then splash water on my face after washing my hands. My reflection shows the bags under my eyes. Thanks to the bathroom lighting, I look like a fucking ghoul. Whatever. It's not like I need to impress anyone. I just need a good night's sleep. Two hours more; I can do that.

Back at the car, I unload the extra provisions I've just bought. Chris has done an excellent job of eating everything in sight. He's like a bloody goat. I'm starting to worry for the car upholstery. I can't have him gnawing on the furniture, so here I am, with an armful of food, hoping it satisfies his appetite. Remind me to never have kids. Christ, they cost a fortune.

Chris is snoring in the back seat. Daisy is fully awake, looking at me intensely as I slide into the driver's seat. "Let me drive for a while." She isn't asking me. I look at her, wanting to argue for some reason. I always drive; it's my job. "Callie, you look exhausted. Let me drive." Her hand slips into mine and she squeezes. I nod. What's the point of arguing?

"Stop in Valencia. We can grab a motel for the night. It's been a long day for everyone." She nods, unbuckling her seatbelt to trade places with me.

It's been half an hour since Daisy took over the driving duties. I want to rest my head and sleep, but I can't. My mind won't settle. I fiddle with the radio until it lands on a soft jazz station. Now I can feel Daisy's eyes on me every so often. Is she upset with me? Probably. Will she listen to me? I hope so.

"Where are we?" Chris's sleepy voice pulls me out of my never-ending cycle of questions. I check the SatNav again.

"Nearly in Valencia. We're going to stop soon."

"M'kay." His head hits the headrest again, and he's out. I chuckle. Daisy flips the indicator on to turn off the highway. She's spotted a motel that will suffice for the evening. It doesn't have to be posh.

The rooms are everything you expect of a cheap motel. Thank God there were three single rooms available. I think I would have lost my shit if I were forced to share with Daisy again.

We all mumble a tired "good night" to each other after agreeing to meet by the car at 8:30 a.m. I sling my bag down and head for the bathroom. The shower is surprisingly powerful, and I stand under it until I prune. The bed is calling me, like a siren, when I finish in the bathroom. My head hits the pillow and I slip into a vivid dream.

My phone wakes me up. Every part of my body hurts. I need to move and get the blood pumping. The fitness app on my phone hasn't seen much action lately—a bit like me. Time to crack it open and get my heart rate up.

Twenty sweaty minutes later, I sit on the bed with a terrible motel-room coffee. I should be drinking water to rehydrate after my workout, but my brain still feels tired. The caffeine is needed, even if the beverage tastes like shit.

The motel doesn't provide breakfast, but there is a restaurant next door. It's only 7:45 a.m., so I have time to grab a decent meal. The road trip food has long lost its allure. My skin will thank me for eating something healthy.

The restaurant is nearly full, but I manage to get a table. The waiter pours me a large coffee and gives me the menu. I already know what I'll have: a Spanish omelette. The bell over the door jingles. Daisy walks in, her eyes on me. I wave her over. Before I overthink, I shoot a message to Chris, asking him to give Daisy and me a chance to talk. I tell him I'll get him some breakfast. He returns my message with a thumbs up.

We sit in silence for a minute. The waiter asks Daisy what she would like. She looks at me for help.

"Do you want an omelette?" She nods. I order for her and wait until the waiter has moved away. "Can we talk?"

"About?"

God, she is infuriating sometimes.

"About our make-out session the other night." I'm done fucking about. I can't stand the atmosphere between us.

"What's to talk about? You changed your mind, or you didn't like what you heard. It's fine, you're not the first hearing person to freak out."

I honestly have no idea what she is talking about. Why wouldn't I like what I heard? She was sexy as hell, moaning under me, and her breasts were something from...well, my fantasies, I suppose.

"What do you mean? Why wouldn't I like what I heard?"

Her face has flushed, and I can see how badly she wants this conversation to end, but it can't—not until we are okay.

She massages her forehead. "Look, I know I sound funny when... I can't control how I sound when I'm turned on like that. It's okay if my voice freaked you out. I'm just upset you left."

"What are you talking about? I left because my first time with you, Daisy, wasn't going to be in a musty farm house after I'd just had a breakdown. You deserve more than that." I shake my head. I can't believe she thought that's why I stopped things. "You sounded sexy as fuck. It took everything I had to pull away. You're not just some girl, you're Daisy—*my* Daisy."

My heart is pounding in my ears. I just overshared, didn't I?

Saved by the Spanish omelette. The waiter puts our breakfast down and I ask him to add another order, to go, for Chris. My face is hot, and I can't look at her. The fork I have just picked up is shaking. I feel her hand rest on mine, stilling it. Her eyes are imploring me to look at her. I can feel them on my skin. Daisy is one of the most expressive people I know. Her eyes and face can tell you everything she is thinking, without a word or hand sign.

I close my eyes and take a deep breath, before raising my head to meet her gaze. What I see in her eyes steals the oxygen from my lungs.

Twelve

Daisy

I'M A MIXED BAG of emotions. Callie has just told me I'm *her* Daisy. She also said I sounded "sexy as fuck" when I moaned. That's the first time anyone has ever said that and I believe her. The look in her eyes tells me everything I need to know. Now it's my turn. I need to be brave.

She has no idea how crazy I am for her. Even with all the years that have passed between us, my heart runs right back to Callie. We have a lot of catching up to do. Her life has been anything but ordinary, and I know going through everything she has will have changed her. But I know, no matter what, I will always want her.

"And you're *my* Callie." Her eyes widen at my statement. "You were right to stop us. I didn't like it at the time. I thought my voice disturbed you." She goes to speak, so I hold my hand up to stop her. "What we did the other night was something I've wanted since we were teens. I never thought it would happen, though."

"Really?"

I have to chuckle because her eyes are *so* wide.

"Yes, really. Look, we are in a really fucked up situation right now. We haven't seen each other in a decade, and it would be too easy for me to go all in with you. But I can't... Not yet. We have to finish this thing and bring you home. Then, I want us to try, if that's what you want too?"

There. I've put it all out on the line. I've had time to think, really think, since Callie walked out of that bedroom. Being with her would be a dream come true, but my logical, reasonable brain has kicked in. Starting a relationship under these conditions would be an error. It's not real life. Okay, for Callie, this has been her life for years, but it won't be her life forever. I have a life and a job to go back to. Callie will need to rebuild herself and find her home, wherever that might be.

Jumping into bed with her would be fantastic, I'm sure. But I can't do that without the emotions that come along with sex. I've done it for every other liaison I've had because they didn't mean anything to me, but I couldn't switch my feelings off with Callie. The most important thing right now is that she is back in my life.

"Okay, so what do you want to do now? Because honestly, now I know you feel the same as me. I'm struggling not to bend you over this table and have my way with you."

Her admission makes me blush, and I hope no one near us can understand sign language.

"Callie!" I admonish.

She laughs, then grows serious. "Daisy, I meant what I said earlier. I was joking about the table... Kind of. You are special and I want it to be done right."

I'm not sure what "it" means. "So let me clarify... Is it sex or more you want?"

I have to get straight to the point. We both need to be crystal clear about what is happening between us.

"So much more, Daisy. If we get together, it's for real. But I get what you're saying, too. We *are* in a God-awful mess right now and we need to focus on that problem first," she answers.

"Okay, but now I can openly ogle your bum, yeah?" I smirk. Honestly, I ogle her perfect arse every chance I get. She barks out a laugh. My smile broadens, because watching Callie laugh is the best.

"Ogle away." She winks at me, and I thank all the deities I'm sitting down, because holy hell, that wink slays me. "Can I just hold your hand for a minute?"

The vulnerability on her face knocks me back. I slide my hand onto the tabletop and wait for her to take it. She caresses my hand with her own. We sit for several minutes just looking at each other, our Spanish omelettes forgotten. Our moment is obliterated by a very panicked looking Chris, who runs into the restaurant flushed.

"We have to go, now!"

I look at Callie. My surprise mirrors hers.

"What's wrong?" Callie asks, dragging Chris into the chair next to her.

"There was a guy snooping around your door. At first, I thought he might have just got the wrong room, but I watched him try to pick the lock."

"Fuck. Did he get in?" Callie's eyes are furiously scanning the restaurant.

"No, the housekeeper came round the corner with her trolley before he could crack the lock. He scarpered, but I doubt he went far."

"Fuck, fuck, fuck." Callie's face is pinched.

My breathing is rapid. I've never really been in danger before. My line of work has some risks associated with it, but nothing like this. Callie has her head in her hands.

"Callie?" I need to know she's okay. If anyone can get us out of here, it's her.

Chris looks at me. He needs reassurance, but I can't give it to him. I have to get back to the room. I can't leave my laptop.

Suddenly Callie raises her head. "Okay, kids, this is what we're going to do."

There's the Callie I know. She looks confident and sure. Now I can start to relax a little.

"Chris, how are you at starting fires?" she asks.

"No idea. Never tried, but I'll give it a bash!"

"Good enough. Daisy, how do you feel about being a maid?"

My head goes to a very inappropriate vision of me as a maid, servicing Callie. *Not helpful, Daisy.*

"I'm game." I'll do whatever is necessary to get us out of this situation. Dressing up as a maid isn't really that bad.

"Okay, first you need to acquire a uniform. The housekeeper will be moving from room to room. As soon as she's done, the bloke will probably try again. I need you there to keep him away." I nod. "Chris, you need to start a small fire at the back of the kitchens. That way, it will get noticed quickly. It has to be big enough to call the fire brigade. I don't want to cause damage, but we don't have much choice."

"What will you do?" I ask. Is she going to do something dangerous?

"I have two jobs. First, I need to get eyes on this guy and try to figure out if he's alone. Second, I will break into our rooms from the bathroom windows. They are woefully unsecured. Once I have our things, we'll meet at the back of the restaurant."

"Okay." Chris has a look of determination on his face. "Why do we need the fire brigade here if you're just going to break in through the back?"

"We need everyone to be kept back. The fire department will set up a perimeter. Whoever is here will have to wait until the fire is cleared. It will take roughly five minutes for the fire brigade to arrive—"

"How do you know that?" I ask.

"I checked last night. It's always a good idea to know response times of the services. You never know when you might need their help."

Can you imagine living your life like this? It's second nature for her to figure this kind of shit out. I would bet everything I own, she already had several plans ready to go, in case this happened before we even arrived last night.

"Okay, let's go. Chris, get that fire started as soon as you can. Remember, it has to be big enough a fire extinguisher won't be able to douse it. Be careful, and make sure no one can get hurt. Got it?"

"Got it." With that, he leaves.

"Daisy, put your hair up in a bun. If they caught sight of you this morning, they would have seen you with your hair down. Don't do it until you're in the motel, though. I doubt he, or they, will be waiting inside. It's likely they're in a car. I'll spot them easy enough. The maids will keep their uniforms in the staff room. You have to get in and out of there quickly and then get to our rooms."

"Be careful, Callie." I lean over and kiss her on the cheek. There isn't enough time for sentimental feelings. Chris will be getting the fire going soon, and I need to do my job for Callie. I walk out of the restaurant, careful not to look like I'm scouring the area for some douchebag man-hunter.

Callie was right. There isn't anyone in the foyer when I enter the motel. Hell, there isn't anyone anywhere, or any cameras. I swiftly check around me, before pushing through to the staff room. It's the only door marked *Private*. An educated guess that turns out to be correct.

The room is dingy. Five lockers rest against the back wall, with a small table surrounded by mismatched chairs in the middle. To the left is a kitchenette with a fridge. Now I just hope there is an open locker which also contains a uniform. Unsurprisingly, the lockers are broken. I raid each one until I find the dishwater-grey dress I've seen the maids wear. Not quite the fantasy I first had when Callie suggested I take on the role.

I put my hair up in a bun using a beige hair tie I find in the same locker as the uniform. I cringe as I put it in my hair. *Please, please, please don't let me get lice.* The thought makes me shudder and I almost rip it out. Once I have my gag reflex under control, I grab a maid's cart. The people who work here really don't give a shit about protecting the motel's property.

If Callie was taking on the role of "hard-working maid" as I am, I know she would do a much better and more convincing job than me. Maybe I should have swapped tasks. In fact, I definitely should have. *I'm* the one who can go about unnoticed. Callie is the actor. Shit, I'm going to screw this up.

Something is off. Callie would know she's the better choice to go undercover. Why did she give me the job? She sent Chris away too.

Crap, she's going to leave us. If I know one thing, it's that Callie Compton would never put the people she cares about in danger. Someone being here, getting this close, qualifies as Chris and me being in danger. I think she plans to lure them away, leaving us behind. Not a fucking chance—not if I have anything to say about it.

Ignoring what Callie told me to do, I head back to the restaurant. Callie is gone, but I can smell smoke in the air. The alarm in the restaurant is wailing and people are filing out into the parking lot. I turn to see several motel guests leaning out of their doors, trying to see what's going on. There are sirens in the distance. Callie was right. The emergency services will get here quickly.

Chris runs up behind me, grabbing my elbow and making me shriek. In all the chaos, I've lost my bearings. Where is Callie?

"What are you doing?" Chris asks, looking slightly petrified at the commotion around us. He must be scared. I am.

"I think Callie is going to do something stupid." And it would be stupid. We all need to stick together, but Callie is used to doing things on her own.

"What do you mean?"

I go to answer, but I'm stopped by a firefighter ushering us away from the buildings. Two engines have arrived, and there are so many people I'm starting to feel claustrophobic. The firefighter pushes us through the crowd until we are free from everyone. My heart rate spikes because the firefighter is still leading us away. Soon, we will be out of sight. Fuck, I think we are being kidnapped.

"Don't worry, I'm not kidnapping you." Who knew Spanish firefighters could sign?

Hang on. I bring myself to a stop, grabbing the helmet of the person who is leading us to a motorhome. Callie's beautiful face is beaming back at me when the helmet and face mask are removed.

"Hey you two, nice job." She sticks her thumbs up at us both.

My body is feeling a lot of things right now: relief we are not actually being kidnapped, anger because Callie didn't tell me the whole plan, anxiety over this fucked-up situation, and lust. That's right. Lust! Callie Compton, in a fucking firefighter uniform, is a lesbian's wet dream.

Callie is stripping away the uniform, one article at a time. If I carried cash in notes, I would be sticking them down her trousers right now. Am I dribbling?

"Jump in the camper. We need to go," she says, ripping me out of my fantasy. "Daisy?"

Callie is waving in front of my face with a grin. Shit, she caught me staring. Chris has noticed too, if his smirk is anything to go by. I roll my eyes. Whatever. I own my lusting, thank you very much!

I point to the RV. "Whose vehicle is this?"

There's no way we are *stealing* a bloody camper van. The door to said vehicle swings open. Out step two of the most ordinary people I have ever seen. They have to be English. I imagine their house is beige and full of doilies.

"Ah, Laura, you're back," the man with the beige cardigan and comb-over says, talking to Callie.

Must remember her name is Laura now.

"Derek, thanks so much for this. We owe you big time."

Derek; of course that's his name. What does she mean "we owe him."

What is happening?

"This is my girlfriend, Poppy, and my little brother, Bobby."

I struggle to not glare at her.

"It's lovely to meet you all, and I'm very sorry to hear about your troubles. Not to worry though, we'll get you to safety."

I am completely lost.

"Oh, aren't you pretty?" The beige woman is talking to me now. I smile and thank her. She notices my voice. "Oh, are you deaf, dear?"

"Meryl, that's not very polite," Derek says.

"I'm sorry, I didn't mean to offend."

Alright, I'm over this already.

"No offence taken." I put on my most polite voice.

"Do you think we could go, Derek? I'm not feeling great about sticking around much longer." Callie has taken a step forward, backing Derek and Meryl into their van. Chris follows. He's been silent throughout it all. I'm the last one to board.

The vehicle is one of those huge motorhomes, the ones that are the size of a coach. Sure enough, every surface has a doily on it. I smirk to myself. Meryl sits us down on the sofas. Derek climbs up front and settles into the driver's seat. In a few seconds, the RV roars to life, and we're off.

Meryl pats Callie's arm. "I'll put the kettle on. You all relax."

Thankfully, the kitchen is at the other end of the vehicle. I turn to Callie and raise my eyebrows in question.

"Derek and Meryl think we're on the run from our homophobic dad. I told them he found us, and I was worried what he would do if he got hold of us."

Smart.

"How the hell did you know that would work?" Chris asks. He must be whispering because he's got closer to us both and has hunched his back. He clearly doesn't want to be overheard.

"They have a rainbow flag in the back window. I spotted it last night. This morning, I heard them talking in the restaurant. They're nice people. My gut said they would help us." Callie glances at Meryl to make sure she's not in earshot. "It's better we tell them something as close to the truth as possible. That way, it's not difficult to keep track of the story."

She's right. We are being tracked and we would be in danger if we were caught, so we aren't lying, really.

Honestly, I don't care what story we have to spin, as long as we are safe and together.

Thirteen

Callie

THAT ALL WENT PRETTY well! Nothing like a good escape from danger to get the blood pumping. It chaps my ass I didn't get to finish my Spanish omelette. Why can't bad guys be more considerate? Like, I know you have a job to do, evil goon, but at least wait until I've had my coffee and breakfast.

To Daisy and Chris, the situation probably seemed pretty dangerous, but in all honesty, I'd had a "planned get away" from the moment we arrived at the motel last night. It comes naturally to me now, to scope a place out and have an extraction plan ready.

It was unsettling to see Chris so worked up when he came into the restaurant. The poor kid looked scared to death. As for Daisy, well, she looked concerned, but not overly panicked. I like to think she had faith in me to get us out of it.

For a moment, I considered sending Daisy and Chris far from me while I lured whoever was after us away. I can't stand the thought of them in danger. The thing is, though, I need them... Not just because they're both helping me get the book, but because I can't be on my own again. Not now.

While Chris and Daisy set off to do their part in the plan, I did mine. That involved me slinking out another toilet window. I hate that is becoming my thing. It's not very James Bond, is it? Anyway, it took me all of five seconds to spot the guy who was looking for us. It wasn't a nephew, that was for sure. This guy was a professional, but I'd wager, new to the job. Someone should let him know, sitting in his car with a pair of binoculars is a dead giveaway.

It took me ninety seconds to break into our rooms. I like to time these things; it keeps it entertaining. Thankfully, we are all travelling light. I stashed our stuff and moved on to the next stage of the plan.

I'd already banked on Daisy ignoring my instructions. She's too cerebral, and I knew she would think I was going to do a runner, leaving them behind. I just needed her out of the way and safe, for a little while. I can't get us to safety if my head is worried about her.

Once I'd identified Captain Obvious in his spy wagon, and got our belongings, I approached Derek and Meryl. It's true what I said to Daisy. I had spotted their motorhome last night. This morning, before I spoke to Daisy, I happened to overhear them talking. They're the kind of people that any gay person could only wish to have as parents. Derek was discussing their son and his upcoming nuptials with his boyfriend. He spoke with so much pride, I nearly welled up. That's when I knew they could be our saving grace.

My initial plan was to get us away from the motel and hitchhike. The car was burned. Whoever the guy was, I'm sure he would have noted the make, model, and licence plate of our rental. Stowing away in a luxury motorhome definitely seemed like a better idea than thumbing it across Spain. So, in that moment, I became Laura, a runaway lesbian with her girlfriend and little brother, trying to outrun our evil father. I hope Chris doesn't mind I stole his story.

Derek and Meryl hadn't hesitated when I asked them for help. I bet they would be the type of people to show up at a gay wedding and walk the groom or bride down the aisle in lieu of their absent, homophobic parents.

Chris had done a fab job with the fire. He'd made sure the bin he lit up was far enough away from the building there was no major danger, but it was big enough the restaurant couldn't put it out by themselves. As soon as smoke started clogging the air, our mystery man gave all his attention to it, just like I wanted.

The firefighters turned up much quicker than I expected. I hedged my bets I could get a spare uniform from one of the rigs. I entered chameleon mode and slipped in without anyone noticing.

How did you dress so quickly? I hear you ask. Well, I had a fabulous long weekend with a firefighter a few months ago and we did a lot of role play. I can don the uniform just as quickly as a professional, now. And thank God, because Daisy didn't leave me much time. I'd just finished putting the trousers on when I saw her exit the motel in the world's worst maid outfit. Seriously, all my fantasies went right out the window.

Chris wasn't far behind, so I got into character. No one stops a firefighter to check credentials when there is an emergency. A quick look over at Captain Obvious told me he was distracted by the chaos. That allowed me to get to Daisy and Chris. I need to have a word about their

"Stranger Danger" awareness. Neither of them questioned being whisked away.

Derek and Meryl knew to expect us. I hadn't filled them in on the plan, just that I would create a distraction and would meet them at the motorhome. As far as escapes go, it wasn't very complex or dangerous. My adrenaline did spike, but nothing to get my knickers in a twist about. Hopefully, we would be far away by the time the dude in the car realised we're not there.

Back to our current situation and this beast of a van. The first thing I'm going to buy when I'm home, is an RV. They are fucking awesome. Derek and Meryl have everything they could ever need. It's a literal house on wheels. According to Meryl, there are two double bedrooms and a single, a full bathroom with an add-on to the master suite, a beautiful kitchen area, and a lounge section sporting a fifty-inch TV and motorised recliners. This thing must've cost a friggin' fortune.

"Here we go. A nice pot of tea to settle everyone down," Meryl chirps. She busied herself with tea making whilst I filled in Daisy and Chris about what had just happened. They seem to be happy enough to go along with my story.

"Meryl, thank you so much." I really am grateful there are still such good people in the world.

"Oh, no need to keep thanking us, dear. As long as you're safe, that's all that matters. Now, you and Poppy can have the second double room. Bobby can take the single. We're heading for Italy, so feel free to stay with us as long as you need."

Fucking perfect! Finally, we're catching a break. Touch wood, we can stay with Derek and Meryl all the way to Italy.

"May I use the bathroom?" Daisy asks.

"Of course, love," Meryl shouts. I need to talk to her about that. Daisy nods and heads to the back of the bus.

"Meryl, you don't need to shout. She won't be able to hear you, but she can read your lips. I can even try to teach you some sign if you like?"

"Really? Oh, that would be wonderful. I'm sorry if I'm upsetting her," she replies sincerely.

I pat the seat next to me and she sits down. "Let's start with your name."

I take her through her name in sign. Chris has perked up, too. Maybe a sign language lesson is a good way for us all to decompress. Daisy exits the bathroom and stops. She has a slight blush on her face. I wish she didn't feel as if someone learning to speak to her was something to feel embarrassed about.

Meryl beams like a floodlight when she turns to Daisy and signs her name. Daisy smiles widely and sits with us. For the first time in all the years of knowing Daisy, she actually participates in teaching. Maybe that's who she is now? Someone proud of her differences. I hope so. She did the right thing leaving ten years ago. It gave her a chance to find her confidence, and I love that.

We're two hours in and Derek announces he's pulling over to stretch his legs. I'm hoping that some food is going to be on offer, because I could eat a scabby horse. No one wants to see a hangry Callie.

I spend a few minutes with Derek discussing our location. Right now, we are just outside a town called Amposta. Another hour and a half and we will be near Barcelona. I don't love that we are close to Barcelona, not after being there not so long ago. Derek assures me we won't be stopping again until we hit the French border. I'm fine with that.

Now we are safe, I want to talk to Daisy. We have a conversation to finish. Before that though, I need food. Meryl saves the day with a plate full of sandwiches. Chris starts to salivate, and I laugh, because I have seen that lad eat. Meryl will need a few more loaves of bread if she's going to keep up with his metabolism and appetite.

Daisy screws her face up after taking a bite of a cheese sandwich. I laugh again because there is only one thing that makes her pull that face, and it's Marmite. She is a hater, whereas I am a firm lover of the black goo. Naturally, she hands the rest of it to me to finish. It's almost as if no time has passed and we're teens again, sharing our lunch.

Millie, the motorhome, is parked across two bays at the rest stop in Delta de l'Ebre National Park. We all fill our lungs with some fresh air. It feels really good to have a breather. My mind wanders back to the discussion I had with Daisy this morning. I understand she doesn't want to start anything just yet, but, my God, I can't help but think about it.

Daisy Simpson is into me, and has been since we were teens. Talk about breaking news! I could kick myself. If I had just told her back then, we could have been together. She would have been my first and only. Yeah, yeah, I know everyone will bleat on about young love never lasting and all that crap, but I know in my very essence, she was put on this earth to be with me.

I want her in every way, especially biblically. Daisy is hot, and she wants to ogle my bum. Her words, not mine.

Or did *I* say that? Whatever. Ogling will happen, and if I get my way, so will some much-needed sexy times. Let's see what happens when we share a room tonight.

The sun is shining, and there is a light breeze. Derek is off taking photos with Chris. That makes me smile. Chris needs it. I think he's been starved of enough love to last him a lifetime. Good man, Derek! Daisy and Meryl are setting up the rest of the sandwiches on a picnic table. It looks like Meryl raided Tesco before setting off. Ooh, she bought Quavers!

When Chris is done taking photos, I will check in with him. He was really quiet after the whole restaurant fire thing and I'm worried. This is probably all too much. Maybe I could speak to Derek and Meryl, ask if he can stay with them for a while? Cheeky, considering we hardly know them and they're already doing so much for us, but hell, you have to be cheeky sometimes, especially if it involves protecting your family and Chris is a part of my new family.

Now that the adrenaline has worn off, my arm aches. I wasn't as graceful getting out of the restaurant toilet window as I thought. I have a graze on my elbow, and it's slightly puffy. Blood has stained my T-shirt, which is a pain in the ass. I only have so many clothes to wear. I'll clean myself up later.

Meryl has put on a great spread. She's made enough sandwiches to feed an army, or one Chris. Daisy has relaxed now. I think Meryl's attempt at sign broke through some of her walls. The two of them are chatting away like crazy. Chris and Derek are in a heated discussion about The Wombles. I don't even want to know.

I finish off the last of the cheese and Marmite sandwiches. I could do with five minutes on my own to decompress. It's a bizarre feeling being surrounded by people again. Daisy looks at me as I get up from the bench. I let her know I'm going to have a quick walk. She doesn't try to follow.

Breathing exercises have always worked for me. Deep breath in, count to five... Slow breath out, count to eight.

Alright, Callie, time to figure out how the hell that guy found us!

Actually, what I should be trying to work out is *who* the guy was. If he wasn't a nephew, then there is someone else involved now. I'm stumped if I know who. It's possible one of Betty's business partners is sending their own henchmen. She hasn't exactly done a fab job of finding me herself.

My Spidey sense tells me it's something else; something I haven't considered. I should talk to Daisy. She's the one who is good at thinking outside of the box. Chris too, actually. He's proven to be a very smart cookie.

We have to work it out soon. It's no good changing locations if we're going to be found each time. Daisy needs to do a sweep of all her electronics again. Could it be Chris that is being followed? He told me he's switched his phone off, but is that sufficient? I have no clue.

The walk has helped a little, but not enough. Bypassing my comrades, I enter Millie—yes, I snigger at my own dirty thought—to take a quick shower. Meryl was quick to tell us we should treat the place like home. I'm not going to argue. I need to clean my cut and put on some fresh clothes. For a motorhome, the water pressure is pretty good. I don't want to use up all the hot water, though, so I'm quick.

The bedroom I will be sharing with Daisy is nice. The bed is a little smaller than a double, but it looks comfy. My duffle is on the floor. I rummage around, taking everything out and placing it on the bed. Finally, I find a pair of pants and a bra. I successfully have underwear on, and I'm putting everything back in my bag, when I hear the door behind me open, and then close. I turn around to find Daisy staring at me, eyes wide, and blushing. That's when I look at the items in my hand.

Fourteen

Daisy

CALLIE IS STANDING IN the bedroom in her underwear, clutching a dildo and a tube of Durex Sensitive lube. I have lost all cognitive function. Black lace, creamy skin, and a dildo. Am I hallucinating? Doubtful. If I were, Callie wouldn't be staring at me with such a panicked look on her face. We just stand gawping at each other. Seconds tick by and we're still staring.

I can think of only one reason she is standing there in underwear, holding a dildo, and now I feel bad, because I've clearly interrupted her "alone time." I'm no stranger to self-servicing; a girl's got needs, you know. If Callie needed a bit of time to decompress with her silicone buddy, who am I to judge? I just don't know how to extricate myself from this very awkward and silent moment.

I'd only come into the room to check my laptop. I wanted to do another security sweep on it. Plus, I should contact my boss. My job still needs doing, even if it is from the road. Jesus, why am I babbling on about that? Callie Compton is standing in front of me with a fucking dildo and I haven't said one word. I clear my throat because it's as dry as Penny's Victoria sponge cake.

"I...I'm sorry, I'll just..." I hook my thumb over my shoulder to indicate I'm going to leave her to it.

"It's not what you think." She practically throws her toy on the bed behind her and grabs a T-shirt. That's disappointing.

"It's none of my business." But oh, how I want it to be.

"I was just trying to find some clothes in my duffel, and I was re-packing when you came in. You have the worst timing," she chuckles.

At least it's not so tense in here anymore. My eyes wander to the toy. I can't help it. She catches me and smiles. But this smile is devilish in the most delicious of ways.

It was only this morning we said we would wait before trying to be more than friends. Now, at this moment, I want to forget I ever thought those words. My body is at odds with my rational brain.

My body wins out as it draws me forward a step. "Meryl and Derek took Chris for a walk around the reserve. They said they'd be about an hour."

Why did I just tell her that? She didn't need to know, not in this second anyway. I could have waited until she was dressed and outside of the bedroom.

"Well, that's interesting. We're alone then?" Her fantastic eyebrow lifts and she smiles. No, no, no, this is not a good idea. But I want her so much.

"I can't sleep with you, Callie." Ah, my brain is kicking in again. Her face doesn't change. She's still smiling, which is odd. She moves to the bed and climbs on, crawling on all fours. My heart is in my throat. I'm getting a world class view of her arse in those black lace knickers. Her body twists around and she leans against the pillows.

I watch her hands as she slowly signs to me, "Just watch then."

The T-shirt is ripped off. Her thumbs hook either side of her knickers. I think I might have a stroke if she removes the... Holy shit, she's removing them! Slowly and confidently, I watch her glide the fabric down her toned legs. I am captivated. Nothing short of a nuclear attack could get me to move from this spot. I never thought myself a voyeur, but damn, I am enjoying this show.

Her eyes never leave mine, even as she reaches for the toy she discarded a few moments ago. The lube is left where it is. Obviously, she is wet enough already. I feel that in my own pants too. I'm clenching like a drug mule in an airport security line. This is the hottest thing I have ever participated in.

Callie brings the tip of the dildo to her chest. She slowly glides it down between her bra-clad breasts. I follow the trajectory of that toy like a damn hawk. Her legs open and I am given my first look at her. I feel like a treasure hunter who has just cracked open a chest full of gold. And, just like that treasure hunter, I want to claim that gold as mine.

Gently, she rubs the dildo through her folds. My mouth waters. She's struggling to keep her eyes open. I can see how much she wants to let her head fall back in pleasure. Her breathing is laboured and her nostrils flare. I contemplate whether to break my stance and go to her, or keep watching.

The toy dips into her. She begins to pick up rhythm and I moan. This is the sweetest torture. Fuck it. I won't sleep with her, not this time anyway. Instead, I'll give her something to watch, too. I flick the button of my shorts open and slide down the zip. Callie's ministrations pause as she regards me. I see a flicker of surprise, but it's quickly replaced by unbridled lust.

My finger glides easily through my slit. I avoid my clit to begin with because I'm pretty sure I'll come immediately, and that would be embarrassing. I am aching for release.

We spend a few minutes edging. Callie then picks up the rhythm, so I finally circle my clit. I have to grab my nipple. My need is taking over control and I'm not sure how long I can hold off. I don't need to worry, though, because Callie is writhing. Her chest is dotted with red patches as she comes. I let myself go, and it is magnificent!

Goodbye friend zone. There is no way we can remain "just friends" after that. Callie has collapsed entirely. The toy is still in place, and I am itching to go over to her and play. Instead, I pull up my zip and refasten my shorts. Carefully, she takes out the dildo, and then starts giggling.

"What is funny?" Laughing wasn't the reaction I expected.

"Nothing, nothing."

I was clearly missing something. "Tell me."

"Okay, but please don't be offended or anything."

Oh, sure, because saying that is a great way to ensure I'm not offended. I scowl at her, because I can, and she won't take it badly. Callie knows my scowls, and this one is "mildly irritated," not "I'm deeply offended."

"Alright, stop scowling. So, you know how I name things."

I nod, because of course I do. I watch her gaze travel to the toy and then I realise...what name goes next to Dildo?

"Are you kidding me? You named your fucking dildo, Daisy?"

Her hand covers her mouth as she laughs. "I swear it wasn't intentional. I wasn't sat there thinking 'Oh, I'll call this Daisy after my first love.'"

Did she just say I was her first love, as in L.O.V.E.

"You were in love with me?" I don't give a shit if her toy is named after me. At least I was always on her mind. My question takes her aback. She's just realised what she said. I can see her cogs working. She takes a big breath in.

"Daisy." She gets off the bed, and I have to will myself not to stare. I can see her red curls and, wow, I want my face in them. "You were everything to me. I loved you with everything I had."

I feel a tear run down my face. Shit, I'm crying. Callie cups my face and swipes the tear away. I haven't said anything yet and I won't get the chance to because she is leaning in. Her lips touch mine and it's so soft; so tentative. It feels like my very first kiss all over again.

My ability to see reason has left me. Callie Compton loved me. Past tense though, what about now?

Shh, Daisy, for fuck's sake, just enjoy this!

Her lips begin to move, and her hand goes from my cheek, to the base of my neck. She's pulling me in, and now our bodies are flush. My hands drop to her hips. Her skin is soft and warm. There is no rush. We're taking our time, enjoying each other.

I feel her filling me with desire. We don't know what's going to happen tomorrow. We could get hit by a bus. I know that's a popular adage, but in our case it's true, we really could kick the bucket any day now. If something happens to me, and I miss out on being with the only woman I have ever loved, I will be so pissed at myself. Time to seize the day and all that.

With little effort, I walk her backwards towards the bed. It's not like the room is massive, so it takes us two steps and we're there. My tank top is lifted up and over my head, and I'm glad I didn't wear a bra today. Not to toot my own horn or anything, but I have killer boobs. They're C cups, and they're perky little buggers.

Callie continues to kiss me thoroughly. Our tongues are having the time of their lives. Her palm massages my left breast, and it's everything. As well as being perky, my tits are very sensitive. Her massage becomes firmer and I moan. A part of me goes stiff, and not in the good way. I know she said I was sexy when I moan, but it's difficult for me to believe.

At my sound, her hand shifts so she's pinching my nipple. Oh Lord, I want to cry out in pleasure, but I keep as quiet as I can.

Please let Derek, Meryl, and Chris be far, far away from this bus.

I grab her ass, because, why wouldn't I? I've spent long enough looking and fantasising about it. It's firm and delicious. I will be biting that backside before the day is done.

God knows when she undid my shorts, but they're now falling to the floor. I push her away, so she falls on to the bed. Her hair is a wild mass of curls. Thank you, humidity. I love her hair like that. She reaches round and unclasps her bra. I discard my knickers, and now we are both fully naked.

This is a monumental moment, and I want to take a second to really feel it. I have no doubt we will be fire between the sheets. Callie scoots up the bed as I climb on and stalk towards her. I have so many things I want to do to her I can't decide where to start. I run my hands over her legs as I reach them. Everything about her is perfection in my eyes.

Her hand cups my face again. She wants me to lie on her. I have no idea if Callie has slept with a deaf person before. If she's used to whispering sweet nothings in her partner's ears, we may have a problem. I've had three women express that sleeping with a deaf person was "no big deal," and each one of those women ended up getting frustrated because they couldn't talk dirty to me in bed.

I shake my head to dispel my mind of those memories. Callie stills my head and looks at me with concern. She hasn't broken our contact to sign, and she hasn't let a word pass her lips. She's using her hands to touch me, to ask me if I'm okay. I lower my head and kiss her deeply.

My thigh slips between hers, and I begin to move. This feels like the most natural thing in the world. Her body fits mine; her touches are everything I want without having to ask. Even though I had an orgasm, minutes previously, I can already feel myself building. From the way Callie is grabbing my arse, I think she's also close. We grind harder and kiss deeper until I feel her body begin to shudder.

Feeling her orgasm tips me over the edge and I come in a wave of ecstasy.

Hours could have passed for all I know. Time is irrelevant when you are in a post-orgasm haze. I've collapsed on her, and she's holding me. I rise every time she breathes, and I adore it. Hopefully, I'm not too heavy.

Her hand lazily strokes my back. Did she enjoy it as much as me? I lift my head and look down at her. Her head lifts and her lips capture mine once again.

With ease, she rolls me onto my back. Her lips slip to my neck, and she nibbles at my pulse point. I can feel her nipples brush against me as she descends. I don't have the heart to stop her, but I don't think I can go again. Honestly, she's lucky she got two orgasms out of me. It's a first.

Callie is a confident lover; she takes command and doesn't falter in her quest to reach her goal; My pussy. That's her goal now. She slides her tongue into me, and I almost buck her off the bed. I am ridiculously sensitive, but not in a sore way. To my astonishment, my clit is gearing up for another round.

Slow, long licks get me to the point where I'm ready to beg. In one fell swoop, she sucks on my clit and clamps my nipples with her hands. I'm gone. What I'm experiencing is nothing short of heavenly. My body spasms and lights zip across my eyes. This orgasm is going on forever and Callie is coaxing me through it with soft licks and gentle squeezes. It's possible I passed out.

Three orgasms in a row is a record for me in one night, but I shouldn't be surprised it was Callie who was able to get me there. Her kisses tell me she's making her way back up to me. I want to reciprocate, but my body is jelly. Finally, I see her beautiful face over mine. Her pupils are wide, and she looks ravenous, still. Christ on a cracker, she has one hell of a sexual appetite.

Foolishly, I think we are done. I'm wrong. I squeal as she flips me over to my stomach. Her weight shifts and for a moment she gets off the bed. I haven't got the energy to look at what she's doing. My eyes close and I'm drifting to sleep, but when my hips are lifted into the air, I become fully conscious. My energy levels spike and I look over my shoulder. Callie is on her knees behind me with her toy strapped into a harness.

Our eyes meet. She's silently asking me if I want this. My answer is to back my ass into her.

Fifteen

Callie

IF I DIE TOMORROW, I will go to the next life a happy woman. Daisy is on all fours in front of me, waiting for me to fuck her. So much for not sleeping together. I grip her hips, steadying myself. I'm so turned on, I can barely see straight.

I slide inside her and she jolts forwards. The toy isn't too big, so I doubt she has a problem accepting it. I see her hands ball into fists and her head drops. I massage her lower back as I gently move. There is no resistance. She's so wet, I can glide in and out easily.

The wonderful thing about Daisy the Dildo—I cannot believe I had to admit to Daisy she has a sex toy named after her—is that it has a pocket for a bullet vibrator at the base. Whilst Daisy the Human was recovering, I slipped it in when I donned the harness. Let's party!

With the flick of a finger, I get the little bastard buzzing. A few quick breaths, and I manage to stop myself from coming prematurely. The bullet is effective.

The moan that radiates out of Daisy is fantastic. I pick up my pace. The little vibe is making me tremble, but I will not come—not until I hear Daisy cry out. Her hand is now slamming against the headboard.

I'm struggling to keep my concentration. Every vibration is like a bolt of electricity to my clit, and I can't stop from crying out. I look down at the toy entering her and I can't believe I get to see this. I slam into her a little aggressively, but she only moans louder. Her ass is pounding back into me. She wants it fast and hard. When I hear Daisy scream, I explode. My hips are thrusting maniacally, and I know a second orgasm is about to wipe me out.

My body curls over Daisy when I've ridden out the second climax. I can hardly breathe. Daisy collapses onto the mattress and I follow. I'm still inside her. Quickly, I stop the bullet before it fucking kills me.

When I can breathe like a regular person, and not an emphysemic pensioner, I slowly remove the toy from her and take off the harness. Daisy rolls over and I take her in my arms.

There is only silence. I think we both need a bit of time to come to terms with what has just happened. It's a monumental occasion...well, at least for me. Our friendship is changed irreparably. Even if we decide not to start a relationship, we can never go back to being friends.

Now I've had her, I can say with all certainty I want a relationship. The problem is, I don't know if it's possible. Let's be realistic. Collecting the pieces of the black book is one thing, but once that's done, once we have all the pieces, what then? Surely, it can't be as easy as handing it over to the police. I don't believe for one second Queen B will go down without a fight, or at least, exacting some revenge.

My chest tightens at the thought of Betty, my own flesh and blood, harming Daisy or Chris. I need to keep them safe. Betty going to prison doesn't guarantee that. It will take months to disband her organisation. I've looked at some of the names in that book and I know they won't go quietly, either.

Sometimes I think I should just wait it out. Betty isn't getting any younger. She can't outrun time. If she hasn't got an heir, who will take over once she's gone? Would it be easier for everyone if I just stay hidden for a little while longer? Daisy could go back to her life. I could send her back with the book. Maybe Betty will leave me alone if she has that. I internally roll my eyes, like that would ever happen.

Daisy rests her hand on my chest. In all my reverie, I haven't noticed my breathing has become somewhat rapid, and not in the "just had lots of sex" kind of way. I can feel the blood rushing in my ears.

How could I have been so reckless? I've invited danger into Daisy's life because I was lonely. I should have kept running. I should ditch her and Chris, and go far away. I have everything I need stashed away. It wouldn't take much for me to slip away. Daisy would be hurt, but surely she would understand. But what about her brother?

Fuck my life, I'm going round in circles. I've already gone through this thought cycle, and I got nowhere. No matter what I do, I feel trapped.

"Stop." Daisy's face is directly over me. One hand remains on my chest, the other is cupping my face. It's the first break in silence since we came together. Her eyes are sparkling, which makes me breathe easier. "Stop thinking, just for a little while."

I nod, because what else can I do? She lays her head over my heart and I feel her sigh. It's just dawning on me; Daisy has probably felt the same way as me for just as long, and I'm ruining our moment by panicking. The shutting of the main door makes me jolt. Daisy must have felt it close, because she sits up like her arse is on fire, causing me to laugh because it's ridiculous. We're acting as if we're going to get caught doing something naughty.

I laugh again, because if the door had banged shut ten minutes ago, they would have *definitely* caught us doing something very naughty.

Not the time, Callie.

Daisy scoots off the bed and starts redressing. I take a second to watch her because... *Damn!* Daisy at eighteen was hot, but Daisy at twenty-eight is mind-blowingly sexy. I want to throw her back on the bed and have my wicked way with her all night. Too bad that won't happen.

The bedroom door rattles as someone knocks. I huff out an exasperated breath. "Hang on."

I scramble off the bed and stick on some shorts and a vest top. Daisy looks at me and smiles. We haven't even had a chance to discuss what's going on between us now.

"Meryl said we're leaving. Said she's put the kettle on," Chris calls through the door. I tell Daisy what he said and we head to the living room area. Meryl and Derek are still outside, tidying up. Chris greets me with a shit-eating grin. "Have fun, did you?"

I want to smack him upside the head. Little shit.

"Shut up." That's my fantastic comeback. I can feel my face go red. Shit, did they all hear us?

"Ready to go?" Derek calls. We all nod and settle down on the sofa. I should probably take another shower, but it will have to wait.

"The next part of the book is in Orvieto. It's a town in Umbria. I hid the book in a cave—"

"In a cave? Jesus, I hate caves!" Chris blurts. I look around to see where Meryl is. Thankfully, she's up front with Derek. I trust them, but they don't need to know everything about us, especially the location of the book parts. I glare at Chris.

"Keep it down." He mouths "sorry" to me, and I nod. "The caves are accessible to the public. I hid the pages when I was on a guided tour. This time we won't need to sneak anywhere, okay? It's totally safe, but I understand if you want to wait for us in a café or something," I say to Chris, who is looking queasy.

"I think I will. I get claustrophobic."

I can see in his eyes there is a story behind his feelings. Should I push it?

"Do you want to talk about it?" He shakes his head. I leave it at that. Daisy has stayed silent. I'm starting to worry that what happened between us is freaking her out.

Netflix entertains us for a while. Derek parks after four hours. We've cleared the border and are now in France. I've never been to this area, so a little part of me is excited. Derek tells us we're staying for the night.

I step out of the motorhome and nearly squeal in delight. I'm not a squeal-y kind of person, but the view is breathtaking. We are high above the sea. The carpark is just a dusty bit of land, but there are a couple of other smaller vans pitched up for the night. Further down the road, I can see a town. The lights of buildings are twinkling in the low summer light.

"Nice, isn't it?" Derek comments, as he joins me by the railing of the carpark.

"It's beautiful."

"The town is Cerbère. It's a bitch to drive the van around, but it's worth it."

I can't believe Derek has just said "bitch." That makes me grin.

"So, you know the place well?" I'm chatting with the man like I haven't got a care in the world. It's refreshing, but so untrue.

"Oh, yes. Meryl and I have travelled here several times. The town isn't big, but the views are stunning. I was going to suggest we all take a walk to the closest restaurant. It's been a while since we've eaten out. What do you think?"

I think I want to cry. I know it must seem stupid, but this all feels so normal, I can't cope. The last time I went to a restaurant was with Daisy, just before her eighteenth birthday. I'm not sure you can call Pizza Hut a real restaurant, though. We didn't care, because, you know, the ice cream machine. That's what it's famous for, right?

"Sounds perfect." I hope my voice doesn't betray the fact that I could start bawling at any second. Derek squeezes my shoulder and leaves. I take a few calming breaths. Suddenly, I feel out of control. Everything in my life has changed so quickly. I may not have liked being alone for six years, but I was in control, always. Now, not so much.

We walk down to the nearest restaurant, which is perched on the side of the cliff. The sun has almost set, but the outdoor terrace offers a spectacular view of the town. We sit at a table like we're a family about to enjoy a nice meal on holiday. It's surreal.

The food is delicious, and the conversation is light. I know Derek and Meryl have questions, but they haven't pushed anything. The reality is, their questions will go unanswered. We need to leave them. As much as I would love to stay in that motorhome, it's not an option. From what Derek has told me, they are heading to Florence. We need to go farther south. It's going to be much easier if we have our own transport. I plan to talk to Daisy about it tonight in bed. Wow, I can't believe I just said that. I will be in bed tonight with Daisy Simpson.

The evening was thoroughly enjoyable, but now we need to get serious. Chris seems happy to go along with whatever Daisy and I decide. I had a brief chat with him on the walk back from the restaurant. We agreed to talk more in the morning.

Daisy is already in bed by the time I've finished having a quick shower. She looks adorable all tucked up. I want to hold her all night, but I have to focus.

I slip under the duvet and prop myself up. "We need to get a car. I think we should leave Derek and Meryl before we get to Italy. They don't know our destination and I think it should stay that way."

"Okay." The way she's looking at me tells me this isn't what she wants to talk about.

"Right, so we fucked." *Well, that was blunt, Callie!* I have no idea why I just blurted that out.

"Fucked?" Her eyes betray her hurt. I've just made our experience sound like it was just another fling.

"Sorry, that came out wrong."

"Did it?" She sighs and then rolls over.

What the hell is wrong with me? Okay, so in the literal sense we fucked, or I fucked her or whatever, but that certainly isn't how I want to describe the experience. Call me cheesy, but in my eyes, we made love. So, if I feel that way, why in the name of Christ did I just say that to her?

I roll her back over. I can't leave her feeling like that. She stares at me. There is a mix of hurt and anger stamped across her face. I'm a fucking tool sometimes!

"I did *not* mean that. What we did together, Daisy, means so much to me. I'm sorry."

She sits up. I hold my breath. "That was thoughtless of you, Cal." I nod. "I've been thinking about it—us. Maybe we should hold off on sleeping together again." I want to do the absolute opposite. "Let's get to know each other again. If this is to work, I want to know you. Our lives have changed. We have changed."

I want to argue that she's wrong, that we should be banging like rabbits now we've finally found each other, but I can't. All those worries I felt after we'd had sex are still there. Having my head in the clouds won't help any of us, so I agree with her.

"Can I still kiss you, though?" I can't imagine not touching those lips again. She smiles, leans forward, and kisses me. If only we could stay locked away in this room, sharing kisses. I would happily live like that.

Daisy is sound asleep. I'm staring at the ceiling. It's been hours, but I can't switch off my brain. I think being with Derek and Meryl has given me too much comfort. I've allowed myself to start looking forward to things. Just a simple meal at a restaurant has me brimming with hope and happiness. That's dangerous for me. Bloody hell, are you as bored as I am with my self-pitying, worrying bullshit?

The vibration of a phone catches my attention. It has to be Daisy's. Mine is on silent, on the table in the kitchenette. My curiosity is piqued. It's wrong, and I know Daisy will be super pissed if I snoop, but I can't help it. It hasn't escaped my attention that Daisy is over-the-top secretive about her occupation.

I love how she tried to fob me off with "I do tech." I mean, what the fuck does that mean? Plus, you don't have a laptop that well-protected if you're just a regular old IT consultant. No, she's into something big, and I want to know what.

I lean over to grab her phone. She doesn't stir. Turning away, I hit the home button. The notification shows a message from "Queen Bitch" and my heart begins to pound. There is a second vibration and a new message that displays a photo.

I think Betty has just killed her brother.

Sixteen

Daisy

THERE IS NOTHING LIKE a good stretch in the morning. The bed in the motorhome is surprisingly comfortable. I arch my back, elongating my spine. My arm sweeps across the bed. Callie isn't there. I feel the end of the bed dip. Raising my head, I spot Callie with her head in her hands, elbows on knees. This can't be a good sign.

Feeling me shift, she turns to me. Her face is pale. Her eyes are swimming with unshed tears. What the hell has happened? Before I get the chance to ask, she hands me my phone. There are two messages, both from Betty. I read the first one.

Queen Bitch

Consider this your final warning. You can have two more weeks.

I click on the second, which has a photo attached. It shows my brother lying in the foetal position, his face a bloodied mess. I presume he's alive.

"I'm sorry. I'm so sorry." Callie's hands are trembling. "Daisy—"

"Hey, hey. Stop. He's alive." I need her to calm down. No doubt she's imagining the worst and blaming herself.

"How do you know?" She has tears streaking down her face. I wonder if this is the first time she has allowed herself to break down. Callie is one of the strongest people I know, but she's only human. Can you imagine the toll her life has had on her mental health?

"Betty wouldn't take away the only bit of leverage she has on me. Daniel is badly beaten, but alive."

"What the hell do we do, Daisy?" She looks so defeated it shocks me. Callie always has a plan; hell, she normally has plans from A-Z. This Callie has no more to give.

"Right now, we get up and have breakfast. Then we talk. We will figure this out, Cal." I hope she sees the sincerity in my eyes. My blood is boiling under my skin at the thought of Callie suffering as she is. Betty-Fucking-Compton will pay dearly for what she has put her only granddaughter through, I swear it.

It takes a few minutes, but eventually Callie pulls herself together. She doesn't want to show weakness in front of the others, which secretly makes me feel good. Yeah, it's a bit twisted, but I like being the only one Callie is vulnerable in front of.

The morning sun is only just peeking over the horizon when we head into the main area of the RV. The other three are still sleeping soundly. I prepare the coffee and take it out to Callie, who is leaning against the railings, staring out to sea. She takes the cup. I want her to open up to me, but I need to wait for her to feel comfortable. I doubt she's had anyone to open up to in a long time.

"I just want this to be over, Daisy." She's put her mug on the railing and is now facing me. My heart breaks a little because she looks like a scared child. "I should have just stayed. Maybe it wouldn't have been as bad as I thought. At least then I wouldn't be putting the people that mean the most to me in danger."

"That was never an option, Callie. You're not her. You could never have done what she wanted you to do. You had to leave and I am happy you did. I'm sorry I left you and never looked back—"

"Fuck, Daisy, I could never blame you for getting out of there. I just wish I could have gone with you to university. Imagine how different our lives would have been."

"I do need to apologise, though. You were my world, Callie, for years, and I just left. The only excuse I have is, for once, I felt as if I fit in somewhere. I wasn't ignored, made to feel like a freak, or made to feel less than. When I got to university, it just felt so good to be free, I never wanted to look back."

"Good. You were always too good for that place. You deserve to be seen as the magnificent woman you are."

"How can you say that, when I practically abandoned you?" Tears are streaming down my face now. The guilt I have carried for all these years is drowning me from the inside. I did leave her, and look what happened.

"Sweetie, you did the right thing. Betty was never going to let me go. I was always going to have to run away. Do you think, for one minute, this is the life I would want for you? Skipping town every couple of weeks, changing your appearance? No, Daisy, I wanted you to go to university. I wanted you to forget about your wankshaft of a dad and my sociopathic Nan. I just hate that you're here now."

The statement cuts me. I understand what she means, but it still hurts. I can't think of anywhere else I would rather be. I love my job and I love my life in Scotland. I have friends, but all of that pales in comparison to being with Callie. I wish we were at the place in our relationship where I could confess how deep my feelings are; how they've always been, but it's not fair. I need to bide my time. I just hope Callie doesn't push me away before I get the chance to tell her exactly how I feel.

"None of this is either of our faults. I think we both need to let some stuff go. What is important, is that we are together, and we are going to bring you home. Callie, what happened to Daniel isn't your fault. He was always going to find himself on the wrong side of Betty. Each one of her lackeys will find themselves either beaten, killed, or locked up, if it means she survives. Even my dad isn't safe, and he's one of her most trusted 'employees.' Together, we can end this. We're not kids anymore."

She's turned to stare out to sea again. I know she's mulling over what I've said. Hopefully she agrees and we can move on. I want to crucify the old witch, and I need Callie's help to do it. I turn to look at the rising sun. If Callie needs time, that's what I'll give her. Our silence is broken by a noisy Chris, stumbling out of the RV looking like he's been dragged backwards through a hedge. His hair is sticking up and his T-shirt is half in his boxers.

"Hey, guys," he waves. He approaches us and throws an arm around each of our shoulders. He takes a deep breath in and smiles. He looks from Callie to me and then wiggles his eyebrows. "So, are you pair going to be giving each other googly eyes from now on?" He has a smirk on his face. Callie starts to laugh.

"Shut your face," she says, shoving him playfully, but looking at me. I will happily make googly eyes at her if it makes her smile like that.

"Hey, you two were the ones giving rabbits a run for their money yesterday! It's a good job I'm not impressionable, you could have scarred me." He's laughing.

I start to feel my face burn. Shit, I think they actually heard us!

"You didn't hear shit." Callie rolls her eyes. She is acting much cooler than me right now. I want to put my hands over my face and hide.

"Like hell we didn't. We came back to the van because Meryl forgot her sunscreen. We turned right back around once we saw that whole vehicle rocking. Damn, Callie." He punches her shoulder and turns to me, winking. I want to fucking disappear. Callie puts her hand to her mouth, then throws her head back, laughing. I know she's mocking my reaction.

"You're both assholes!" I direct it to both of them and then start laughing. Why should I be embarrassed? Yeah, it's a fucked-up time in our lives, but I can't deny that she definitely rocked the van, and my world. "Can we be serious for a second? Are we leaving Meryl and Derek now, or later?"

"Why are we leaving them?" Chris looks surprised at my question. I think he's become attached.

"I don't want them in harm's way, Chris. The longer we stay with them, the more likely they're going to get caught up in all this shit."

"I get that, Callie, but I don't see why we can't stay with them until Florence. No one knows we are here—"

"That we know of, Chris," Callie interjects. She's right, we still haven't figured out who the guy at the motel was, or how he found us.

"It's a couple of days. Surely we can stick with them for that long?"

I can see the concern in Callie's eyes. If it were just her, she'd have gone by now. Her name would have changed, as well as her appearance. She looks at me, searching for an answer. I put my arm on Chris's shoulder to get his attention.

"Why don't you stay with them, Chris? I'm not trying to get rid of you, but Callie and I aren't happy that *you're* involved, either. Meryl and Derek would be happy to take you in for a while, I know it. They're good people that can keep you safe. Just until we're done, and then if you want, you can come to us."

I hadn't meant to say all that, but it makes sense. I understand Callie took him in because he needed someone, but now, with all the uncertainty, I don't think he should stay. Derek and Meryl have treated him like their own since we met them. I have no doubt in my mind they would be more than happy to look after him for a while. They strike me as empty nest people. I look at Callie. I can see she agrees and is thankful I was the one to suggest it.

"You don't want me with you?"

"Chris, you know that's not what Daisy means. Can you honestly tell me you want to leave the security of this van to trek around Europe, hoping we don't get caught by people that will do unspeakable things to us? *I* don't want to fucking do it myself, mate, but I have zero choice. You do. I want you safe. As Daisy said, after all this is over, if you want to come and stay with me, I would love it. We might not have known each other for long, but you are very important to me. I want to protect you."

Chris looks between us. He's conflicted; it's written all over his face. I think he feels a deep connection to Callie and is afraid to lose her, but I can also tell he wants to be safe. He needs stability after having such a shitty time of it. "Derek and Meryl might not want a tag along."

Callie turns her head. Something has caught her attention and I follow suit. Derek is standing just outside the van door. "You can stay with us as long as you want to. We'll keep you safe until you can go home to Callie and Daisy."

Shit, fuck, and arsehole. Derek must have heard the entire conversation if he knows our real names. I look frantically at Callie, but she seems calm.

"I'm sorry we lied about our names, Derek."

"No, no need for apologies. I get you three are trying to protect yourselves. I completely understand. Can I tell you something?" We all nod. "Meryl and I adopted our son when he was thirteen. He came to us because he was being abused by his dad. Beaten regularly because he was effeminate. His biological dad didn't want a gay son, so he thought he could toughen him up with violence. Thankfully, his behaviour was reported. Glen ended up in foster care. We'd been foster parents for years, but when Glen got placed with us, we knew straight away we should be his forever home. We were meant to keep him safe. I have that feeling with you, Chris. I understand you're not a young kid who needs parents, but you still deserve to have people who will love and support you. Callie and Daisy are two of those people, and I believe Meryl and I could be, as well."

Well, fuck me, I'm bawling now. How I wish I'd had parents like Derek and Meryl. Chris's throat is bobbing, so he's trying to stop from blubbering too. Callie is the only one who has a gigantic smile on her face.

"I knew you were good people when I saw you, but wow! Derek, I can't thank you two enough. Really, I can't even—"

"Say no more." Meryl says, stepping up next to Derek. "We are honoured to help. Everyone deserves love and safety, and if that's what you need from us, Chris, you got it."

My legs are moving before my brain registers what I'm doing. I pull Derek and Meryl into me and hug them with everything I have. I wouldn't say I'm a pessimist; maybe more a realist. Can you blame me, after growing up where I did and being treated the way I was? But here, right now, I'm so happy the universe is giving me a reason to be hopeful; that there are still good people in this world who are only motivated by kindness and love.

Meryl hugs me tight. After a few moments, I feel pressure all around me. It's the good kind of pressure; the reassuring kind. I tilt my head and see that Callie and Chris have joined us in a big group hug. We stay like that for a long time. I think all three of us needed to feel this. We've all been let down by the people who were supposed to love us the most in the world. We were dealt a shitty hand. Derek and Meryl can't make up for all those years of hurt and neglect, but they can give us what we need now.

We eventually pull away and start laughing. "Let's get breakfast and talk some more," Meryl says with a smile and a wink.

Callie pulls my hand and holds me back whilst the others go back inside. "Can I just hold you for a little longer?"

Damn, I'd let this woman hold me forever. I nod. She moves in and wraps her arms around me. I bury my face in her hair. One day, I will bring her back to this stretch of coastline and hold her like this. That thought gives me hope and I cling on to it. For now, we are okay. For now, we have each other, and we can dream about the future.

Seventeen
Callie

WE STAYED WITH DEREK and Meryl until Florence. Thankfully, we had no run-ins. It seems we really did give the guy at the motel the slip. My heart feels lighter knowing Chris is with Derek and Meryl. It sucked major balls having to say goodbye to him, but I know in my gut it was right. We all bought burner phones. He's got our contact details and we have his, plus Derek's and Meryl's. I meant what I said to him. If he decides he wants to stay with me when it's all done, I will welcome him with open arms.

Seeing the photo Betty sent really drove it home for me. Running isn't an option. I can't let her get away with what she's doing. I dread to think how many other families have suffered at the hands of that woman. And for what? Power? Money? None of it makes any sense to me.

Betty never gave me her origin story, so I have no idea how she came to be the woman she is now. Does it matter, though? She's done what she's done, and now she has to pay for it. I feel empowered by Daisy. For once, I believe we can actually achieve what we've set out to do.

Three more pieces of the book, that's all we need. Daisy has told me she will figure out who we need to give the information to. I'm guessing she works for MI5 now. She's definitely working for the government. I really hope she's some bad ass spy. Can you imagine the role play? Oh, if she calls me Money Penny...

Sexy times will have to wait until we get to our next hotel, though. Daisy said she wants us to wait until this shit with Betty is finally over with, but I can't, and actually, I doubt she can either. What's the point? We might as well screw our way through this—at least it will lighten the mood. Being in a perpetual state of fear and anxiety is exhausting. I'm twenty-eight. I don't need a fucking ulcer just yet.

I've decided to take Daisy to see the sights in Florence. The pages in Orvieto aren't going anywhere, and we have been nonstop from the moment Daisy found me. We need to talk about what she's going to tell Betty. We may as well have that conversation over a bottle of wine and pasta.

"Have you been here before?" I'll feel a bit of a tit playing tour guide if she's already visited.

"Nope, never. I went to Rome once with a girl, but just for the weekend."

I hate that sentence. Who was this girl? Ugh, I bet they probably did stuff all weekend. I think my face has just given me away, because Daisy is now laughing at me, shaking her head.

"Yes, Callie, I had girlfriends, and shockingly, had sex before you."

"You don't have to point it out." I shiver at the thought of another woman having her hands on Daisy. I know she's not mine. She can be with whomever she wants. I'm certainly not one to judge. I lost count of how many women I've been with, but it still claws at me. Did they treat her right? I hope so.

"Callie, I literally found you because you left a string of women behind."

"Can you not remind me?" Even though this is an awkward conversation, I'm just glad to be having it with her.

I take her to a couple of museums, which she seems to enjoy. My favourite part of the day is when we grab some gelato and chill by the river. Although, twenty euros for a scoop of ice cream is a tad excessive. A girl's got to budget, you know.

The hotel is tiny, with only a dozen or so rooms. I'm more than happy to be sharing a bed with Daisy again—this time with nobody to interrupt us. We head to a restaurant that's a few streets away. It's cosy and inviting. To the outside world, I'm sure we look like any other couple going out on a date. I'll pretend too, just for this evening.

Daisy picks the wine, because I have no idea what is good or not. It's friggin' grape juice. How different can one bottle be from the next? Daisy gives me a death glare when I share that bit of wisdom with her. I order wild boar pasta. Daisy has something with truffles—it looks nice. We eat in relative silence. Maybe it's just the day catching up with us?

"I need to message Betty," Daisy signs when she's finished her main course. I knew we would have to talk about it, but I kind of hoped we could have one night off.

"What do you want to tell her?"

"The truth... Well, as much of the truth as possible. If she knows I've found you and we are retrieving the book, I think that will get her off my case for a while. She doesn't need to know we're planning to fuck her over. I think mentioning that would be a little counterproductive." Her cheeky grin makes me smile.

"Tell her what you need to. I'm cool with whatever. By tomorrow evening, we will have the second part of the book. We'll then need to make our way to Copenhagen for the third. After that, well, one more stop in the Scottish Isles and we're home free."

Oh, how I wish it were as simple as that. In a way, it should be. The pages in Orvieto should be easy to pick up. Copenhagen might be a tad more difficult, but I don't want to tell Daisy that yet. As for Scotland, well, I hope she doesn't mind getting dirty, and not in the fun way.

We sit in the hotel room after our meal and a walk. I think Daisy enjoyed the day, even if the conversation got a bit stilted after we started talking about Betty. One day, we might be able to converse like regular people. Wouldn't that be nice?

I'm not going to try anything on with her tonight. Best to leave it for a while, or at least let Daisy make the first move. I sink into the surprisingly comfortable mattress and practise some deep breathing whilst Daisy uses the bathroom. I picture the underground section in Orvieto where I hid the pages. There's no reason to think they've been disturbed, unless there's been a major catastrophe down there. I cross my fingers and pray that won't be the case.

At least this time, I know I won't run into any women I slept with. Orvieto was a day trip for me, three-and-a-half years ago. I love Italy and have visited many cities, but Orvieto always stuck with me. I think it was the way the town sits high up. It's superb to see when driving, like a fairytale city in the sky.

The door to the bathroom creaks and Daisy gets in bed. I don't move; I'm still trying to deep breathe my way to sleep. I'm laying straight, with my hands down by my side. I feel the quilt move and Daisy takes my hand. She intertwines our fingers. That's all I need to relax. I shut my eyes and visualise my happy place.

The smell of coffee wakes me up. Wow, I feel great. I can't remember the last time I slept so soundly. I woke up once in the night, which isn't unusual for me as I learned to be a light sleeper after going on the run. Daisy was curled up against me, her head buried in my neck. That was nice. It didn't take me long to drift off again.

I'm not trying to be a soppy mare and usually I wouldn't be caught dead snuggling with a woman, or talking about my feelings, but Daisy is different, so you might as well get used to it. Anyway, back to my current reality, which is the smell of Italian coffee permeating my senses.

I shift myself into a sitting position. I am positive my hair looks like a bird's nest because I forgot to tie it up last night and now I have to suffer the consequences. Sitting on the bedside table is a to-go cup of coffee and a cornetto. I know what you're thinking, and no, Daisy did not bring me a wafer cone ice cream for my breakfast. A cornetto is an Italian croissant, and I fucking love them. Did I tell Daisy that?

Sometimes I forget living alone has diminished my social skills. I shouldn't be surprised when Daisy raises her eyebrows at me as I shoved half the cornetto in my gob, like the Neanderthal I am. Flaky pastry is falling all over my tank top and the bed covers. I realise my mistake too late. I try to chew with my mouth closed, but it's difficult, considering it's bursting with buttery pastry. I give her a smirk.

Once breakfast is finished, I inhale the coffee vapours. Italian coffee is like having your brain kicked by a mule. It wakes you the fuck up! Daisy has eaten her food with a lot more grace and delicacy, but at least it looks like I have amused her.

We need to sort out a vehicle, and I'm ready to shake things up a little. Daisy is not going to like what I have in mind, but that's half the fun. It's less than two hours to Orvieto if we take the highway, but I plan to go the scenic route. Rural Italy is friggin' stunning. I know a place, not too far away, where I can acquire what we need. In fact, I have a stash bag on the other side of the city. I'll grab it to give us a bit more cash.

All my stash bags have the same things in them. Money—cash only, fake IDs, and a disguise of some sort. Since Torreguadiaro, I haven't worn a disguise. I can't see the point anymore. Not having my hair pinned up is a relief; wigs are really uncomfortable.

The clock on the wall reads 8:30 a.m. We should probably get going soon. I look over at Daisy, who is now engrossed in her laptop. That's new. Usually she asks me to leave the room when she's on it. I *so* want to ask her if she's Jane Bond. She'll tell me when she can, and *if* she can, I suppose. I sign to her that I'm going to take a shower. She nods, and then gets back to whatever she's doing.

Smelling better, and thoroughly caffeinated, I am ready to get on with it. It's not uncommon for me to feel restless. I usually counteract that feeling with being efficient. Once I know I need to be somewhere, I don't mess about. Now though, I have to wait for someone else, so it's difficult. Daisy takes half an hour in the shower! Half. An. Hour. What the hell is she doing for half an hour? Okay, so my mind went places for a moment, but I doubt she's actually doing *that*.

I'm just about to bang on the bathroom door—because I'm getting impatient—when she strolls out, smelling fresh and wonderful. Her hair is silky and hangs down by her shoulders. I forgive her completely. From now on, she can spend as much time as she wants in the shower. She'd tell me to go fuck myself anyway, if I complained about her bathroom time.

The bags are packed and are by the door. I leave Daisy to collect her laptop. We hit the streets of Florence with some newfound energy. The place I need to go to get our transport is twenty minutes away by foot. First though, I want my stash bag.

Daisy follows me without question. I ask her to wait outside whilst I go in and collect my bag from the luggage storage I use. We only need the money, so I shove that in my duffel. I hesitate, before taking the ID, too—you never know when we might need something like that. I don't need the disguise, so it gets left in the bag and shoved back into the locker. I need to make a note to cancel the rental.

Once this is over, I'll have no need for any of my stash bags. I can't wait for that to become a reality.

Daisy is waiting on the other side of the road when I come out. She doesn't ask me what I collected, and I don't offer an explanation. We continue winding through the streets until we come to a motorbike dealer I know. I want to laugh at Daisy's furrowed eyebrows.

Alberto is a cool guy. I once rented a Vespa off of him, and we ended up chatting for ages. He left a lasting impression on me. I think it was our shared admiration of naming inanimate objects that really solidified our bond.

We enter the shop and head for the counter. Alberto is clacking away on his keyboard. I clear my throat and hope he remembers me. The bright smile he gives me tells me he does. A few minutes of me conversing in broken Italian gets us where we need to be: standing in front of the prettiest motorbike and sidecar that I have ever seen. I reel back when something hits me in the shoulder. Daisy has just thumped me, and her face does not look amused.

"No," she says hotly.

That's it, just "no," from her. I turn back to Alberto and tell him we will take it. I've only rented it, and have every intention of returning it in two days' time.

"Please," I beg Daisy. I'm not prideful. I really want to drive Maggie the Motorbike to Orvieto. I deploy my puppy eyes—Daisy could never say no to those bad boys. She is full-on scowling at me, but I see the cracks forming. I double my efforts. These are the best puppy eyes I have ever given, and boom, she wilts like a leaf in autumn. Well...she throws her hands in the air, huffs, and storms out, so I'll take that as a "Yes, Callie, by all means, let's drive Maggie to Orvieto."

Score.

To make her feel better, I also rent helmets that have dog ears attached. They are going to look so damn cute, flapping about as we drive. Shit, I wish I had a leather jacket now. Ah well, I have aviator sunglasses, so those will have to do.

With the rental agreement signed, I drive Maggie out from the parking lot, to the street. Daisy takes one look at me, and then my helmet, and covers her eyes with her hand. I think she's impressed. The sidecar has a little boot, which is too fucking adorable. Luckily, we are travelling light, and everything fits inside. With great reluctance, Daisy slides into the padded sidecar. I hand her the other helmet and wait.

It's like we're in a showdown. Daisy is glaring at me, and I'm smiling back at her. One of us will have to break because we can't stay here looking at each other all day. A growl leaves Daisy's throat, and she slams the helmet on. I silently laugh, because I was right; she looks awesome in her dog helmet. I kick the bike back to life again, and set off. Orvieto, here we come.

Eighteen
Daisy

Let me define for you, the word "mortification." It's a noun meaning "great embarrassment or shame." A couple of other words you could use to describe the feeling are "humiliation" and "chagrin." It doesn't really matter, just pick one, and that's how I am feeling right now.

I'm sitting in a sidecar attached to a motorbike. The vehicle is bright orange, and quite frankly, my part of the ensemble is shaped like a bullet vibrator. Let's add my open-face *dog* helmet to the mix, and I'm hoping you are getting the level of mortification I'm feeling right now.

Callie is loving every second, and if it wasn't for that fact, I would be throwing a tantrum right now. I'm not too old to stamp my feet and scream in frustration. It's difficult to do that, though, when your travel companion is grinning like an idiot, wearing her own dog helmet and aviator shades. I guarantee she would kill for a leather jacket right now. I'm guessing she thinks she's Steve McQueen from The Great Escape, although I think we resemble Wallace and Gromit, if I'm honest, especially with the fucking helmets.

What was wrong with a nice comfy car? Hell, I would take one of those Smart Cars over this. I've lost count of the amount of people who have overtaken us with their phones pointed in our direction. We're going to be a fucking meme; I can feel it. One consolation, is that Callie didn't insist on me wearing the goggles that were tucked in the sidecar. I'll stick with my Ray-Bans, thanks.

We've been driving for almost two hours. I have to say, Callie certainly knows how to show a girl the sights. We've been weaving around country roads and the views have been fantastic. If this were a real holiday, I would have asked her to stop, several times, especially when we drove past an olive farm. I bet their oil is out of this world. But it's not a holiday, so we plough on.

Callie seems more determined now. After the photo incident, I really thought that she was going to lose it a bit, but I was wrong. If anything, the threat against my brother—and therefore me, by proxy—has ignited something in her.

Chris leaving us was a blow, even though it was absolutely the right call. Derek and Meryl are fantastic, and I can't wait for all this to be over so we can see them again. Whether they know it or not, I've adopted them as surrogate parents. Actually, I think all three of us have.

Just three more stops and the book will be complete. I will definitely be going through it with a fine-tooth comb before I hand it over to the law. Callie has left the task of finding the right authority to me, and I've decided to bring my mentor in on it. I trust her, and I know she will point us in the right direction.

A sudden jolt snaps me out of my thoughts. Callie has slammed on the brakes because an Italian driver on the other side of the road is overtaking and heading straight for us. Nothing gets your heart pumping like being twenty centimetres off the ground in a vibratormobile, whilst a car speeds at you on the wrong side of the white line.

If I ever return to Italy, I will *not* be driving. They are fucking crazy here. I watched a woman, in something that looked an awful lot like a Playmobil car, harass a BMW for twenty kilometres. She was up his arse the entire time, until eventually, she overtook him, cursing wildly. Bonkers, all of them.

We crest a hill and the breath is stolen from my lungs. In the distance is Orvieto. I did a little reading up on it before we set off. It's a city that's perched on the flat summit of a large volcanic tuff. There is definitely a fairytale feel to it. I cannot wait to get there. A: so I can exit this bloody sidecar, and B: because even though we have to get the pages, I want to explore this gorgeous city with Callie. She says they have phenomenal gelato.

Callie parks the motorbike in a carpark at the lowest point of the city. Apparently, the walk up is a must-do, and who am I to argue with that? I jump out of the sidecar, rip the helmet off, and walk in the other direction as fast as I can. Callie catches up to me seconds later, laughing. I'm so glad she finds my humiliation funny, although by now, even I can crack a smile.

We walk together slowly. Neither of us are in a rush. Now and then our hands brush, and all I want to do is lace our fingers together, so that's what I do. If she's surprised, she doesn't show it. The little smile she's trying to hide tells me she wants it just as much as me. We wander through the streets, and I am captivated. Sandy buildings tower above us. Creeping plants adorn the walls. The streets are medieval, with cobbled roads.

I follow Callie as she shows me different parts of the city. She hasn't indicated she wants to get the pages and for once, I think she's actually enjoying herself. Her hands are flying as she signs rapidly with excitement. I can't help but smile. We sit down for the famous gelato she was raving about. After the first bite, I know I could polish off my body weight in the stuff.

We hadn't planned to stay. In fact, Callie was the one to suggest we grab the pages and head back to Florence in one day, but I can now see she's regretting the plan.

"We could grab a hotel for the night?" I know she wants to, so I don't mind being the one to suggest it.

"Really?"

"Why not? Let's get the pages so it's done with, and then we can enjoy our night and head out tomorrow."

We find a nice boutique hotel and reserve a room. It's already past lunchtime, so we sit and eat. The pizza I order is ridiculously good. It's a simple tomato and pesto with thin crust and it is *orgasmic*. I could marry this pizza and have its babies. Callie gets a four cheese version, and by the face she's pulling as she bites into a slice, I would hazard a guess it's good.

The tickets for the underground tour are booked and we're standing in line. There's a crowd of about twenty, which is good. We can stick to the back of the group, making us less likely to be caught. Callie told me the hiding place requires her to climb a little. This should be interesting.

I hate caves. I'm not a fan of small spaces, but I'm not exactly claustrophobic. It's the cold I detest, which is funny, considering I live in Scotland, where it is arguably like the fucking Artic most of the time. My Scottish-born friends love to rib me because my wardrobe is stuffed with big wool jumpers, gloves, and thermals.

We start to descend. Callie is interpreting what the guide is saying, which I wish she wouldn't—only because it's causing people to notice us. I tell her to stop, and she looks a little put out. I see her glaring at the couple in front of us who keep shooting looks over their shoulders. I stifle a laugh, because Callie, in protective mode, is adorable. I think she's about as intimidating as a Care Bear, but hey, maybe others find that terrifying.

The tour continues. The underground is a labyrinth of grottoes. It's hard not to feel the history as we walk. So far, we've been down here for forty-five minutes, meaning we have around fifteen before it's done. The pathway veers to the right and I feel Callie tense. Her eyes are slightly panicked, and I know something has gone wrong. The end of the tour drags out, until finally we exit and head to a café. I sit at a little table and wait for Cal to get back with our coffees. She sits down, and her leg instantly starts bobbing up and down with nerves.

"What's happened?"

"They've cordoned off the path. We weren't supposed to go to the right. The normal route should have taken us straight on."

"Shit."

"I think the section where the pages are hidden is undergoing work. We have to get down there and retrieve them. Fuck, for all I know, they've been found and tossed."

"Then let's go." I'm ready to down my coffee and set off.

"Hang on. We can't just nip down there and access a restricted area. We're going to need a plan."

"Well, that's your area of expertise."

She nods and sits silently for a few minutes. "Can you access the database of the tour company and make me a fake ID?"

Yes, I can, but I'm surprised she's asked me. I haven't given anything away about my talents where computers are concerned.

She rolls her eyes. "Don't look at me like that. You've got a laptop that looks as if the dude from James Bond built it, you're secretive to the point I'm guessing it's a case of national security, you would have to kill me if you told me anything about your work, and I know how smart you are, Daisy. I think hacking into that system would be child's play to you."

Well, shit, she's got me there. I'm not confirming or denying the part about my work being a case of national security. My laptop is top-of-the-line, not something that can be found outside of a secure building, and yes, the system she wants me to hack is far too easy. I don't know why I'm so surprised—she was raised to be observant. I just never thought she'd be able to read *me* so easily.

"Put me in their system as a new tour guide. I'll steal a work shirt and I'll go back in tomorrow. All I need, is to get past security and access the tunnels. I know my way around. Hopefully, I won't run into any workmen, and I can grab the pages."

"Yeah, sounds like a cinch. No worries." My arched eyebrows show how ridiculous I find her brazen attitude. If we've learned anything, it's that our little adventures always go tits up.

"No point worrying about it until it happens, right?"

I sigh and nod. Callie has been made to do far more dangerous things than sneak into a cave, but I still worry. I nibble on the pastry she bought and sip my coffee. Callie's back goes ramrod straight and her eyes go as wide as dinner plates. I have no clue what is wrong. I look around, frantically expecting a S.W.A.T. team, or hired guns, to come bursting through the crowd. The only person I can see waving in our direction, is a very busty Italian woman shouting something.

Callie looks genuinely terrified, but not in the "I'm going to die" kind of way. Then the woman is on her, pulling her up from her seat. The woman goes full contact; I'm talking full-on body slam. Her hand grabs Callie's face, and she plants a messy kiss on Callie's lips. I must look like a gawping fish, because my mouth is opening and closing, in sheer shock of what I'm witnessing.

Callie hasn't moved a muscle. I can't make out what the Italian woman is saying. Her face isn't angled my way, but I can see her jaw moving rapidly. Her hands are wandering all over Callie, in a way that tells me they have been intimate.

I clear my throat, which causes Callie to whip her head in my direction. I don't need to sign to ask her what the fuck is happening. Finally, she grabs the woman's arms and stops them from practically groping her. I read Callie's lips and find out the woman is called Gabriella. Callie gestures her hand to me, causing the woman to turn her head, and I finally get a good look at her.

She is definitely beautiful. Her body is curvaceous, like Sofia Loren in her heyday. She has thick, luxurious hair that curls around her face and hits just above her shoulders. Her lips are painted with a vibrant shade of red that accentuates their plumpness. Big brown eyes lay underneath fake eyelashes and dark eye make-up. I'm a little intimidated.

Like a dork, I wave. Her eyes scan me up and down, and then she turns back to Callie. Again, I can't see what she's saying, which pisses me off. Gabriella's hands start groping again, and I can see Callie getting more and more flustered. I have no idea what to do. Does she need saving, or is Gabriella someone she *wants* to have groping her, and she's just embarrassed that I'm sitting here watching the whole thing?

That's when I see Callie's stress tick. It's a little nerve in her right eye that pulses when she's super stressed. She's uncomfortable, and the advances from Gabriella are unwelcome. Time to jump in and save the day. I stand and move to Callie's side. I thread my hand through hers and look Gabriella square in the face. She's not turning away from me this time.

"I'm sorry, but who are you?"

"Gabriella Bianchi."

"Hi Gabriella, I'm Daisy, her wife." I feel Callie squeeze my hand. I know it's gratitude, and not surprise, she's conveying.

"Wife?" Gabriella is pissed, no doubt about it. "Since when?"

You don't have to be a hearing person to know she's getting louder. I can see a little vein in her temple pulse. Callie flinches as well, telling me she wasn't expecting the volume of Gabriella's voice.

"For six months now. This is our honeymoon. We had to wait a little before we could make the trip, but it's been worth it." Gabriella is looking from me to Callie. "I take it you are a friend?"

I don't know what name Gabriella associates with Callie. A smirk forms on Gabriella's face. I know that look. She thinks she's going to shock me as she confesses she fucked Callie. I gathered that much, all by myself.

"Oh, Rachel and I go way back. We had a night of passion that was unforgettable."

I internally roll my eyes.

"Well, she is very unforgettable," I say, looking at Callie with adoration.

Gabriella narrows her eyes at me. She was expecting me to flush or get upset at her little revelation. I don't think so, lady.

"Anyway, it was lovely running into you," I say with a perfunctory smile before turning back to Callie. "Rachel? Are you ready? We have a hot tub to enjoy, baby."

I have no idea if there is a single hot tub in Orvieto, but the look on Gabriella's face was worth it. Callie nods, and I pull her hand so we can walk in the other direction of Gabriella, who is still standing there, looking as if she wants to kill me.

Nineteen
Callie

Gabriella Bianchi. Gabriella. Fucking. Bianchi! I think the Universe is a cruel asshole. Of all the people to run into, Gabriella Bianchi is the absolute worst. She is, by far, the scariest woman I have ever met. Now, I don't mean she's nasty or violent. No, no. Gabriella is... Shit, I don't even know how to explain it.

I met Gabriella in Rome. I'd arrived in the city, only planning to stay for the weekend. Huge cities, like Rome, make me nervous, but I still wanted to check it off my "On The Lam Bucket List" of places to visit. Anyway, I'd done all the sightseeing shit every tourist does. It was cool. I especially liked the amphitheatre. I decided to hit up a club. I needed to blow off some steam, and that's where Gabriella caught my attention. She was dancing like there was no one else in the room. Plus, her ass is amazing, so, you know, there was that.

Simultaneously drinking and making reasonable decisions, was never my strong suit, so you can guess what happened next. I sidled up close, danced, and propositioned her for a night of fun. She accepted, but insisted we went back to her place. No worries, I never liked taking women back to the places I was staying, anyway.

So, we get to her little flat...and then...well...then Gabriella came alive in the most terrifying of ways. I am no prude. I like to think I'm adventurous when it comes to sex. I don't even mind a bit of Dom/sub action, but Gabriella was on another level.

I'm not a small person, by that I mean I'm tall and have a decent amount of muscle, but Gabriella picked me up, like literally picked me up, as if I weighed nothing, and threw me on the bed. I remember looking into her eyes and seeing something more than lust; she was animalistic.

My clothes were ripped—literally—from my body. The tank I was wearing ended up being one long piece of fabric. Thank fuck that jeans are hard to destroy. My knickers were not so lucky. Once she'd stripped me, she pounced—once again, literally! I'm not sure if you have ever had a grown woman roar at you. I'm not talking a sexy, cute roar, like an "it's foreplay and things might get a bit rough" kind of thing. No, I mean a full-on realistic roar, like an actual fucking lion. Let me tell you, it is unnerving.

I'm not embarrassed to admit, I lay there like a slab of meat. I was so shocked, I kind of froze. Once she'd stopped roaring, she momentarily slipped off of me. Naively, I thought she was done with me. Maybe I wasn't doing it for her, which I would have been happy with. Nope, I was so wrong. She grabbed me with one hand under my arse, whilst the other shimmied a harness up my legs, sporting the biggest dildo I had ever seen.

If you cast your mind back a few days, you'll remember that I like strap-ons. I have my own in my duffle. I've messed about using one with plenty of women—of all shapes and sizes, with no issues. Hey, I love it when a woman goes a little nuts when I'm fucking her with a strap. With Gabriella, though, it was different.

Imagine a very sexually aggressive woman bouncing on a bouncy castle, and that's what it was like. She straddled me and bounced from her knees onto the toy. No lube! From then on, she just bounced, like fucking Tigger, clawing at my chest, roaring again. I have to hand it to her; the lion impression was impressive. I can only surmise she's a massive fan of NatGeo.

Once she was done riding me like a fucking mechanical bull, she ripped the harness off and sat on my face. We'd had no conversation about limits or consent since walking into her flat. I can only describe the experience as something akin to being waterboarded with a vag. Gabriella bounced her way through *that*, too.

As well as a great ass, Gabriella has very large breasts. I like boobs. I think they are a great gift to this world. When I first noticed Gabriella at the club, I saw her boobs first, and was looking forward to having some alone time with them. I changed my mind about that when Gabriella slid down from my face, leaned down, and almost suffocated me with her tits.

You're being dramatic, I hear you say. I swear on my life, I am not. For the first time since I ran away from my sociopathic nan, I feared for my life. If you polled a million lesbians and asked them if dying while being screwed was a fun way to go, I guarantee the results would lean heavily on the side of yes. I am here to tell you, categorically, it would be a horrendous way to go. Boobs should be comforting and sensual, not a set of weapons that can inflict deadly force.

Before I passed out, Gabriella released me. She climbed off my body, thanked me in Italian, and threw my clothes at me. I think my brain registered then that I could escape, so I ran out that door like I was fucking Usain Bolt, and never looked back. That was the only time in my sexual history I felt used. I did *not* like it at all.

Let's cut back to me and Daisy, sitting at the table at the delightful café in Orvieto. Imagine my absolute shock and horror when I saw Gabriella. Then imagine my sheer panic when she came over to us, grabbing my face, kissing me, and running her hands over my body. God, even the memory sends shivers down my spine.

What must Daisy have thought? I froze when Gabriella was in front of me. I tried to stammer out a few words. I think I managed to tell her I was on holiday and I said Daisy's name at one point, but my brain was scrambled. Gabriella was talking so fast, I struggled to keep up. What I did translate, was that she wanted me to go back to her hotel room with her for a repeat of that night.

To my absolute joy and relief, Daisy saved me. She told Gabriella I was her wife—which sent very pleasant feelings through my body—and then told her we were on our honeymoon. I remember seeing Gabriella's eyes bulge and her vein pop out. Daisy didn't seem scared of her, though, and before long, she'd whisked me away.

Currently, I'm sitting at a bar with a drink, wondering how to explain all that to Daisy. When we planned to come to Orvieto, I'd been so happy. First, because I could play tour guide to Daisy, and second, because I hadn't slept with anyone here, thus, no risk of drama. Like I said, the Universe is an asshole.

Daisy is looking at me, concerned. "Are you okay?"

I imagine my face had taken the pallor of a Victorian child, sick with cholera. I nod and take a sip of my drink. The alcohol burns my throat and it feels good. Another sip, and I'm starting to come out of my shock.

"Cal, you don't look okay. Who was that woman?"

"Someone I met in Rome." Not a lie.

"Someone, huh?" Daisy isn't going to let this drop. I sink the rest of my drink and signal the bartender for another. I sink that one too before spilling everything to Daisy. When I finish, I can't make eye contact with her. I don't want to see that look in her eye. As much as she's tried to reassure me my sexcapades aren't an issue, I can't help but worry she'll see me in a less than favourable light. What woman would want to start something serious with a lesbian that's fucked half of Europe?

"Jesus, Cal." Yeah, what she said! "I hate predatory lesbians like that." Her face is clouded over with anger.

"She wasn't predatory," I say, "just enthusiastic."

"No, Callie, she was a predator. At no point did she ask if you were comfortable. There was no consent. She took what she wanted from you. She's a predator."

Okay, I don't like this conversation anymore. I'm sure I can bring it up again when I'm home, talking to a therapist that I most definitely need.

"Let's change the subject, please." Daisy nods and sips on her wine. "Should we go back to the hotel so you can sort out the ID for tomorrow?"

"Sure. It won't take me long, though," she shrugs. Confidence is oozing off of her, and I love it.

"You go back to the hotel and do that, and I'll go get a uniform."

My plan for tomorrow is simple, really. There are plenty of people who are not Italian that take groups of people on guided tours. It's an easy way to make money. I plan to turn up tomorrow when they open, tell them I'm a summer employee, and that I was told to shadow an experienced guide to get an idea of how it all works. I know there is room for it all to go tits up and at this stage, I kind of expect it. We have no other choice, though.

With Daisy on her way back to the hotel, I stealthily make my way to the tour office. I do *not* want to run into

Gabriella again. The tour office will close soon, so I need to be quick. Thankfully, there are still plenty of tourists buying tickets, so sneaking past the front desk should be easy. Finding a uniform is the hard part. Hmm, maybe sneaking is the wrong way to go.

Looking at the staff here, I would bet only one of them is a full-time employee and the rest are interns or just part-time. If I can get to an intern, they might be more likely to buy the story I've concocted.

I see my mark—a young lad, maybe early twenties. He's spent more time looking at his phone than he has at the many people he is supposed to be helping.

"Excuse me," I say in my sweetest voice. I flick my hair over my shoulder. Yes, I'm setting feminism back a few decades, but tough shit. I need this clown to drool over me. I clear my throat. Eventually, he looks up, and I almost laugh when he finally registers me. Bless him and his little red flush.

"Hi, yeah, hello." He's not Italian—I'd guess German. He's also got a long way to go before he's as smooth as he thinks he is.

"Hi, I'm Yolanda. I'm due to start here tomorrow, but I haven't been given a uniform."

Note to self: call Daisy ASAP and tell her my name is Yolanda.

"Right, erm, okay. I'm just a front desk guy. I can call over, er, the guy who works here properly."

No, I don't want that.

"Oh, no, he's busy. He sent me to you," I say easily.

"Oh, right, okay." Come on kid, just get me a fucking T-shirt or whatever. "Yeah, alright, just a sec."

I watch him slip in the back. I'm praying he's not talking to anyone else and is just retrieving the shirt. A few minutes pass and I'm starting to get twitchy.

"Sorry about that," he calls as he walks back over to me. "I couldn't find them and then I didn't know what size to get."

Can he see the wave of relief that's just washed over me?

"Oh, no worries. Thank you so much. Will you be here tomorrow?"

He nods frantically. The poor thing thinks I'm interested. Great.

"Yeah, just me in the morning, actually."

Fab-fucking-tastic. Maybe the cunty universe is ready to give me a bloody break.

"Wonderful, I'll see you tomorrow..."

"Hanz."

"See you tomorrow, Hanz." I leave quickly and head to the hotel, still in full stealth mode.

Daisy is in the shower when I get back. Her laptop is open and on the bed. I don't snoop. I close the lid and wait for her to come out. I wish the room had a minibar because my nerves are shot for the day. In a cloud of steam, Daisy emerges from the bathroom in just a towel and my world stops turning. She is stunning. Her long hair is wet, hanging down her back, and her cheeks are red from the hot water.

"How did it go?"

"No problem. All set for tomorrow. I closed your laptop but I didn't look."

"I know. Shall we go out for dinner?"

"Would you mind if we ate in here? I'm knackered."

"Sure, let me grab some clothes and I'll nip to get something."

Music to my ears, although I do feel a little guilty. I'm sure Daisy was looking forward to seeing Orvieto at night.

"No, hang on," I blurt. The words are out of my mouth before I know it. I shouldn't let my past fuck ups stop Daisy from experiencing things. I had planned to take her to this little restaurant at the edge of the city. It's a little hole in the wall that overlooks the valley and the food is excellent. "Give me half an hour to shower and we'll go out."

"But you just said you wanted to eat here?"

"No, I changed my mind."

"Sure?"

"Sure." A small smile graces her perfect lips and I know I made the right choice. I just hope we're not in for any more surprises.

Exactly thirty minutes later, we head out to the restaurant. I can't help scanning my surroundings every ten seconds. It's ridiculous that one woman has made me act like this. We arrive at the restaurant, sans problem. It's not packed. In fact, we are one of only four couples seated on the terrace. Daisy is taking in the view with wonder in her eyes. The sun is setting, and it's perfect.

After I tell her what's on the menu, we both order pasta dishes. I order us some fried vegetables too, because they're awesome. We share a bottle of wine, and I finally feel the stress and nerves melt away. I'm not even worried about tomorrow. Being around Daisy grounds me and makes me feel safe. It's as simple as that, really.

When the sun has disappeared and the mosquitoes are going to town on my legs, we call it a night. The bed feels wonderful when I slip under the covers. Daisy is still in the bathroom. Rolling over to my bedside table, I set my alarm because I must get to the tour office as soon as it opens. The door to the bathroom opens and closes. I wait for Daisy to get into bed, but she doesn't. Curious, I peer over my shoulder. Daisy is standing there, stark bollock naked.

"I don't want you to have the memories of that night plaguing you. Let me give you new ones," she all but purrs. Gobsmacked and dumbstruck is my current state of mind. "Would you like that?" Fuck yes, I would like that. I nod, and she climbs into bed next to me. "Can we go slow?"

I nod again.

And then she kisses me.

Twenty
Daisy

If nipple sucking were an Olympic sport, Callie Compton would win gold every damn time. I never knew I could get to the point of climax just by having my girls played with. It's ridiculous, but here we are, the proof's in the pudding. My clit is about to combust and she hasn't laid a finger on it yet, just her mouth on my nips.

I was standing in the bathroom getting ready for bed and I just finally gave in. All this "waiting until it's the right time" shit was just that...shit! There is no "right time" and, quite frankly, I'm sick of my own excuses. Callie wants me, and I want *her*.

We had a setback today with our plan, and then there was the whole Gabriella thing. I think giving each other pleasure is a brilliant way to turn the day into a win.

Oh, she's adding her hands into the mix now. God, she's good…I mean really good. I kind of hope she's only this good because it's me and her, but that might be wishful thinking.

Isn't that how it's supposed to be, though? If every romance novel ever written is believed, the best sex of your life is with your soulmate…and all that jazz. I've had good sex, but with Callie, it's phenomenal. Maybe she'll whip out Daisy Junior again, although that feels a bit creepy now. I need to ask her to rename the dildo.

I can feel the orgasm building. Callie is stroking me and sucking my nipples at the same time, and it's fabulous. Yep…yep…here it comes. Holy shit, it's never-ending. I think I just tapped out of reality. My head is buzzing and my heart is pounding.

I am spent.

Callie looks down at me. Her lips are swollen and her eyes are shining brightly. It's more than lust peering out of those perfect blue eyes. I hope I'm mirroring that look, because I feel it too. I stroke her cheek and kiss her slowly.

Learning about how Gabriella treated Callie made me furious. No one deserves to be treated like a piece of meat, especially when they didn't give consent. That's the bit that gets me the most. I know Callie has only ever had one-night stands, but I know she would never treat a woman the way Gabriella treated her.

Tonight, I want to remind her how she should be treated. I push her shoulder gently so she's on her back, and slip my thigh between hers. Her hair is splayed across the pillow, and it is magnificent. I dip my head and kiss her again. There's no rush. Our tongues dance together and I begin to rock my hips. We are both wet; her want is being painted on my thigh.

I see her chest begin to rise faster. Her skin begins to flush. Her nostrils flare. I don't want her to come, though—not yet. This moment needs to be savoured. Slowing my hips, I kiss the side of her mouth, then her chin. I push my fingers through her thick locks. She grabs my arse, pulling me closer.

If this were a romance novel, I would tell her I love her. Maybe I will one day, but not now. Now, I just want to make her feel spectacular. My hips begin to move again, grinding harder. Her hands dig into my arse cheeks. Her head rolls back, she's losing control, and it's a glorious thing to watch. Her mouth opens and I feel the scream through her body. She's shaking and gripping me harder.

My orgasm hits a second later. My body crashes to hers and we hold each other. Only for a second or two though, because we're not finished. Actually, tonight is just getting started.

The sun shines through the open curtains. We forgot to close them last night. I am in a state of bliss. I roll over and my heart soars. Callie is facing me, fast asleep, with her arm draped over my waist. My movement doesn't disturb her. She looks so peaceful.

We get the second piece of the book today, and then we are heading back to Florence to drop off the rolling vibrator. After, we're heading to Copenhagen, which means the next few hours are going to be long and tiring. So for now, I want Callie to rest. I hope she's peacefully dreaming.

The coffee shop down the road is packed when I go in. It takes me a good twenty minutes to grab two coffees and that croissant thingy Callie likes. I hope she's still sleeping. I didn't leave a note and she will panic if I'm gone when she wakes.

No danger; she's softly snoring when I get back. I place the coffee down and grab a shower. I really wore her out last night, which makes me a little proud. I feel the shower door open and close. Turning round, I'm met with Callie's lips on my neck. All the times I fantasised about Callie taking me in the shower, and here I am, living it.

After the water has turned cold and we're both thoroughly sated, we sit on the bed, cuddled together, as we eat breakfast and drink the rocket fuel that is Italian coffee. My nerves are tingling as the time draws closer for her to leave. There shouldn't be a problem. I set up Callie's ID in their database, so she should be in and out.

We finish our coffee and Callie springs out of bed to dress. She's ready to get this over with and so am I. Smoothing down the shirt she acquired yesterday, she pulls her hair into a bun, and kisses me. Just that one little act, has me daydreaming about our future and all the goodbye kisses we will have as we set off to go about our days.

"I'm off," Callie says, kissing me a second time.

"Okay, be safe. Call me when it's done."

She nods. There's no point in me tagging along. I have other things to attend to—my day job, for example. I've really dropped the ball recently.

Five minutes have passed since Callie left and I need to get into work mode. I have several emails waiting, but only one grabs my attention. It's from my boss. Yesterday, I spoke to her and filled her in—kind of—on what I was doing. I didn't give her any information that would identify Callie. I told her I was helping a friend, and that was it.

If you knew the specifics of my job, and the people I work for, you wouldn't be surprised to know my boss didn't bat an eye after I told her what was relevant for her to know. She's still on a need-to-know basis. The email I receive back gives me the name of the man we will hand over our precious information to. I commit it to memory and then erase any evidence I received the communication.

Thirty minutes go by and still no Callie. I don't want to be the type of person that worries, but it's Callie. How can I not? I contemplate going to grab another coffee but decide against it. I don't want her to get back and me to be gone.

A total of fifty-five minutes has passed since she left and finally, the door swings open. I gasp, because Callie is soaked from head to foot.

"What the hell happened?" I shriek.

I feel we ask that question a lot.

"Well, I figured out why they were having to do work. The chamber was partially flooded."

"Shit, the pages?"

"All good. I'd hidden them in a compartment, high up. The water hadn't reached it, but I had to go swimming to retrieve them."

I hate to think what was in that water.

"Shower! Leave the pages, and go get cleaned up."

Without protest, she dumps a wad of pages on the little table by the door and heads to the bathroom. Chris left me with the first part of the book, so I collect the second part, too. I flick through the pages and note all the names. Some I have heard of, some I haven't.

Using my phone—which is secure again—I scan the pages, automatically uploading them to my virtual vault, just as I did the first part. We need a copy in case something goes wrong.

Looking a hell of a lot better than when she got back, Callie joins me on the bed. "Ready to go? I think we need to get moving."

"Ready when you are." I can understand why she doesn't want to stick around.

"Come on then." She stands and takes my hand to help me up. I can't resist giving her a kiss. She kisses me back with force, and we stay that way for a few minutes.

Our bags get packed and we're ready to go. The walk to the bike is short—shorter than I wanted it to be. I can't believe I have to get back into that sidecar again.

We arrive in Florence and return the motorbike. I can't say I'm going to miss it. Callie had fun, though, so that's all that matters. We decide to stay one night in Florence, before setting off for Copenhagen.

"I think we should forego another car," I say with a sigh. I don't know about Callie, but all the driving is exhausting.

"Okay, how do you want to get there, then?" She doesn't seem upset that I'm changing her plans.

"Train. Look, we can leave from Florence tomorrow morning. The train will stop off in Bologna, where we will need to change. From Bologna, it's a couple of hours to Milan. Then we change at Lugano, then at Arth-Goldau. A change at Basel to Hamburg, then—"

"Okay, okay, I get it. There are a lot of changes," Callie laughs.

"Yeah, but it means you get to rest on the journey. Driving from here to Copenhagen is a lot, Cal. By train, we will be in Copenhagen in under twenty-four hours. We won't have to keep pulling over for gas and snacks, or to sleep."

"Hey, if you're game, I am. I love trains."

That bit of information surprises me. I guess there are plenty of things I still need to learn about Callie.

"I'll book the tickets and then we can head out for dinner. Deal?"

We seal it with a kiss. "Deal."

Sorry for the Jason Donovan reference.

It hasn't escaped my notice, that Callie is being very tight-lipped about the location of the third set of pages. I should just ask her, but something is stopping me. We've been sitting on the train to Hamburg for an hour, and she's drifted off to sleep again. I can't settle. My phone vibrates and I see Penny's name flash across the screen. Shit, when was the last time I contacted her?

"Hey, you," I say with far too much enthusiasm. I manage to prop my phone up on the little service tray attached to the seat in front of me.

"I thought I should confirm you're not dead."

Oops, she's pissed.

"Sorry, Pen, I lost track of checking in. I'm fine; no harm done and healthy as a horse."

"Where are you?"

I disabled my phone tracker after the whole Gary debacle.

"On a train."

"That's it, that's all you're going to say?"

I wish I could fill her in, but that would be reckless. The fewer people who know, the better. It's vital we have an element of surprise. Betty might look like a church-going, cardigan-knitting, sweet old lady, but she's fucking ruthless. I have no doubt, she would hurt every single person, who had the slightest inkling we were coming for her if it meant she could save her own wrinkly hide.

"Pen, it's better you don't know."

"Well did you catch up to Callie? You can at least tell me that."

"I did. I'm with her now."

"Wow, okay. So when will you be home?"

"Not sure. Don't worry, it won't be too much longer. Did you feed Walter?" Walter is my goldfish, that has lived a surprisingly long time in my care. I could kill a cactus, so he's doing really well.

"Of course. Right, I'll let you get on then. Please be careful."

"Will do. Bye."

I hate that a little part of me is suspicious Penny called. Is that how it's going to be now? Am I going to question everyone's motives? Jesus, it's exhausting. I would love to be at home now, snuggled on my lumpy sofa with a pack of bourbon biscuits and a cup of tea, binge watching something on Netflix.

I look over at Callie, who's still sleeping. She is really wiped. I doubt she's got this much sleep in the six years she's been running. Will she come back to Edinburgh with me? What does she want to do when it's all over? I huff out a breath. I want her with me more than anything.

The train slows, ready to stop in Hamburg. Call me paranoid, but something, or should I say someone, catches my attention. A woman sitting four rows back is glancing at us. When did she get on the train? Was it at Florence, or after? Our seats are facing backwards, so I have a clear line of sight. I nudge Callie awake. Blinking rapidly, she looks at me, disorientated.

"Callie, I think that woman is looking at us," I whisper hiss. I can't say she's following us, because I've only just noticed her.

Callie discreetly looks. "When did you notice her looking?"

"Just now, when I finished on the phone with Penny."

"I didn't see her in Florence. She must have gotten on later."

"Do you think it's someone to worry about? I could be mistaken." I'm no expert. My mind could be playing tricks. Callie looks again.

"There's only one way to find out. The train is going to stop soon. You need to be ready to go. I'll grab our bags. Don't look back, just run to the exit."

"You want to get off the train?"

"Yup. We can catch another one if we are wrong. But if she is watching us, I don't want to lead her to Copenhagen."

I have to trust Callie. She has the experience and I trust her gut completely.

We sit and wait for the train to stop. Callie holds my arm, signalling I should wait. Suddenly, she squeezes me hard, and I shoot out of my seat. I don't look back, I just head for the door, which is about to close. I understand that Callie had us wait until the last second before getting off. I leap onto the platform and run. The adrenaline is surging through my body, and I pray to any and all goddesses, that Callie is behind me.

I can't stand the not knowing any longer, so I slow my pace and turn around. My heart bursts in my chest as I see Callie weaving in and out of people on the platform. She has our bags. I look at the train that is now pulling out of the station.

"Run, Daisy." Callie is mouthing. "Run."

I look past Callie's shoulder and my stomach rolls. The woman from the train is chasing Callie. She's also chasing me. I turn and sprint. I have no idea where we are, or where we should go.

Twenty-One
Callie

My feet are loudly slapping the concrete of the train station platform. Daisy is a few metres ahead of me. She keeps turning her head, making sure I'm still behind her. I do the same, but for me, it's to check if the woman is still chasing us. She is. I need to do something. We can't outrun her forever.

Impulsively, I stretch out my stride and easily catch up to Daisy. Thank God I keep up a good level of fitness. Adrenaline is surging through every muscle fibre. My heart is pumping strongly, pushing me on. I feel like I could outrun anyone in the world right now.

I look ahead. There's a building coming up. I think it's the platform coffee shop. I reach for Daisy and steer her around the corner of the building. I then stop, lean against the wall, and count to three. I stick my arm out to the side and pray. The sickening thud of a body hitting the floor confirms I have successfully clotheslined our pursuer. Eat your heart out, Brodie Lee. That's a wrestler, FYI.

Splayed out on the floor, the woman is completely dazed. She hit the ground hard. I take advantage of her temporary disabled state and roll her over to her front. On her belt is a set of handcuffs. Shit, she came prepared. Have I just taken out a member of law enforcement? With my knee pressing her hands to her back, I search her pockets. No ID, but there is a phone. I hand it to a very stunned-looking Daisy.

The woman has unwittingly given me the very thing I need to restrain her. I pull the cuffs out of their sheath, wrapping one around her wrist. I shift backwards, and in a feat of great effort, I wrangle her leg up so her ankle can be cuffed to her wrist. She's hogtied. Now I can take a breath. We can't stop, though. The scuffle has no doubt earned the interest of the station security team.

Daisy is shaking when I reach for her. I wish I could take her in my arms and comfort her, but we don't have time. My experience and instincts have kicked in. We must get off the street—now. I grab her shoulders, steering her to the stairs that lead to the exit. She's moving willingly, but I don't think she's completely with it.

So far, there have been no police or security guards. Maybe we avoided them by coming this way. The street is busy when we exit. I have never been to Hamburg, so I'm like a fish out of water. We start walking, just needing to get some distance.

Finally, I spot an InterCity Hotel. This will do. Daisy is still letting me steer her and I'm getting worried she's gone into shock. I carefully sit her down in one of the reception area's chairs. I book a room for the night and order lunch for us both. The room is nice, located at the front of the hotel, so we can look down to the main street.

I look Daisy in the eye, trying to get her to focus on my face and hands. "Daisy?" She's looking pale and her eyes are fixed forward. "Daisy, honey, look at me. Look, we're safe."

I take her hand and kneel in front of her. She'd deposited herself on the edge of the bed when we entered the room. She blinks a few times and then launches herself at me. We stay locked together for a while. Daisy is crying on my shoulder and all I can do is grit my teeth.

I can't break down now; she needs me to be strong. Hell, I need me to be strong. This is the first time someone has chased me like that. I've never let anyone get that close to me in all the time I've been running. Daisy was the only exception, and now this woman.

"Are you hurt?" I ask Daisy. She shakes her head.

"Just shaken. That was insane, Callie. Who the hell was that?"

That's the million-pound question, isn't it? A knock on the door startles me, but then I calm down. It's just our lunch. I paid extra to have it sent up. I don't think sitting in a restaurant or hotel dining room is something either of us wants to do right now.

Daisy spends ten minutes pushing her sandwich around the plate.

Placing my hand on her leg, I catch her attention, which seems to have wandered. "Daisy, you need to eat."

Reluctantly, she takes a bite. I tuck in, because I'm suddenly starving. Once I've finished, I take out the phone the woman had on her, and put it on the bed. I then take Daisy's bag and remove her phone and laptop. I knew the mobiles looked the same.

Whoever is after us, is using the same type of hardware Daisy uses. That can't be good, or a coincidence.

"You have to get rid of your laptop, Daisy."

She looks at me as though I'm asking her to give up her firstborn.

"I can't, Cal—"

"You must. Daisy, look at this, they're the same model. It's not me they're tracking: It's you."

"That's not possible, Callie."

"Well, it is. I have the burner phone, and that's it. I dumped my original phone in Florence."

Daisy rakes her hands through her hair.

"If that's the case, we have a big problem, Callie. No one, and I really do mean *no one*, should be able to hack my phone or laptop, which indicates someone from my work life is tracking me. It's not Gary; he was booted after what he did."

"Daisy, what do you do?" I think the time for secrets is over. I've been nothing but open and honest with Daisy.

"I can't tell you, Callie."

"Well, that's fucking fabulous." My anger is rising. It's probably due to the panic I felt earlier. I'm not sure, but either way, I'm pissed. "I've trusted you from the start. You show up out of the blue, spouting a story I gladly accepted. Now people are catching up to me left, right, and centre. The only common denominator is you!"

"Are you accusing me of something, Callie, because if you are, spit it out."

I don't know what to say, because I don't know what to think. I would never have thought Daisy would ever betray me... Not until today. It's not a coincidence the woman from the train has the same tech as Daisy. Does that mean the man at the motel traced us because of her, too?

I have too many questions and no answers. Daisy refusing to give up the thing that is allowing these people to track us speaks volumes, in my mind. "Give up the laptop and phone, or we part ways here."

"You think I'm working for Betty, don't you?" Her eyes are laced with anger and hurt, but I won't fall for it. Ever since Daisy Simpson showed up, my life has been on the line. I'd done a great job of hiding, for six years, and now, suddenly, everyone and their dog knows where I am.

"I don't know, Daisy. Are you? These people that keep finding us, clearly work with you. Maybe they were just supposed to observe us, keep an eye on us to make sure you were safe, until you could hand me over?"

"Fuck you, Callie!"

"Yeah, you did that. Was that your surefire way to keep me around?"

Daisy visibly pales and recoils. "How could you ever think that?"

"How could I not? You've been secretive with me from the beginning about all this—" I wave to her laptop, "I trusted you without question."

"I am not working for Betty. I would never work for her. I want what you want, Callie. I want you to be able to come home."

"Then tell me what you do. Tell me who these people are."

"I can't!"

"Then I can't stay with you."

"You're just going to leave me here?"

"I doubt you'll have any problems. Just give your friends a call. I'm sure they'd be happy to pick you up. Hell, you can debrief them on the way home."

I'm being a snarky bitch, which is out of character for me. Later on, I'm going to collapse under the weight of it all, but not now. Now, I need to get away from her, and to safety. If being a royal arsehole is the way I need to act so I can cope, then so be it.

"No, I won't let you leave." Daisy moves to stand in front of the door. "I am not a traitor. I am *not* working for Betty. I am here for you, to help you, and that's it. I know you're scared, Callie, but running from me is not the answer."

"Move, Daisy." My face portrays my mood. "I won't ask you twice."

To my utter astonishment, she backs up to the door and slides down to the floor, completely blocking the way out. I will have to physically remove her if I want to leave.

"If you want me to move, you will have to make me." God, she's so fucking stubborn sometimes. "I will get rid of the laptop and phone, but I can't tell you what I do, Callie. That's for both our safety."

Is this a ploy? Is she giving me just enough to keep me fooled? Shit, what should I do? I won't manhandle her, so if she won't move, I need to wait her out.

"Pass me my laptop," she says.

"Get it yourself."

"So you can dash out the door? I don't think so, Cal. You want me to destroy it, you can pass it to me." She's pigheaded and stubborn as a mule. I might as well do it, because I have a feeling she's not moving anytime soon. As soon as I hand it to her, she starts tapping away. "I've transferred the stuff I need to my vault. Now I'll ghost the drive. If they are tracking it, or my phone, we can use that to help us escape further detection."

"You want to use them as decoys?" I hate that she is suggesting something I think is a good plan.

"Yes, let's send them to Timbuktu or somewhere. I don't know."

"Or we could just leave them here, hidden."

"Wouldn't it be better for them to still think they are onto us?"

She has a point. I agree, and formulate a plan to get the laptop and phone as far away from us as possible. Daisy still hasn't moved from the door. I wonder if she's going to sleep there all night. My anger is ebbing away, and I regret some of the things I said. How can I apologise, though, when a small part of me still thinks it's true?

"When this is over, we're going to have a talk about everything you said to me," Daisy signs furiously. She's hurt, I can see that, but I don't know if I can trust what that means. She seems genuine, but can I trust her?

"Okay." That's my brilliant answer.

I go into the bathroom and shut the door. I need space. The water is scalding, and it's just what I need. I hate that my head is so fucked up. Just yesterday, I was almost happy—content even. Daisy was with me, and we were travelling through Europe. Okay, it wasn't under the finest of circumstances, but it's as close to normal as I've felt in years.

Has this life broken me? Am I always going to be looking over my shoulder, questioning the people around me? That's no way to live, and that's not something I want to subject Daisy to. God, I'm back to being a right fucking melt.

Jesus, Callie, get a fucking grip! You're alive and you're healthy. Find a silver lining, for Christ's sake.

I walk into the bedroom stark naked. Daisy does a double take and looks me up and down. She wants me, and I'm pissed that I want her.

Finally, she looks away and sighs, "Are you going to leave if I have a shower?"

"No."

I'm not lying. My heart won't let me leave, not now the initial shock and anger have dissolved. I'm just tired and confused. Daisy nods, stands, and goes to the bathroom. I find a set of clean clothes to wear. It's the afternoon and we have plenty of daylight left. Ideally, we would nip out and see the sights, but that's out of the question.

Copenhagen is waiting. We have to get there, but the train is out. The only option is to get a car again. Do we leave immediately, or wait until tomorrow? Indecisiveness is not a problem I usually suffer with. Saying that though, this is the first time I've been so close to being caught. I'm questioning everything.

"Hey," Daisy's voice shakes me out of my head.

"Hi. Feel better?"

She looks good fresh out of the shower. My body doesn't know when to quit. I mean, this isn't really an appropriate response to someone who could be a potential risk to my life, is it? My brain has no say in the matter, because my heart and soul belong to Daisy; they always have. God, pass a sick bucket! When did I get so gross and mushy?

"Yep, now we need to talk. What do you want to do?" She's all business, which I appreciate.

"First, we ship out the laptop and phones. Can you first see if there is anything of use on the one we picked up from our pursuer?"

She nods. Although she wiped her laptop and phone, she didn't touch the one we nabbed off the woman.

"There's only one number listed. No calls going out or coming in, but there is a message thread—one-way, by the looks of it. That woman has been sending updates on our location. The last one was when she got on the train. She confirmed that she'd located us again."

"Okay, is there anything we can do with that number?"

"Not if I can't use my laptop, no." It's a catch-22. If we use the laptop, we are still traceable, but if we don't, the number and its owner remains a mystery. "I think it's best if we stick to our original plan. Get rid of the hardware, and get to Copenhagen. Once we have the rest of the book, we can work out who is behind the number."

Honestly, I'm happy Daisy is taking the lead. My brain is fried. I stamp down the little niggling thoughts that are still percolating. If she's lying, I'll find out sooner rather than later, I suppose.

"Okay, we'll head out tomorrow. I suggest we wait until we're ready to leave before sending the laptop and phones. Once we're on the road, I'm only stopping for petrol. It's a straight run to Copenhagen, okay?"

"Fine by me. I changed my mind. I'm not waiting for this to be done before delving into that crock of shit you accused me of. At some point before we get the other piece of the book, we are going to have it out."

Jesus, this is going to be a long fucking journey.

Twenty-Two

Daisy

I spent the five hours it took us to drive to Copenhagen, stewing on everything Callie had said to me in Hamburg. I get that she was upset. Both of our emotions were running on high, but fuck, to accuse me of sleeping with her for nefarious reasons sliced me to the bone.

Without sounding super dramatic, what Callie said to me felt so much more painful than any of the cruel jibes my dad would throw my way. Maybe it's because he meant very little to me and Callie means the world. I'm not sure, but I know I never want to hear such things from her again.

Being chased by that woman was terrifying. For the first time, I actually thought we could come to harm. Yes, we've had some close calls and none of this has been plain sailing, but to have a person chase us with the intent of harming us is something else.

When I was a child, I used to have a recurring nightmare about being chased, but in my dreams, I couldn't run properly. Every time I tried to move my legs faster, they felt as though they were glued to the floor. Having the woman chase us made me feel just like I did as a child. If it weren't for Callie urging me on, I think I would have frozen.

I was very impressed with the way Callie took out our hunter. It was super fucking hot, if I'm being honest. How did she know to do that? I wonder if she's had to tackle someone before. All the hotness left as soon as Callie uncovered the woman's phone.

Just like Callie, I was also shocked to find the woman carrying the same kind of phone I have because, I know, for a fact, the phone I have is only issued to my company, because I helped make the fucking thing. There was no way she could have access to it unless she was an employee. Her being in possession of it raises so many questions, and I can't answer any of them yet.

I guess I can understand Callie making the leap that I'm somehow involved. If the shoe were on the other foot, I may have thought the same thing, but I can't say I would have accused Callie of fucking me into staying with her. Hell, I didn't even initiate it the first time! Yeah, I kissed her in that manky bed in the rundown farmhouse, but it was Callie who felt herself up in front of me, and really took it over the line.

Side note: If this all works out and we live happily ever after, we have to radically change our story, because our future kids cannot know any of this!

What we have shared on this… Shit, what do I call this? It's not an adventure; it's the opposite. A misadventure? Yeah…that about sums it up. Anyway, what the two of us have shared on our misadventure is nothing to scoff at. I thought we connected. I wasn't just fucking her. Is that what she thinks this is? A quick fuck to get us by until it's all over and done with?

See, that's what I'm ruminating on, and usually I'd have no problems having it out with her, but this time I can't. I'm hurt and I'm scared. Somehow, my company is involved in all this shit. They can't possibly be working for Betty, so why are they sending people after me and Callie?

To figure that out, I need my equipment, which isn't possible now, not after getting rid of my laptop and phone. It was the last thing I wanted to do, but I knew Callie would run from me if I didn't do that for her. To be fair, she's right. The laptop was compromised, and keeping it would have been foolish. Still, getting rid of it felt like cutting off a limb.

We arrive in Copenhagen and I'm immediately cold. Did I mention I hate the cold with a passion? I have one jumper and a pair of jeans in my bag, to change into. I'll do that after taking a scalding shower in the hotel room. Callie made us a reservation before we left Germany, and I wondered if she'd stick us in separate rooms considering her feelings.

After depositing our bags in the room—I'll spare you the description—we head out. It's just another hotel room, in another town. I never thought I'd get sick of travelling, but with the mood I'm in, I just want to stop moving from place to place and go home. Callie still hasn't told me the location of the third piece of the book. I follow obediently because I can't handle another showdown with her.

Tivoli Gardens is a place I read about on a travel blog, ages ago. I always wanted to go—in winter, to be precise—because it's supposed to be magical. This visit is *far* from anything resembling magical. It's just one more thing to be pissed about.

Callie buys two tickets, but we don't enter. Instead, she takes me to a pub. Now this is what I'm talking about. I don't even wait for her. I go straight to the bar and order two pints. The beer feels heaven sent as it makes its way into my bloodstream.

Come on, alcohol, do your thing.

The pub is busy, but not in a way I'm used to. In England and Scotland, most pubs get a bit rowdy. Here, there are tables packed with people, but they're laughing and playing board games. It's a bit bizarre, but I'm for it. I'm also for the open fire that's churning out wonderful heat.

We haven't communicated in hours and it's horrible. I'm starting to get upset again as I look at Callie, who is watching a table next to us play a card game. I nudge her foot with mine. She turns to look at me, and I hate that I see the mistrust she has developed for me shine through so clearly.

"Are we just going to ignore each other from now on?"

"No."

Oh goody, monosyllabic answers. I suppose that's one up from no answers at all.

"Good talk, Callie." I roll my eyes at her and shake my head.

"What do you want me to say?"

"I want you to say you believe I'm not involved in this. I'm not working for your fucking nan. Christ, Cal, she's threatening my brother, and I was honest with you from the start about it. If I *were* working for her, why would I tell you any of what she's said to me?"

"To gain my trust," she shrugs.

God, she's being so serious right now, I don't know what to do. I drink some more of my pint. Callie turns her head back to the table next to us. I feel tears sting the corner of my eyes.

No! No fucking way does she get to see me cry.

I have to concede I can't say anything right now that's going to get her to trust me. Weighing my options, I come to a devastating conclusion. I should have let her leave me behind in Hamburg. Having me here with her now isn't going to work. She's so paranoid that she'll keep me at arm's length, possibly forever.

Decision made, albeit painfully. I'm done with this. I found her, which is what I set out to do. I'll take the info from my vault and pass it on to the name that was given to me, and then I'll get on with my own life. I can only hope and pray that Callie comes back to me.

Downing the rest of my drink, I stand and put on my coat. Callie watches me, but doesn't say anything. I shuffle past her and lean down to kiss her on the head before leaving.

I feel broken.

The hotel is a short walk away, and I have my own key card. I scold myself as tears start to form. *I won't cry. I won't cry.* Does it say something about me that I'm walking away? I was so sure I would ride this out with her. Whatever. I'm going to drive myself insane if I keep churning it over in my head.

My luggage isn't even unpacked. I set the key card down, hoist my bag onto my shoulder, and leave. The last thing I want to do right now is travel, but once I'm home, I can take some time to sleep, and process what a heap of shit everything has turned out to be. God knows how I'm going to explain this to Betty without getting Daniel shot in the face.

I step out of the hotel and into the street. There's a taxi rank just up ahead. With only two people ahead of me, the wait isn't more than a few minutes. The taxi driver puts my bag into the trunk, and I open the rear door. Before I can slip into the back, the door is slammed shut. I wheel around, ready to spit venom at the rude fucker that did that, but I stop, because looking flustered with tears streaming down her face, is Callie.

Pulling me back to the curb, she retrieves my bag out of the car boot. She still hasn't spoken, and I have nothing to say. I let her steer me back to the hotel room, where she throws my bag to the floor. I watch her pace from the bed to the door.

"You were just going to leave? No goodbye? Nothing? After everything?"

Her hand signals are erratic, she's shaking, and her tears are pouring now. I'm so fucking confused.

"Callie, it's best I go. After Hamburg, you're not going to trust me. I won't stay with you to be ignored."

Callie grips her head like it's in pain. Her eyes are frantic and I'm getting concerned. Suddenly, she drops to the floor in a heap. I rush to her because I think she's passed out. She hasn't; she's just sobbing.

"I... I c-can't do... do this w-without you, Daisy." I hold her as tight as I can. Her body is almost convulsing, as she lets out years of pain and fear. This is the meltdown she's needed to have.

In all the years I have known Callie Compton, I have never seen her look so broken. Once she started crying last night, she couldn't stop. The proverbial floodgates had opened.

I stayed on the floor with her for hours as she sobbed. Honestly, I was at a loss for what to do.

Eventually, I was able to coax her into the shower, where she stood limply as I washed her hair and body. After, I tucked her into bed and lay with her until she fell asleep. I managed to leave the room long enough to get us some food.

To me, Callie is strong and unwavering. She is calm under pressure, and always one step ahead of everyone else. This Callie, the one sleeping next to me, is a stranger. This Callie is so vulnerable, I could cry. I know I have to be the strong one for now, but I'm not sure how to do that.

Look, I'm not some bloody wuss. I'm a strong, independent woman. I look after myself financially and emotionally. I've never needed anyone. Alright, maybe that's a lie. I needed Callie when I was younger, that's for sure. Not now, though. I learned to look after myself as soon as I left for university.

But I'm not alone anymore. I also have Callie to look after, and that isn't something I'm used to doing. There's a reason—apart from Callie being the only woman I've ever loved—that I haven't pursued relationships with women. I don't know how to be there for someone like that. I think it's scary having another person rely on you.

Callie has slept through the whole of yesterday afternoon, and the night. I've struggled to sleep, too worried about her to settle. It's 8 a.m. and I finally feel her stir. A surge of panic runs through me. I don't know how to act. Should I ignore her breakdown and wait for her to say something, or should I talk to her about it? Why am I being so weird about it?

"Hey," I sign when she rolls over and looks up at me. I give her the warmest smile in my arsenal and hope I don't look super creepy. Her eyes are puffy and bloodshot, but she returns my smile. That's got to be a good sign, right?

"Hey," she replies. I can only imagine her voice must be croaky. She cried for hours.

I pass her a small bottle of water that I put on my bedside table earlier. She takes it and drains half of it. Score one to Daisy. I totally called that right. Maybe I can look after her, after all!

"How are you feeling?"

"Like a truck ran over me!" I bet she does. "Thank you," she adds. I don't want her thanks; I want her trust. "It all just felt too much last night." I nod and place a kiss on her head. "When I saw you leaving, it was like something in me broke." I don't want to say anything until I know where this is going. "I've been alone and scared for so long,

Daisy. When you found me, it was like my world started turning again. And then I felt like I had to keep you and Chris safe, but no matter what I did, people found us. I've been terrified that you would get hurt."

Her eyes well up again and my heart almost breaks.

"I felt a bit better when Chris found a place with Meryl and Derek. But then we were chased by that woman, and I thought you would be hurt which… It's too much to bear, Daisy. I know you're not in league with Betty. I should never have said all that. I'm so sorry. My head is a mess. I can't think straight. It's all just too much."

She's sobbing again and I can't stop my own tears from spilling this time.

When Callie has stopped crying—probably because her tear ducts have dried up—I sit in front of her. "I would never betray you, Callie. Never!" She has to know that's the truth. I need her to know, without a doubt. "Callie, I have been in love with you for so long. No other woman could ever match up. I would do anything for you. *Anything.*" I see no point holding back anymore. "No matter what happens, I will be by your side for as long as you will have me!"

"You love me?"

"Yes. I always have, and I always will. I fell in love with you the day we met, Callie Compton."

Well, it's all out there now. I feel squirmy, because Callie is looking at me so intensely, she might burn holes into my eyeballs.

"I love you, too. Always have."

"Kiss me."

You might want to go and make a cup of tea or something because this is going to go on for a while.

Twenty-Three
Callie

RIGHT, SO I HAD a major breakdown! I'm talking a full-on, losing-my-shit kind of thing, and I said some really fucking bad things to Daisy. My eyes feel like balls of sandpaper after crying for hours on end. Is it possible to get dehydrated from spilling too many tears?

Betty always told me that Comptons should never cry. No one should see a Compton acting weak, because that's what crying is, a weakness. As much as I tried to forget a lot of the bullshit she spouted, that little nugget of fucked up wisdom always stuck with me. I can't remember the last time I cried properly. Possibly not since my mum died.

So twenty-odd years' worth of tears was bound to take a while to get through. Daisy was amazing, which makes me feel like garbage. I'm not sure how I'll make it up to her. I hope she understands how fucked up I was feeling when I accused her of those awful things.

I really wasn't expecting her to declare her undying love for me! I definitely wasn't expecting to say it back. I sure as shit didn't expect us to be getting hot and heavy after the turd of a day yesterday, but hey ho, here we are!

What started off as a make-out session, soon turned into hands grabbing and pinching. There is no way on earth I look sexy right now, not after all that blubbering. I'm guessing my face resembles that of a bee sting victim, to be honest. Daisy doesn't seem put off, though, so I'll shut up and leave her to keep massaging my breasts.

There is definitely a lot for us to unpack and talk about. Jesus, there is so much we need to work through, which, for such a new couple, isn't ideal. I'm calling us a couple now, because, let's face it, Daisy and I are it. Take all the shit away, and what you get are two people in love. That love is my light at the end of this shit tunnel. That thought is what's going to get me through what needs to be done.

I plan to fuck Daisy until she can't remember her name. After that, I'll go and get the third piece of the book, then we'll leave for Scotland. I feel lighter and more focused for unloading everything last night. It's what I needed. I'm ready now. No more fear. I'm coming for you, Betty!

Well, actually I'm gonna come for Daisy first, because she is doing wonderful things with her tongue. Oh, and she just added fingers! Lord above, I can't hold on. This woman is outstanding. My throat is a little hoarse from last night, but I still let out a loud moan as my body trembles under her touch.

When I'm finally coherent enough to focus on Daisy, I take her in my arms. I draw strength from feeling her body close to mine. Of course I'm going to reciprocate, but I just need a minute.

I lift her head from my chest so I can look into her eyes. "Is it okay to call you my girlfriend?"

Don't mock me. I know how lame and prepubescent it sounds to ask her that, but give me a break. I never got to ask her when I was a teen. I'm playing catch-up.

I see her eyes mist a little before she kisses me tenderly. I'll take her kiss as a yes. Daisy Simpson is my girlfriend. Win! Now, back to the job at hand... I roll her over and make my way down her exquisite body. It's been far too long since I've had my mouth on her. I dip between her legs and gently take her clit between my lips.

I've always enjoyed oral, but with Daisy I could do it all day. Her taste is addictive, and the moans she makes when I play with her clit are music to my ears. I love that she grinds against my face, seeking purchase because I'm teasing her. When she growls in frustration, I have to slip a hand through my own folds because it turns me on so much.

My own orgasm is building, so I stop teasing her and get serious. I suck on her clit and tongue her entrance. Her hips are moving feverishly, and her thighs are shaking. Her head snaps back as she tumbles over the edge, and it's glorious. My own climax is raging through me, and I see light behind my eyelids. Sex has never been this intense for me. I'll call it the "Daisy Effect."

We lay together for a while. I love that we don't feel the need to fill the silence; we can just be. I am feeling so much better mentally, and as much as I want to stay locked up in the hotel room with Daisy, I need to get moving. It's difficult, though, when she's so fucking warm and soft.

I sit up and look down at her. Her cheeks have a faint red glow, and my ego loves it, because I did that to her. "I need to go and get those pages."

"How long will it take?"

"That's the thing. The pages are in a space that isn't exactly accessible in daylight."

Her brow scrunches adorably. I'm willing to hold my hands up and admit I screwed the pooch this time. We haven't picked up the parts of the book in the order I hid them. The pages I left in Copenhagen are actually the end pages.

By the time I got round to hiding the last section, I was in a dark place. I just wanted to get rid of the bloody thing. There's nothing like carrying a memento of your fucked up life, everywhere you go, to make you feel constantly shitty, and to remind you of what you left behind.

So, I wrapped the pages up, stuck them in an airtight container, and dumped them in a water feature in Tivoli Gardens. It was a rash move, and I certainly didn't think it through. I just figured no one would think to look in water. It made sense to me at the time.

As you can imagine, I can't go wading through the water fountain to get the box in the middle of the day. Also, I have to be prepared that the fountain has been emptied out since I deposited the pages. If that's the case, our trip here could be for nothing. I explain all that to Daisy.

"So, how do we get them?"

"Well, we go to the park as late as possible, find a place to hide, and then wait until everyone has gone home."

There are cameras everywhere in this park. I'm a tad worried we could end up getting arrested. However, I have a plan if we get caught. It's a weak-ass plan, but still, a plan. Daisy is not impressed we're having to do this at all. Even the promise of mind-numbing sex isn't stopping her from scowling at me. I told her she could wait in the hotel, but that went down like a lead balloon. It's a no-win situation for me. I give up.

We are currently hiding in a bush!

[Please insert joke here]

I desperately want to say something funny, but I'm a little scared Daisy will beat me to death. Considering she's just furiously signed she has a literal stick up her arse, I don't think she would appreciate the humour.

The park closed ten minutes ago, but there are still a ton of staff around. When we go for the pages, we need to be fast. I forgot how fucking freezing it can get here. Daisy looks like an icicle, which is another reason she hates me right now. Her lips are starting to go blue, proving she should have stayed in the hotel room, like I suggested. I'm mad at myself for not insisting, because I know how much she detests the cold.

Alright, it's now thirty minutes since the park closed and I think Daisy is getting hypothermic. We need to go. Now.

I think we can sneak to the fountain without getting caught. There are plenty of places we can duck behind to avoid the security man. It's dark, so we might be able to stay off the camera monitors by keeping to the shadows as much as possible.

And we're off!

So far, so good, I haven't spotted anyone. I memorised the map of the park. We aren't too far away from the fountain. Daisy has her head on a swivel. She knows what she's doing. A few more rounds of run-and-duck, and I have our target in sight. I'm just about to leave the safety of the shadows when Daisy hauls me back. I missed the security guy walking in our direction. My heart is pumping hard. He doesn't seem to have seen me.

I blow out a breath of relief when he trundles by, whistling to himself. Daisy gives me the green light to make my run over to the fountain. This has to be quick. Unlike most of the park, the fountains are still illuminated. I'm going to be completely visible.

Come on, Callie, you got this.

I nod to Daisy that I'm going. I run as fast as I can to the fountain. Paddling through water is *not* a quiet activity, so I just have to go for it. The fountain is made up of three separate jets. They are in the shape of flowers. I threw the box in the closest flower. I hope to God it's still there.

My feet are freezing by the time I make my way to the correct flower. I thrust my hand into it and search. My anxiety rises. I can't feel the box. Fuck! I take a beat to calm myself. So far, there are no alarms wailing, or men with bats running at me, so I don't think I've been spotted. After I feel my heart rate chill, I start my search again. Finally, my fingers brush against the familiar plastic box. Yanking it out, I send a thank you to the Universe.

All we have to do now is exit the garden without being spotted, and we're home free. There is a staff entrance at the other end of the park. My feet are numb as I try to walk. This sucks major fucking balls. I'm fond of my toes, and losing them to frostbite would really piss me off. Daisy has taken the lead. She's so quiet as she moves, it's a little freaky.

Daisy points to the staff entrance. We are so close, I can almost feel the warmth of the bath I'm going to take when we get back to our room. Obviously, I've just jinxed us, because there's now a security guard chilling by the gate we need to go through. He's having a smoke, scrolling on his phone.

I'm going to lose an appendage if I don't get warm soon, but this fella isn't moving. I need to do something. I turn to ask Daisy if she has any idea what we should do, only to find she's not there. Jesus, she's like a ninja. I scan the area to see where she is, but nothing. Great, now what do I do?

There's a loud crash to my left. The security guard immediately shifts from his position to check it out. I watch him approach the building where the noise came from. Daisy is suddenly behind me, pushing me forward to the gate. We are ten feet away when I hear the guy shouting at us. I grab Daisy's hand and pull her through the exit. I really can't feel my feet, so running is proving hazardous. I trip several times.

We are both breathing heavily by the time we make it back to the hotel. The security guard didn't chase us for long. I doubt he's paid enough to make it his mission to track us down. We do need to leave Copenhagen, though. It's very possible our faces were caught on camera, and the last thing we need is to be hauled out of bed by the Danish authorities. I think the worst we would get is a charge of trespassing, but neither of us wants that.

Daisy takes the box and puts it in her pack. I jump in the shower and try to get the feeling back in my feet. All in all, we are ready to go within the hour. Now, we didn't get round to discussing the next leg of our journey, which will take us to Scotland. Driving there will be hideously long, and I'm just ready to get this shit done with.

"Where to?" Daisy asks as we exit the hotel and head for the rental car.

I want to give her a solid plan, but I can't. In fact, recently, I've started to lose my ability to plan ahead. Back in Tivoli Gardens, when we came across the security guard at the gate, it should have been me suggesting a distraction, luring him away from our exit. My mind was blank. Something in me has changed, but I'm not sure what it is.

"Let's just start driving. We need some distance before we plan anything."

You know, I never enjoyed being called The Chameleon. I hated I was able to pull the wool over people's eyes. It always felt wrong. I used some of the skills I'd learned from Betty, whilst on the run. It was a necessity. Since Daisy turned up, though, I can't think like The Chameleon at all. Every day, it's gotten harder and harder, which is really fucking inconvenient, because now more than ever, I could do with being that person.

I think Daisy brings me a sense of calm. She is my home, and when I'm at home, I don't want to be a charlatan or a crook. Whether I like it or not, The Chameleon is both of those. I've had to be those things to survive, but I can't do it anymore. We still have obstacles to overcome before we succeed, and I'm worried that the person Daisy needs me to be to get the job done...is gone. I can't bring her back.

"What are our options?" she asks me after an hour of us driving.

"We could drive all the way. It would mean heading to Calais and going through the tunnel, or we can grab a flight. Either way, you will have to use your passport, and that means you will be flagged. I presume your company has it on some sort of watch list."

"Oh, they definitely will. What do you think is our best option?"

"If we fly, we can land in Aberdeen. From there, we can drive or charter a smaller plane to get us to the islands. To be honest, Daisy, I'm done driving."

"Then that's what we do."

My gut twists. I haven't been to any part of the UK since leaving Scotland all those years ago. I wonder if Betty can sense me getting closer?

Twenty-Four
Daisy

It feels like we have a ticking clock hanging over us. Ever since I stepped through airport security, I feel as if time is counting down. There is no doubt my company will have flagged my passport. After all, I did just disappear.

The big question is if my company has alerted Betty? Someone within the organisation must be on her payroll. I can't think of any other reason they would've tracked me and sent someone after us. I find myself questioning everything. All the people I've ever worked with could be potential Queen B employees, and I never knew. Shit, Penny could be one! No, surely not. She's my best friend.

This still isn't the time to be contemplating all that, not when we are so close to the finish line. One more piece of the book and then we hand it all over. After that, well, I don't know what happens.

We arrived in Aberdeen two hours ago. I'm exhausted, but Callie doesn't want to stop. I guess she's right. If anyone is looking for us, it would be stupid to hang around. I guess I will just sleep in the car. Callie agreed to do one last bit of driving. I offered, but I think she needs to remain in control for now. Her behaviour has been worrisome since Copenhagen.

It's a couple hundred miles to Skye. We have a boat chartered to take us to the Outer Hebrides. I'm not looking forward to it at all. I never grew sea legs, so I'm going to hurl, and that's not attractive. My mind wanders to Edinburgh. I feel like I'm so close to home, yet so far away at the same time. I haven't been away for long, in reality, but after everything we have been through, it might as well be years.

Edinburgh will have to wait just a little longer. I look out of the window and sigh with happiness. I do love Scotland. Callie decided to drive through the national park, which was a great idea. It's so beautiful and peaceful. Just for a little while, we can pretend we're still on holiday. Honestly, that's what I've been doing this whole time.

Callie is so intense right now, I don't know what to do. She obviously needs time to herself, so I need to occupy my mind. I think about the pieces of the book. I have studied the two pieces we picked up in Spain and

Italy. Unsurprisingly, it's full of shady-ass people. Some I've heard of, some I haven't, but regardless, they're all scumbags in my mind. Whether they push drugs, steal, or simply do accounting for one of her dodgy businesses, they all deserve to go to prison.

For the most part, it has been Callie who has got us to where we are, using her skill set. Mine is about to come into play as I open the watertight box to survey the third section of the book. Callie told me it is, in fact, the end of the book. What I see excites me. These pages aren't full of names, they're full of letters. No spaces, just lines and lines of letters. It's a puzzle, and I'm going to solve it. Something in my gut is telling me this piece of the book is our smoking gun.

With Callie still concentrating on the road, I pull out a pad and pencil. The code doesn't seem too complex. At first glance, I would say it's a letter-for-numbers code. I need a key. I'm betting the key to the code is in the book somewhere. If Betty was daft enough to write down all her contacts, it's safe to say she noted down the key to the code—probably to make sure she didn't forget; she's not getting any younger.

So far, nothing. The first two pieces hold no clues. It's possible that I'm wrong, and Betty hasn't noted the key down, which will make it harder for me to crack the letter code. I can feel myself get frustrated. I'm pulled out of my bad mood by Callie's hand on mine. I look over and she has a small smile on her face.

"Let's stretch our legs."

She's pulled the car over without me even noticing. That's how wrapped up I was in the code.

"Where are we?"

"About halfway. I need some fresh air, though, and a coffee or ten."

We head to the service station. I grab us two large coffees whilst Callie goes to the loo. There are plenty of tables free, so I pick one furthest away from anyone else. The caffeine feels amazing. It's the boost I needed. Fatigue is rolling through my body, but I won't sleep until I crack the code.

"Here." I push Callie's coffee toward her as she sits. She looks just as tired as me.

Callie points to the coded pages. "Thanks. What's that?"

I explain what they are and tell her about my thoughts on their importance.

She cocks her head. "I bet they're her accounts."

Callie says it so casually, like of course that's what the letters are hiding, and I smile because I think she's right. If we can give the authorities access to her illegal accounts, she would be done for. A list of names is one thing, but alongside accounts of illegal money, is quite another.

I breathe deeply. It's *so* important I break this code. Pressure builds in my chest. It's on me. I need to be able to do this for Callie. For a split second, I waver. Old insecurities are hard to let go of sometimes. Dad told me I would never amount to anything, and that I'd be of no use. I can't let that be true, not when it means so much, and not when it means I could help bring Callie home.

Callie scans the pages. Her brows are scrunched together in concentration, and she is beautiful. I don't give a shit if she looks tired...she's radiant.

"Don't think too much. I doubt the key is complex," she signs.

I take the pages back from her and think. Callie is probably right. Betty has put some effort in to conceal her accounts, but that doesn't mean she did a good job. Maybe I've been overthinking it. What if she simply replaced letters with numbers? So, A=0, B=1, etc. That would work up to number nine, but then what? I can't see how it would work with double digits. Maybe she just repeated the pattern. If J=9, then K would start over at 0.

Before I set about testing my theory, something jumps out from the page. The letter Z. There is a definite pattern. There are eight letters, then a Z, another two letters and another Z, two letters and a Z. That's when I spot the second pattern. After the last Z, there is an X. The pattern then starts all over again. I'm convinced, more than ever, that the letters are account numbers. If I'm right, the Z represents a dash. That means the first eight letters are probably the account numbers, and the next six are sort codes. Sort codes are broken up by dashes. The X represents a stop.

I take my pad and jot down the first eight letters on the page. JUBTEFTHZHHZYHZSDX. Then I factor in my theory: JUBTEFTH-HH-YH-SD. So J through H is the account number, and then the rest is a sort code. It's a start. I can at least break up all the letters on the page. If I had my laptop, I would have run all the info through software that would have cracked the code in a few seconds. Alas, that's not the case, so I'm going to have to do this old school.

"We need to get going. Can you carry on doing that in the car?"

Shit, I almost forgot Callie was sitting there. It's a terrible habit I have once I'm into something. The world kind of disappears on me. She doesn't look pissed, though. In fact, she's looking at me with an affectionate smile. I bet she thinks I'm a dork!

"Let's go." I offer to drive again, and to my surprise, Callie agrees. The code can wait a few more hours. Hopefully, Callie will get some rest.

Two-and-a-half hours later, we arrive in Skye. Callie has been passed out the entire time. I wish I didn't have to wake her, but she is the one who planned the boat journey, and I have no clue where we need to be. Waking Callie is harder than I thought. She is completely out of it. I have to stifle a giggle when she cracks open her eyes and pulls a face, letting me know she's not impressed I've disturbed her.

"Hey, just tell me where we need to go, and I'll drive. You can go back to sleep."

"No, it's fine, I'm awake. Let's swap."

We jump out of the car and trade places. I'm instantly cold. Jeez, how I wish we were back in Spain.

We drive for another half an hour. The landscape is getting more and more wild. There are no villages to speak of. My nerves are on edge. Finally, we pull over to a farmhouse next to a loch. There have been no signs for miles, so I'm completely lost.

"A guy I met years ago has agreed to take us to the island on his fishing boat." Callie is already getting out of the car. I scramble out after her. I knew the boat she chartered wasn't going to be fancy, but a fishing boat. I am definitely going to vomit. The rolling sea, plus the smell of fish! I can already feel my stomach churning.

The door to the farmhouse opens, and a young man steps out. He's not the hardy mariner I was expecting. Honestly, I was picturing an old man with a long beard and an eye patch. I may have watched too many films. The man steps close to Callie and shakes her hand. He smiles at me and ushers us inside. The interior isn't what I imagined either. Whoever this guy is, he has fabulous interior design skills.

"Daisy, this is Ewan."

"Nice to meet you, Ewan."

He nods back at me.

"We're going to stay the night here and then head out in the morning. The weather should be okay. Ewan will stick around and bring us back tomorrow evening."

Oh, thank fuck for that. From the way Callie has described her previous abode on the island, I was not looking forward to staying there.

I wonder how Callie knows Ewan. I'm sure he doesn't know her real name. They are talking, but it's polite and nothing too personal from what I can gather. Ewan makes us tea and offers us shortbread, which I inhale. Damn, I love shortbread.

After an hour of very polite conversation, Ewan shows us to our room. Once again, it's very nicely decorated. He leaves us alone after he's shown us where everything is. I crash on to the bed.

"How do you know him?"

"I used to see him when he travelled over to the island. He had a thing going on with the farmer who owns the shack I was living in."

"So...he's gay?"

"As a rainbow. We would talk, but he never knew the reason for me being on the island. Hell, Hamish didn't either. That's the farmer we're visiting by the way. He didn't ask any questions either. Not after I paid him."

"And that's where the last bit of the book is? In the shack?"

"Not quite, but it's close."

I do not like the look on Callie's face.

"Where is it?" After the whole Tivoli Gardens thing, I could do with this extraction being easy.

"I buried it. We just need to do a bit of digging. It's nothing to worry about."

"How much digging?" I'm not against manual labour, but I'm not keen on doing it in the freezing cold.

"Don't worry, I'll do it."

"I can help, Callie. You need to let me help."

"You have the code to work on."

I huff out a breath because she's right. I want to break the code as soon as possible.

"I'm going to work on it tonight so I can help you tomorrow. Okay?"

"Alright. Look, let's get some shuteye. As much as I would love to ravage you right now, I can barely keep myself upright."

"You can ravage me any time. Sleep."

I settle into bed but keep the little lamp on. Callie is snoring in under five minutes, leaving me to work on the code. I apply my theory, and sure enough, I have a list of account numbers and sort codes, but I can't be sure they're correct. I need my laptop. It's the only way to be sure. Shit, what do I do? At some point, I'm going to have to contact someone to help me.

Hours must have passed by the time I make a decision. Once we have the last bit of the book tomorrow, I'm going to insist that Callie follow me back to Edinburgh. There is only one person I trust to help us, and that's Janet.

Janet recruited me at the end of university. She has been my mentor and confidant, and I know that if anyone can help, it's her. Janet is the one that gave me the name of the guy we will eventually hand everything over to.

Callie isn't going to like it after the debacle with my phone and laptop. I have to convince her, though. Janet will be able to help me figure out who was spying on me as well. That is equally important as cracking the code in my eyes.

My mind is racing. I desperately want to sleep, but I'm too wired. Normally, I would give myself an orgasm, but I'm not sure that's appropriate with Callie next to me.

Now I'm thinking about orgasms, and my body is responding. Great! Callie is facing away from me, and she is a deep sleeper. I bet I can get away with a quickie.

I'm panting hard when I feel Callie roll over. Busted! The problem is, I'm too far gone to stop. I think my clit would rally a protest if I tried.

Not to worry, though, because Callie is replacing my hand with hers. I'm so close to finishing, it only takes her a couple of strokes for me to climax. I have to bite my lip to stop any noise I know I'm making from escaping into the very quiet house. Ewan doesn't need to hear me come.

Once I have relaxed, Callie curls into me and falls back to sleep. I close my eyes, feeling the beat of her heart. It's a rhythm that is so familiar, it acts as a lullaby. Finally, my mind is quiet and I sleep.

Twenty-Five
Callie

Rolling over to find Daisy pleasuring herself was interesting. Not something I've ever experienced before. Usually I leave my partners sated. Saying that, though, we hadn't had sex since Copenhagen, so I shouldn't be surprised Daisy needed a release.

One thing I've learned about adult Daisy, is that she has a high sex drive. I love it. I wish I could have stayed conscious long enough to have carried on, but I was exhausted.

Waking up this morning was a herculean effort. My body feels like it needs to shut down for a year to recover. That's what I'll do when it's over. Now, though, I have to rally. We have a boat to catch and a book piece to dig up.

Ewan hasn't mentioned anything about Hamish. I'm worried something has happened between them. I hope

Hamish hasn't sold the land or done something drastic to it. We don't need another setback.

Daisy has looked green since she woke up. We shared a tender kiss before heading downstairs. Since then, she's not looked at all well.

"Are you okay?"

She clearly isn't.

"I'm fine, just not a huge fan of boats." Shit, why the hell didn't she say? "Don't look so worried, I'll be more than okay. A little sea sickness is nothing."

"You should have said."

"It's fine, Callie, really."

My mood sours. I don't like that she is going to suffer. We sit and eat breakfast with Ewan, who is silent. He was always a quiet guy, but this is a bit much.

"Ewan, is everything okay?"

"Aye, just been a while since I've been to the island, is all." I love his strong Scottish accent.

"You and Hamish?"

"Split a few months ago. He wanted me to move to the island but I cannae do that. My dad left me this house under instructions that I stay here."

Those are the most words I think I've ever heard him speak.

"I get that Ewan, and at the risk of sounding like I'm interfering, your dad isn't here; Hamish is."

Ewan and Hamish made a sweet couple. It was clear as day they were mad for each other. I hate the idea they are throwing something away over a promise to a dead man. That might sound callous, but it's true. Ewan and Hamish have lives to live, and in my opinion, should be living them together.

"I know you're right, lass. I think I've left it too long, though. Hamish won't want to see me now."

"Nonsense. Don't waste what you have with Hamish, Ewan."

Christ, I could write for an agony aunt column. Do they still exist? Whatever. I hope he sees sense. I'm an expert on living with regret. I know what I'm talking about.

He doesn't reply, just nods. We finish our food in silence before packing up and preparing for the trip. The weather is actually nice, which surprises the shit out of me. I remember those first few months on the island as being cold and windy. Not today, though. Today, the weather gods are smiling down, and I send up a little "thank you." Hopefully, Daisy won't feel too sick.

Ewan's boat is small, considering it's only him who fishes. Daisy sits at the back of the boat with her head hanging over the edge. She has emptied her stomach several times since we left. I feel worse when I realise she's going to have to do this again on the return journey.

I see the island, and I have some weird feelings about it. We dock at a tiny jetty. On the hill above us is Hamish's house. Ewan has gone pale now. Jesus, the three of us look like we have some sort of illness.

Daisy is more than happy to be on dry land. It doesn't take her long to bounce back. She must be bloody starving. There can't be anything left in her stomach. I reach into my pocket and fetch out a chocolate bar. Maybe some sugar will help.

Once we are all squared away, we head to Hamish's. The door to the house opens and out steps the man himself. He hasn't changed at all in six years. Work jeans, plaid shirt, and a shocking red beard. He is a bear of a man. He also has the kindest eyes I have ever seen.

Ewan hangs back. The air is thick with tension, and I hate it. Stepping forward, I hug Hamish and introduce him to Daisy. To Daisy's surprise, she is hauled into a hug, too. I laugh.

Ushering Daisy into Hamish's house, I look back over to Ewan, giving him a thumbs up. I hope he's brave enough to swallow his pride and ask for a second chance.

Inside, Daisy has settled at the kitchen table. Hamish has a similar taste to Ewan, so the house is lovely. Everything is modern and sleek, but still looks homey. I wonder how much it cost to have everything shipped over. It's not like he can nip to the local furniture store.

My musings are interrupted by Hamish and Ewan, who walk through the door hand in hand. I can't contain my smile.

"You want a nip?" Hamish asks in his gruff voice. We can't stay long, but I'll never turn down whiskey.

Without waiting for an answer, he pours four generous glasses and hands them out. It's a weird situation. I know these men, but not really. We were a part of each other's lives, but I always had to keep them at arm's length, and yet, I feel close to them. It's bizarre.

"Slàinte Mhath," Hamish shouts. Daisy takes her cue from me and swigs her drink, almost choking.

"There's a spade out back. Just call if you need a hand, lass," Ewan says. I haven't explained why I need a spade and they haven't asked. I like that about them.

Standing at the back door, my eyes land on the shack—the place I called home for a short time. When I say shack, I'm not exaggerating; it's tiny. At the time, it was all

I needed. Hamish did a little work on it to make sure it was liveable and that was that.

I pick up the spade and walk over. Daisy is next to me, surveying my old home. God knows what she thinks.

From the door of my little shack, I turn to the left. I count two hundred paces and then turn right. Another fifty, and I stop.

Oh, shit!

Remember when I hoped Hamish hadn't made any changes? Yeah, he has. Karl, Hamish's prize-winning bull, has taken up residence in the field where the book piece is buried.

Cows I could cope with, but Karl? No fucking way. He's a beast with a terrible temper—at least he was when I was here last. Back then, Karl was all the way over on the other side of Hamish's property.

How in the hell am I supposed to reach the spot to dig, with a literal raging bull hanging around? I look at Daisy and then back at Karl, who has noted our presence, and of course, looks like he wants to eat us.

"Don't tell me it's in there?" Daisy signs, pointing to Karl. I just nod. What the actual fuck Universe? "Okay, so how do we get it without being trampled?"

"Good question." I have no clue, really. My days of planning are over. I think my brain has finally given up.

"Well, we need to distract him." Daisy is taking the reins again, just like she did in Tivoli Gardens with the security guard.

"How?" I have, literally, no ideas; my mind is blank.

"How far is the spot you need to get to?"

I look, and approximate it's about twenty metres away. I point to the spot, leading Daisy to follow my finger.

"Okay, so we need the bull over there," she says, pointing to the far end of the field.

"Yeah, but how are we going to do that?"

"Simple. I'll go over there and antagonise him."

That is the worst idea in the world. Daisy vs Karl, I don't think so.

"No."

"Callie, you're the only one who knows where the bloody spot is. We can ask Hamish and Ewan to help. Surely, three of us can keep the beast occupied long enough for you to do the digging."

I groan, because it's really our only option. I can't exactly ask Hamish to relocate his bloody bull. I drop my head to my chest and sigh.

"Okay," I sign without looking up.

Daisy takes off toward the house to fetch Hamish and Ewan. I can't move without losing my place. I know I need to go twenty-six paces to get to the book section. I didn't bury it too deep, so it shouldn't take long to get to. My concern is that Karl will kill me. Is that dramatic?

With Hamish, Daisy, and Ewan, all at the other end of the field, I roll my shoulders, preparing for what I'm about to do. I give them the signal. All three climb over the fence and start clapping and shouting. Sure enough, Karl gives them his full attention. I hold my breath as I climb the fence and count out my paces. So far, so good. I reach the spot without Karl being any the wiser.

Dig, Cal, for the love of God, dig.

The hole is getting deeper and I'm still not hitting anything. I'm going to be so pissed if I've made a mistake. I keep at it until finally I hear the ding of metal on metal. I cheer, which was a huge mistake. Karl turns his snotty head my way. I freeze.

We're in a standoff and I know I will lose, epically. I look down at the hole. I can see the metal container. Karl has turned to face me. Daisy and the others have doubled their efforts to catch the bull's attention again, but he's having none of it.

Shit, fuck, and bollocks. Karl is doing that thing with his hoof. You know, the thing where they scratch at the ground before running. He's preparing to charge.

I drop to my knees and paw at the box, trying with all I have to loosen it from its muddy cage. I look up, and in that moment, I know I have mere seconds before Karl loses his shit and tramples me.

Finally, the box comes free. Karl makes one of the most terrifying sounds I have ever heard, before he starts running. My stomach almost drops through my arse.

I faintly register Hamish screaming at me to run. A direction I do not need, because my legs are already working double-time. I run as fast as I can.

Now, in the movies, the person running always makes the mistake of looking over their shoulder, therefore falling over something. I'm not that girl. My focus is solely on the fence I need to get to. I can hear his hooves and they are getting uncomfortably close.

I'm metres away from the fence. I know I have no time to think. In a feat that would impress an Olympian, I vault over the barrier, landing heavily on the other side. I close my eyes and wait for Karl to burst through. It doesn't happen.

I can't move. My body is curled up around the tin box like a pretzel. It's only when I feel a warm hand on my face, that I dare move my head. Daisy is leaning over me, stroking my cheek.

Oh, thank the Lord, I'm alive!

Pain shoots through my shoulder. The landing was bad; I think I've dislocated it. Gently, I move, and yelp. I want to pass out the pain is so bad. Hamish is next to me in an instant, supporting my full weight.

Slowly, Hamish and Ewan lift me and carry me back to Hamish's house. They place me on the couch. I must look like shit. My clothes are covered in mud, as are my hands.

I pass the tin to Daisy. We've done it! We have all the pieces. Tears unexpectedly roll down my face. Daisy is by my side in an instant, wiping my cheeks.

Hamish leans down and says, "We need to get that arm back in place, lass."

Joy! I nod, because he is right. Daisy steps back, looking horrified, as Hamish begins to work his magic. It's not the first time he's had to patch me up, so I trust he knows what he's doing.

Ewan passes me a bottle of whiskey. After a few healthy swigs, I nod to Hamish. The process of popping my shoulder back in may be relatively fast, but when it's happening to you, it feels like a fucking lifetime.

I scream and cry, but then I feel it slot back in and it's done. Hamish whisks my arm up into a sling and gives me back the whiskey bottle. The next thing I know, I'm waking up, still in the same position on the couch.

"Hey," Daisy signs. She's sitting with Ewan at the table. "You kind of passed out."

"I'm sorry." I have no recollection at all. We should have been back on the boat already.

She rolls her eyes playfully. "Don't be daft. How are you feeling?"

"Sore. Did you look at the pages?"

"Yeah, more names. It's finished, Cal. I just need to verify the accounts and we can end this."

My brain is feeling foggy. How does she expect to verify the accounts? I ask her, and her face does this thing when she's feeling uncomfortable. It's an expression that lands between a wince and a grimace.

"We need to go to Edinburgh."

That's when I realise what she's saying.

"Are you insane?" I screech.

Okay, that's not the nicest thing to ask someone, but she has to be kidding. Going back to her flat isn't safe, and contacting anyone from her work is foolish.

"We have to, Cal. Look, you need to trust me." That's not fair, is it? I trust her, but this... "Trust me, Callie." Her eyes are fierce, and I know what I say next will determine our future relationship.

"I do. I'll follow you." If I don't trust Daisy, then what is the point of doing any of this?

Honestly, I have no idea what to do next, anyway. If Daisy thinks she's found a way to bring Betty to her knees, then I'll go with it.

Ewan's phone rings. He excuses himself to take the call. Daisy sits next to me and gives me a kiss that portrays how much she appreciates my last words.

The moment is ruined when Ewan marches back in. "We have a problem."

Excellent!

"What?" Daisy asks.

"There was a guy looking for you two. He's been asking around the farms."

We knew it was only a matter of time before they caught up with us. I just wish we knew who *they* were.

Twenty-Six
Daisy

At least I don't have to get back on that awful boat! Now we know there is a creep hanging around Ewan's place, we can't go back. I should be panicking, but I'm not. Am I becoming desensitised to this shit? Possibly. Is that healthy? Definitely not.

Callie looks more worried than me, but that could be pain. I can't imagine how much her shoulder must hurt. I nearly passed out watching Hamish pop it back into place. Not forgetting our time spent with Karl, which got all our adrenaline pumping, it's no wonder she looks freaked out.

We decided to take Hamish up on the offer to use his truck to get us back to Edinburgh. I'm surprised how calm Ewan and Hamish are being. I know they don't know what's going on, but they're not stupid. This isn't a normal situation.

Ewan didn't bat an eye when he found out Callie's real name. I accidentally used it in conversation. I know Ewan thought her name was Jenny. Callie told me this morning.

To be fair, Hamish didn't react either, which I find curious. Here was this woman, who turned up out of the blue six years ago, calling herself Jenny, and they were super cool about it. No invasive questions. Nothing. They just let her crash.

Fast forward to the same woman re-introducing herself as someone entirely different, and still no probative questions. I kind of want to ask them about it. Surely they must be curious?

Callie is asleep again. The whiskey she knocked back is doing its job. Hamish is cooking dinner and Ewan is watching him with heart eyes.

"Why aren't you two asking about all this?" I ask Ewan.

"If Callie wanted us to know, she would have told us."

"But you're not curious? Come on, you must want to know what's going on."

I don't know why I'm pushing it. I should just be grateful they have been so good to us...to Callie.

"Everyone has shit going on, lass. It's not our place to intrude on Callie's life. Not if she doesn't want it. All we can do is offer kindness. When Callie turned up on this island, it didn't take a genius to figure out she was running from something. Underneath her 'tough girl' routine, we could see how scared she was. We weren't going to turn our backs on her. If all we could offer was a roof, and a little conversation now and then to help her out, then that's all that mattered."

"You're not angry she lied about her name?"

"Och, do you really think we believed her name was Jenny? Like I said, it didn't, and doesn't, matter. She needed someone to have her back, and we did that."

"Well, I appreciate it. I couldn't be there with her at the time. I'm just pleased she met you guys."

"Aye, we can see that you mean a lot to each other. I hope one day you can sort out whatever's going on and settle down. That girl needs some normal, I reckon."

Isn't that the truth! Callie does need normal, and I'm going to give it to her.

Callie is still sleeping, so we eat without her. The clock on the fireplace tells me it's almost nine in the evening. I'm conscious that Callie hasn't eaten since breakfast.

Gently, I wake her up. Her face is marred with pain, and I hate it. She manages to eat a little, but she clearly wants to go back to the *Land of Nod*. I take her upstairs and get her into bed.

Tonight I plan to work on the rest of the coded letters. There are pages of them, and I'm keen to have them finished for when we get back to Edinburgh. I find the whole process quite therapeutic. It reminds me of when I first started to work for my company.

It's past midnight by the time I finish, but I'm happy. I was able to quickly work through the pages once I got focused. Unlike the other two sections, I can't take pictures of them and upload them to my vault, which means I have to keep them safe. If anything happens to them, we're fucked. I won't have a copy to back up our claims.

Callie, rolling over, wakes me. There is a sliver of light shining through the crack in the curtains. Judging from the weakness of the rays, I would guess it's just past dawn. It's not surprising Callie is ready to get up. She's slept for hours.

I roll over to face her. I can't help but smile when I see she's watching me. "Morning, creepy," I joke.

She laughs and kisses me. "I'm sorry. I sort of passed out yesterday."

"No 'sort of' about it, Cal, you did pass out. How's the shoulder?"

"Okay. A bit achy. I'm afraid you'll have to do the driving, though."

I'd already surmised that. It's no problem, though. Callie has done thousands of miles in the driver's seat. I'm actually glad she has to hand over the controls to me for a while.

I stroke her face. "We should get going soon. It's early, but we have a long drive ahead."

"Yeah, let's blow this joint," she says with childish enthusiasm. I have to laugh because she's ridiculous and cute.

"What about the guy lurking around Ewan's?"

"Nothing for us to do. Ewan will head back alone and whoever is there will see that. We should have a decent head start."

We descend to the kitchen. Hamish and Ewan are already up. Hamish has made us a cooked breakfast that smells divine.

Ewan tells us he's heading out when we do. He also tells us he's finally moving to the island. I'm so glad for them. They really are great guys.

Going on the run with Callie might be scary, but the one thing I can say, is that we've met some really wonderful people. It kind of restores my faith in the world a little.

Hamish's truck is a big SUV. I secretly love it, even though it is definitely killing the polar bears with its emissions. I'll do some volunteering or something to make up for it when we get home.

Sitting high up in the cab of the truck makes me feel like a giant. I like it. Callie is grinning at me, and I know she is reading my mind. I ignore her and drive on.

The ferry is already docked when we arrive at the port. Thankfully, we'll miss Skye completely. The ferry will dock at Oban. I'm confident I won't need to vomit on the ferry. The trip on Ewan's boat had been horrendous.

It doesn't take long to board. As soon as we're given the all clear, we exit the gargantuan vehicle and head to the café.

With a not-so-bad cup of coffee in front of me, I take the time to look at Callie. She looks better than yesterday, but I'm still worried. I'd like to get a doctor to look at her shoulder. I'm sure Hamish has done a great job, but I suppose you can never be too careful.

The good thing about yesterday's activities is that she was forced to rest. Her skin is glowing again, and her eyes are back to being bright.

"Why are you staring?" she asks.

"Just making sure you're okay."

"Honestly, I feel tons better than yesterday."

"I can't believe you almost got mowed over by a bull!"

Now she's out of danger, I can see the funny side. I wish we had filmed it. Honestly, add a bit of Benny Hill, and we could have sent it in to a video blooper show and got a few hundred quid.

Before I can stop myself, I'm laughing. The absurdity of it all is hilarious. You couldn't write this shit! Callie is quick to join me, and I'm sure we look unhinged to the other passengers.

The ferry ride is uneventful, which is a nice change. My stomach feels a little queasy, but I keep my breakfast down. After we've finished our coffee, we find a couple of comfy chairs. I get my head down for a few hours. I didn't sleep as well as I could have last night.

It's only three hours to Edinburgh once we disembark the ferry. I'm anxious to get there. I'm also excited, which I shouldn't be, due to the danger, but that's where home is. I'm looking forward to showing Callie my flat. I hope she likes it. I miss my goldfish too, which is stupid, because I doubt he even knows I exist.

The SUV will stick out like a sore thumb outside my building, so we agree to park it on the outskirts of the city and take a taxi the rest of the way. Hamish will travel to collect his car during the week. I hope we can keep in contact with them.

Speaking of keeping in contact, it's been a while since we last spoke to Chris. Callie doesn't want to message him until it's over, but I miss him. I want to know he's doing alright with Derek and Meryl. I try to broach the subject with Callie, but it's a no-go.

As well as thinking about Chris, I've also been contemplating our next move. I need equipment and I need to talk to Janet.

Going straight to my flat is probably a bad idea. If we get caught there before I've had a chance to figure out if the account numbers are correct, it will all have been for nothing. I tell Callie I think we should head straight to Janet's. She doesn't seem impressed at all, but what other choice is there? We can't do it on our own anymore.

After some discussion, Callie finally accepts my plan. We are a few miles outside of the city now. Instead of heading to the parking place, I drive us to Janet's house, which is in a nice, secluded area. Her garden is surrounded by tall hedges, meaning the SUV will be out of sight whilst we are there. There's no reason to think anyone knows we have Hamish's SUV, but if I've learned one thing recently, it's to not assume too much.

Callie eyes up the house suspiciously. "What are you going to say to this woman?"

I haven't told her all the details about mine and Janet's relationship. I can't.

"I'll tell her the truth."

Callie looks alarmed. "All of it?"

"Yes, all of it. We need her help, Cal. If she knows what we're up against, she can help us more. I can't just waltz in there and ask to use sensitive software without a good reason. Plus, I need her to look into whoever tracked me through my laptop."

I pull up to the house. Janet predominantly works from home, so I'm confident she'll be here.

"Do you want to wait in the car?" I ask, knowing the answer already. No way Callie will let me go in there alone.

"No, you're not going in alone."

Told you.

I nod and make my way to Janet's front door. She will already know I'm here. The door swings open before I can knock.

"Where the hell have you been?" Janet demands.

To most people, Janet comes across as a bitch. Her face always reads "Danger: Stay Away," but I know better. Callie does not, and therefore takes a step towards Janet, ready to jump to my defence. I place a hand on Callie's shoulder, which stops her. She looks at me and then back at Janet, who is looking between Callie and me.

"Jan, can we come in? It's important."

After Callie has backed off, Janet swings the door open and lets us pass. Her house is gorgeous and gigantic. Everything screams opulence.

Janet takes us through to her den. Yeah, it's that kind of house. No normal house has a den, for God's sake. Anyway, enough of my house envy. Janet sits in an armchair and we take a seat on a small two-seat sofa. Now I just have to try to explain all of this.

Janet sits quietly, waiting. I take a big breath and launch into everything. I'm talking the full whack: everything from our childhood up to our presence in her house.

To Janet's credit, she doesn't once interrupt. She sits listening, taking it all in. I've worked up quite a thirst by the time I've finished. I'm comfortable enough with Janet to take myself to her kitchen and grab some water without asking permission.

Callie is sitting, looking at Janet, when I return. Janet hasn't budged or uttered a word. I retake my seat and wait.

"That's a lot to process, Daisy, however, I'm glad you came to me. I can help."

Relief floods my central nervous system. I've felt like a live wire for the past few days. Callie still doesn't look convinced.

"Where should we start?" I ask. I can't worry about Callie right now. We are on the cusp of finishing this. With Janet on our side, we really have got the end goal in sight.

"First, let's run the account numbers. Once we know they're correct, we can get the ball rolling. The name you were given is solid. He's the right man to take the information to. As for the person who tracked you, that's easy."

"Is it?" I'm surprised.

"Yes, it was me." I was not expecting that!

Callie is on her feet before I can say anything. "We have to go," she signs.

Callie is like a coiled spring. She never wanted to come here, and now I think she might have been right.

Janet is on her feet in a flash. "No, don't go."

I don't get the vibe she's being threatening. In fact, she almost looks pleading.

"Callie, just wait," I say.

"Are you serious?"

"Please, trust me." I look at Janet, imploring her to explain herself. Callie will only wait so long before she bolts.

"This is bigger than you know..." Janet begins.

That's not very clear, Janet! Chop, chop. We need answers. Janet sits back down and looks at Callie.

"Please sit."

Callie looks at me, and I nod.

"Start talking, lady," Callie demands.

I have to stifle a laugh, because I'm sure Janet is not used to being spoken to that way.

"I need to call someone. They need to be the one to explain. It's not my story."

"I don't give a shit whose story it is." Callie is getting ready to stand again. I don't know why, but something is telling me we should stay.

"Cal, just wait."

"Daisy, we aren't safe here." I can see the panic in her eyes.

"Cal, we are, please. If there is more going on, we need to know about it."

"I don't like this." I see her huff, but she remains seated. I nod to Janet, who pulls out her phone and hits a few numbers.

"It's me," Janet says into the phone. "Code Plum."

She puts the phone down, and I have no idea what the hell is happening. What is "Code Plum?" I hope to God I haven't trusted the wrong person.

"She'll be here soon." Janet adds, walking over to her drink cabinet. She proceeds to pour three glasses of brandy.

"Who will be here?" Callie asks.

"You'll see. Let's have a drink."

Twenty-Seven
Callie

WHAT THE HELL ARE we doing here? How could I have let Daisy convince me this was a good idea? I don't know Janet. She's a stranger to me, and yet, I allowed Daisy to bring us here and tell her everything. This Janet woman knows about the book, about Daisy's vault; all of it.

And now we are sitting, waiting for some mysterious woman to show up. Is it a mystery, though? I'm guessing we've just walked ourselves into Betty's clutches. I'm so fucking stupid. Why is Daisy not looking more worried? We should be trying to figure out a way to get out of the goddamn house, not sit here waiting to get a bullet to the head!

"Relax," Daisy tells me.

Relax? Is she for real right now? I know she asked me to trust her, and I do, but I'm slightly more concerned that

Daisy has put her trust in the wrong person. We haven't even addressed the fact this woman sent goons after us. The only thing Janet has told us so far, is it was she who put a tracker on Daisy's laptop. How is she trustworthy?

"Relax? We are in danger, Daisy. How can you not see that?"

"You're not in danger, I promise you," Janet interrupts.

Okay, so Janet can understand sign language. Wish I'd known that a while ago.

"And you just expect me to believe you? I don't know you. Daisy may trust you, but that doesn't mean I have to."

I can feel my body preparing for what comes next. My fight or flight is kicking in, and trust me when I say, I will fight! My running days are over. If Betty wants to walk into this house and attack me, she better believe I'm going to attack back. I've not come this far to fail at the last hurdle.

"My job isn't to bring you or Daisy to harm," Janet adds.

"So, what is your job?" I shoot back.

"To protect."

Protect? Who, me? That can't be right. I have never met this woman in my life. She must mean Daisy, but that begs the question why, as well. Who is Janet, to Daisy?

"How long must we wait, Janet?" Daisy asks. Maybe she's finally realising we are sitting ducks.

Janet looks at her phone. "She's here. I promise everything will be explained. Please, just sit, Callie."

I realise I have risen to my feet, ready to fight. I can't sit back down, not until I know who is walking through that door. Janet tells us to wait whilst she goes to greet whoever the hell is here. My heartbeat is pounding and my limbs feel electrified. I steady my breathing. I'm ready.

Janet re-enters the den. And then my world stops. The woman trailing behind Janet isn't Betty, but she is a younger version.

It's not possible!

I cannot be seeing this person. I look at Daisy, who has gone white as a sheet. No, no, no, it's not fucking possible.

"Callie?" That voice, the one that would read me a bedtime story, the one that would sing to me when I had a nightmare and the one that I haven't heard for twenty years.

"What the fuck is this?" My brain isn't ready to accept what my eyes are seeing! "Daisy, what is this?"

I need her to give me answers, but she looks just as shocked and confused as me. I want to run. This is too much. After everything I have been through alone, I can't deal with this.

"Callie, I know you're confused, but please let me explain."

How the fuck is my mother, who died twenty years ago, going to explain this to me?

"You're not real, you're dead!"

I sound like a scared child. I can hear it in my voice. This woman cannot be my mum, she simply can't, and yet, as I look at her, I know she is. Her hair is the same fiery red as mine. Her eyes are the same blue and they sparkle, just as I remember. Her face is older, but she still looks like my mum.

"Janet, can you get her a drink?"

Janet hops to it and hands me a glass of brandy. I didn't drink the first one she gave me, but this time I throw it down my throat. My hands are trembling. I feel an arm snake around my waist. Daisy is almost propping me up. I hadn't realised I was almost collapsed against the arm of the couch.

"Someone explain. Now!" Daisy growls. She's no longer looking surprised. She is looking fierce; she is protecting me.

My mum slips off her coat and sits in the closest chair. Her eyes never leave mine. "Callie, I'm so sorry." I want to laugh at her. Sorry? What fucking use is that to me? "I never wanted to leave you behind. I tried everything to get you out with me, but your nan had an iron grip on you."

"I don't understand," I stutter. Daisy helps lower me to the couch. I'm not sure how much longer my legs can hold me up. Everything feels weak.

"You know I worked for the business?" I nod. "I never wanted to, Callie. Never. But you know, just like me, that it was never a choice. I spent years trying to figure out how to get us away from her, but it was useless."

"But you did get away. You left me."

"Only because I had no other choice. Your nan never let you out of her sight. Not from the day you were born. You were her heir and the one who was going to keep the business alive when she retired."

"You could have faked both of our deaths."

"No, I couldn't, because she never, *ever*, gave me the opportunity to have you alone long enough. I know you won't remember. You were too little, but even when it was just you and me, we were always watched."

I don't remember that. I just remember having fun with my mum.

"I was expendable to her and I used that to my advantage," she continues. "I knew if I died, she wouldn't question it, as long as it was plausible. Car accidents happen all the time."

"Twenty years, mum! That's how long you've been gone. I've dealt with this on my own for two decades."

"I know, honey, and I'm so sorry. My plan was to escape and then start working to bring her down."

"Well, what the fuck happened then, because she's still going strong, and I have been alone!"

"You've never been alone, Callie. I had people watching out for you. Those people were working towards getting the one thing I needed to finally end the family business. The black book. My people tried for years to find it, but Betty never slipped up. No one knew where to find it. No one but you, Callie."

Her eyes are wet, and she's looking at me with pure love. I hate it's making me feel warm inside. I hate she's able to do this to me after all this time.

"I watched and waited and then finally you made a break for it. Believe me when I say I wanted to scoop you up the moment you ran, but hell, love, you were too good at hiding, even from me. You disappeared completely."

"Like mother, like daughter."

"I deserve that. I know it's going to take time, Callie, and I hope one day you will forgive me. Just know I'm not going anywhere. I'll never leave you again."

Her words should be music to my ears, but I can't trust them. Not yet.

"How does Daisy fit into this?" I feel Daisy sit up straighter, her gaze is solidly on Janet. I can tell she feels betrayed.

"When you first disappeared, we kept an eye on all your associates. Daisy was the only one that stuck out. She was relentless with her search for you. I looked into her deeper, and realised she would be an asset to my company."

"*Your* company?" Daisy asks. I still don't know what company Daisy works for.

"Yes, mine. I squirrelled away a substantial amount of money before leaving. I used it to start my own company."

"What the hell do you all do?" Jesus, this is ridiculous.

"I can't tell you that, love," Mum says. I roll my eyes because...seriously!

"Fine, whatever." Yes, I sound like a sulking teenager.

"Janet, you've known all along, and you didn't say anything." The pain in Daisy's voice is evident.

"Daisy, If I could have told you, I would have," Janet answers.

"Daisy, I asked Janet to recruit you and mentor you. Your skills are impressive, and I'll admit I wanted you close, just in case you were able to find Callie. Which you did."

"Why did you send people after us?" I ask.

"They were never after you. Once Daisy located you, I wanted to make sure you were okay. That you had everything you needed. My people were never supposed to be spotted; they were supposed to be invisible."

"You need new people then, Mum, because they sucked at being covert."

"Maybe you could train them," she laughs. It's strange, because everything—almost—feels normal, as if I haven't had an absent mother. Like we spend all our time chit chatting together. "I thought about revealing myself once Daisy had found you, but..."

"But what?" She could have shown herself in Sweden. Why all this fucking about?

"I was terrified you'd reject me." Her voice cracks and I see tears pool.

"Well, now we'll never know," I snap. Should I be kinder? Possibly, but my defences are up too high for that.

"Where do we go from here?" Daisy asks. She still looks super pissed at Janet.

"We verify the accounts, pass everything on to the name I gave you, and then sit back. Your job is done, Callie. It's over."

I want to believe her. I really do, but until Betty is behind bars, I can't.

"Will you stay here?" Janet asks. "I have more than enough space. You can have your own rooms."

"We only need one room," I say, because I can't think of sleeping without Daisy. I see my mum smirk and I blush a little.

"One room it is. I'll get everything set up. Please stay for as long as you like. You're safe here," Janet says. She shoots Mum a look I can't translate.

"What about my brother, Daniel? Betty has already warned me I'm cutting it close. She will hurt him; you know she will. I can't just sit here and wait. We have no idea how long it will take for the authorities to put her away. Daniel doesn't have that long."

"I have someone working on the problem, Daisy. I promise I'll do everything I can, to get him to safety." Mum talks with confidence. I can see she's used to being in charge. I'm a bit impressed, even if I'm still mad and defensive.

I need more alcohol; more than Janet has, I would guess. I make my way over to the bottle of brandy and pour myself a very generous glass. Down the hatch it goes.

I could do with some alone time. A lot has happened recently—I should stop being so surprised really—and I don't do well with processing big feelings around others.

"Can you show me to our room? I think I'd like some time on my own."

No one argues with my request. I follow Janet up the stairs. Everything in this house looks like it came out of a magazine. I've not had this level of luxury for a while. She shows me into a bedroom that is ridiculously big. It has a canopy bed, for fuck's sake. There is an ensuite and a balcony. Janet makes bank! This house must be worth a few million.

When I'm finally alone, I sink into a chair next to a set of double doors. It's so quiet, I start to feel uneasy. I need to unwind. The brandy is making me feel a bit buzzed, and that's great. I don't feel panicked or filled with anxiety, which is a strange turn of events. You would think, that after all this shit, I would be a bloody wreck. Maybe my capacity to be shocked and surprised has reached their limits?

The ensuite is gorgeous. I only went in for a pee, but now I'm running a bath. It's a clawfoot and I've never been in a clawfoot bath before. I'm going to pretend, for half an hour, I'm a carefree housewife who is living the life of luxury.

It's only after I get in the tub that I find a bath bomb. I add it and instantly regret it. Bath bomb up the arse, is *not* an experience I'd like to repeat. Does it ever stop fizzing?

Once my bum stops feeling weird, I settle down. My head leans back on the little pillow and I close my eyes. Okay, so my mum isn't dead. That's a big one. How do I feel? Happy, obviously, but also detached. I know she's my mum, but she isn't someone I know. I wish I could just fall into her arms and feel everything I should, but I can't. I feel disconnected. That relationship is gonna need some work.

The sound of the bathroom door opening pulls my focus. Daisy walks in and immediately starts stripping. Nice! Slipping into the bath, she lets her head fall back on to my shoulder. We haven't exchanged any words. I wonder if she's okay, it's not just *my* reality that has been impacted. I don't know the full scale of Janet's involvement in Daisy's life, but I'm not blind. Daisy was hurt by Janet's deception.

We remain silent, enjoying the bath. It's the first time Daisy and I have actually been able to stop, and not just for a couple of hours or a night. No, we can properly stop and relax.

I think we are actually safe now. My Spidey sense isn't tingling. This level of normalcy with Daisy is what I've been craving my whole life. Dare I believe, we are going to get our happily ever after?

The bath water is lukewarm by the time we get out and re-dress. It's late afternoon now, far too early to retire to bed, and I don't think either of us has the mind-set to have sex. Later, if I'm lucky.

Now we need to go back downstairs, hopefully to eat, and then talk some more with Janet and Mum. As much as they think my part is done with, they're wrong. I'm not done until Betty is gone.

I had no idea my mum is a lesbian! The way she's snogging Janet, though, is kind of a giveaway. Well, well, well, it really is a case of "like mother, like daughter."

I clear my throat when it becomes apparent they haven't noticed us enter. My mum goes bright red—another trait we share—and Janet looks everywhere but at me as they part.

"No need to stop on our account," I smirk. This day is all kinds of fucked up.

"Sorry you had to see that," Mum mumbles.

"So, how long have you two been together?" Daisy asks. I think this is just another thing she's pissed about. Not them being together, but the fact that Janet, the person she thought she knew, has been keeping things from her.

"Eighteen years," Janet replies.

"Wow, okay," I say.

"We met after I left. Janet has been with me ever since."

"Awesome. I've gone from having no mum, to two mums, in a couple of hours," I joke because I don't know what else to do. Everyone looks awkward, which makes me laugh out loud.

Oh boy, this is going to be a long night.

Twenty-Eight

Daisy

HAVING YOUR DEAD MUM turn up is a tad much, don't you think? I'm starting to believe we've been dropped into a bloody soap opera. Surprisingly enough, Callie seems to be doing okay. I worried a bit when she took herself off to the bedroom for alone time, but I can understand. I wouldn't want to deal with that kind of emotional bomb with other people watching, either.

Even though what I'm feeling, can in no way compare to Callie right now, I'm still trying to wrap my head around Janet and her lies. As I've mentioned several times, I didn't have a great deal of support growing up. Apart from Callie, Penny was the only person to show me that kind of love and support, until Janet came along.

How can I explain what she means to me without divulging what I do? I know, I know, I hear you. It's getting old, all this cloak and dagger malarky, but seriously, I can't tell you. It destroys me I have to keep it from Callie.

Anyway, I'll try my best. At the end of my degree, I was approached by Janet. Obviously, I was super aware she was being really cagey when she offered me the opportunity to work for her. It took several meetings before she disclosed what she did.

Remember, I was young. Okay, so only six years younger than I am now, but hey, that time makes all the difference. All I wanted to do was help make the world a more just place. I was so tired of watching arseholes prevail. Janet offered me the opportunity to do that.

Over many months of mentoring, I came to rely on Janet. She treated me like a capable adult, but also gave me that maternal figure I so sorely lacked. I felt I could tell her everything. Janet was the one person I could go to about anything. It's true that I didn't tell her about Callie, but that was different. That situation was complex, and honestly, I was scared that if I told Janet, she would make me stop looking for her.

Penny only knew a certain amount of detail, and that was because she practically lived with me at one point. There was no way I could hide everything I was doing from her.

As I sit in Janet's den now, I don't feel that trust and comfort towards her I once did. I just feel used. Every time she encouraged me was false. She was only saying those things to make sure I stayed close. My whole career has been curated, and I hate it.

Marie has taken herself into the kitchen. That's Callie's mum, by the way. I'm still in shock that she's here. I remember her fondly, although she was often absent. I always remember her being kind. She adored Callie. There were many times I often wished she were my mum, too. Anyway, Marie has left the room, meaning I'm alone with Janet. I suspect Marie is giving us space.

"Daisy, I am sorry."

I'm sure she is, but what does sorry do? Nothing. It doesn't change the fact she's been lying to me from the day we met.

"You didn't have to lie, Janet. You could've told me, and I would have understood. Hell, I would've come to you sooner for help."

"It wasn't my call. In the beginning we had to be careful; yes, we looked into you, but that wasn't a guarantee you were someone we could trust."

"What about after all the months of mentoring? Surely that told you I was trustworthy. Fuck, Janet, the work I've done for this company demands I'm trustworthy. You chose to lie about this."

"Marie didn't want you to know. Daisy, please, believe me when I say I wish it could have been different, but we are here now. It's almost over."

"True, but I'm not sure I can work with you after this. I confided in you, and I thought of you like a mum, which I now see was a mistake. All along, you were just doing your job. I was just another employee."

"That's not true. Never say that. Daisy, I will spend the rest of my life being sorry for deceiving you, but sometimes we have to make those hard calls. Marie asked me to keep you in the dark and I had to respect that."

We're not really getting anywhere. My rational brain understands what she's saying, but so far, my emotions are winning out and they are pissed off and hurt. I need some time, too. Callie still hasn't come down from the room, so I think I'll join her.

"We'll speak later," I sign as I leave the room.

I jog up the stairs. This isn't the first time I've been in the house. I guess Janet has put us in the spare room that has a balcony. She likes her guests to be impressed. I enter the room and immediately smell an apple bath bomb.

Walking into the ensuite, my shoulders relax at the sight of Callie in the clawfoot tub. I don't wait for an invitation before stripping off and climbing in. All I want is to feel safe in Callie's arms again. We lay cuddled in the warm bath for ages. Only when the temperature drops, do we decide it's time to get out.

The last thing I want to do is go back downstairs, but we have to. There are still things to be discussed, and I wouldn't dream of keeping Callie away from her mum, even for a second.

Callie hasn't said anything about how she's feeling. I have no clue how to handle it. How would I react if my mum waltzed into the room after twenty years of thinking she was dead?

Honestly, I would have probably passed out. I'll wait for Callie to come to me. Pushing her to open up won't help.

Witnessing Janet with her tongue down Marie's throat is a shock. Well, what about today isn't a shock? So... Janet is a big ol' lez. Something else she didn't share. That isn't a legitimate reason for me to be upset. It's entirely up to Janet who she comes out to, but I want to be petulant. It's been a rough few hours.

Once everyone has got over the awkwardness of the situation, we head to the den where we find a tray of sandwiches. Not going to lie, I want to demolish the whole stack. Callie dives in without a care. I see Marie smile at her daughter, and my heart breaks.

I know Callie is hurting, but I can't imagine how Marie is feeling, either. Giving up a life with your child must have been soul-destroying. Once the anger fades, I hope Callie will see they deserve the chance to get to know each other again.

Janet hands me a laptop. I give her a curt nod. That's all I can manage right now. There's no time like the present to verify those accounts. I send up silent prayers to the Universe that I got the letter-to-numbers code correct. With half a cucumber sandwich hanging out of my mouth, I get to work.

Zoning out is something I do when I'm working. I can literally forget there is anyone else around when I get into it, and that's what I do now. Pulling up the software I need, I start adding the first account number and the corresponding sort code. I root through my bag for the book pieces. When the laptop pings with a name, I cross reference it with the names in the book. If that account is linked to one of these people, we have her.

We have a match. I breathe out a huge sigh of relief. I enter a second account and let the software do its thing. Another ping reveals a second match.

Now, not only can I crack codes, but I'm quite good at hacking too. Hacking into these accounts will allow me to see incoming and outgoing transactions. We need to link Betty's account to these coded accounts.

I look up from the laptop and see three pairs of eyes on me. I forgot to tell them what I've found. I was too excited.

"We have matches," I say. Marie looks like she's going to cry. Callie lets her head drop to her chest and Janet squeezes my shoulder, smiling. "We need irrefutable proof Betty is the one sending them money. Without that, she can lie her way out of it."

"The name I gave you can do all that. We need to give him everything and let him do his job," Marie says confidently.

"Who is this guy?" Callie asks. I'd like to know too.

"He is someone I trust. We've been waiting for this for a long time. He knows what to do. I'm asking you to trust me."

Callie doesn't look happy with the answer she's given, but I see it in her eyes that she isn't going to fight it.

"Fine." Callie grabs another sandwich. I'm pretty sure she's eating her feelings.

Using my encrypted memory stick, I add all the information from my vault, plus the book pieces and cracked account codes. I grip the stick hard. This is it. Once I hand it over, everything is out of our control. All we will be able to do is wait.

Marie takes the memory stick and stashes it in her pocket. Now what do we do? We drink, that's what we do. It's not a celebration; that won't happen until Betty is in an orange jumpsuit. No, we are numbing all the difficult feelings that are surrounding us.

I wake up with a crushing headache. We all went overboard last night. I think at one point we were all crying.

Jesus. What a mess.

Callie is snoring next to me. I roll over and get out of bed. I need fluids, ASAP. The alarm clock on the bedside table tells me it's almost 11 a.m. I drink four glasses of water in the bathroom and then head downstairs. Callie doesn't look like she's going to wake up anytime soon.

The smell of coffee and bacon assaults my senses as I walk into the kitchen. Janet is cooking and Marie is sitting at the breakfast bar, reading the paper. I wave at them when they spot me. Janet pushes a cup of coffee and a bacon sandwich in front of me. I want to reject it because I'm still being childish, but my body needs sustenance.

"I've dropped off the information," Marie says.

I'm glad, I want this done with. God knows how long it's going to take this man to act on the information we've given him.

"So, we just wait now?" I ask.

"Yes. I don't think we will be waiting long, though. He has teams of people working on it. I also had an update about your brother."

"And?" I know he's an idiot, but I don't want him dead.

"From what I've been told, he's safe. Yes, Betty is still holding him, but I've had my people create a bit of trouble which is taking her attention away from Daniel. If we attempt to get him before Betty is taken in, she'll know something is going on."

I get where she's coming from, but she's still playing with another person's life. Betty could decide any day now that she's tired of waiting for me to bring Callie to her and make good on her threat to kill him.

"Can I go to my flat?" I would guess they have people watching and would know if any of Betty's guys were hanging about.

"Yes, it's safe for now, but I would still prefer you and Callie to remain here until it's done."

"I just want to check on things. Grab some clothes."

"Okay, I'll have someone take you over."

Our conversation is interrupted by a very sleepy, sexy-looking Callie. Her mane of hair is all over the place. I just want to shove my fingers through it.

"Morning," she clumsily signs.

I lean up from my seat and kiss her gently. I could get used to this—used to having Callie walk into our kitchen, looking all adorable. I hope she wants that too. I hope she still wants that future with *me*.

"Morning, love," Marie says.

Callie freezes for a second, and I realise she's momentarily forgotten that her mum is alive. I see the shock wash over her, just as it did yesterday.

Scratching her head, Callie settles on the stool next to me. Janet slides her coffee and food. Callie wastes no time inhaling her bacon sandwich. No matter what is happening, the woman always enjoys her food. I love that about her.

"Do you want to visit my flat?" I ask her. I think we could both do with time alone.

"Hell yes, I do." It's the first time in a few days I see the excited, carefree Callie, I know and love. I smile and kiss her again.

Breakfast is still awkward, but we all muddle through. I want to get out of the house, sharpish. Marie organises a car to take us to my flat. I suddenly feel nervous.

When we pull up, Callie jumps out of the car, pulling me along with her. I tug her arm, laughing. "You don't know where you're going, you prat."

She grins, and I swoon.

My flat is in the centre of Edinburgh, just above a wool shop. I know the owner and we get on well. He has a daughter that runs the till in the shop and she's nice. She's also a lesbian and has asked me out several times. I hope we don't run into her.

After successfully avoiding anyone else, I lead us up the exterior stairs and open my front door. It's weird, but I feel a bit emotional. My place isn't massive, but it's cosy. I can see Penny has stopped by to water my plants and feed my fish. I'll buy her a bottle of wine. She's a good egg.

Callie takes her time wandering around the living room. She stops at the big-ass map that is still hanging on the wall. I forgot all about my war room situation.

Smiling, she turns around and looks at me. "This is impressive."

"It is. You left quite a trail," I joke. I hope she doesn't think I'm being judgemental, because I'm not. It doesn't thrill me to see all those little pins, but I'll get over it. She's with me now, and that's all that counts.

"Jesus, I didn't realise I was that bad," she laughs, hooking her thumb over her shoulder to the map.

"Mm, yes, you're a regular Casanova, Cal."

Shaking her head, she laughs. I let her continue her perusal. It feels really good to be home. I want to go and hug all my things. I tap on the glass of Walter's tank. He doesn't look impressed. No change there, then.

Twenty-Nine

Callie

IT FEELS TOTALLY SURREAL being in Daisy's flat. Lying on her bed staring at the ceiling, my mind is conjuring all different kinds of things—mainly things that I've missed. I know it doesn't do me any good wishing things had been different for us. A girl can wonder, though...right?

What would our life have been like if I'd had the chance to go to university with her? I don't think it would have taken us long to get together. Maybe after a few too many drinks at a party, one of us would have made a drunken confession, leading to the other one finally opening up when we were sober.

After that, we would have started dating. We would have travelled all over Scotland on the holidays, not able to go too far because we were broke students.

Eventually, we would have moved out of student accommodation and into a flat together...maybe this flat. We would have squabbled about decorating, but then made up with sex in the kitchen. I would have waited until we graduated and then asked her to marry me, because we both know we are a forever couple.

The wedding would take place somewhere hot, because Daisy would want to be in a light dress, feeling sand between her toes. We would have honeymooned in Europe, travelling to different countries in a campervan.

When we got back to Scotland, Daisy would ask me if I wanted to start a family, and I would have said yes. Daisy would carry, and we would have two perfect girls, because, obviously, she had twins.

We'd have bought a big house, with a garden for our three dogs: Chester, Spike and Jet.

Wow, we have an idyllic life, don't you think?

How I wish all of that had happened, instead of this flaming pile of garbage. It's possible I could go to university, and it's possible all those things I've dreamed of *could* come true, but we've lost out on so much precious time that can never be reclaimed. My life has been marked with cruelty and loneliness. How does that fit into a perfect life? It doesn't. I will carry scars forever.

Daisy's flat is lovely. Admittedly, it makes me feel sad and envious. I don't want to be bitter, that helps no one...but I can't help what I feel. Daisy left me and started a life *without* me. I know she would change it if she could, but like I said, it's not possible.

When we were travelling, I let myself think of our future. I let myself dream we could have everything we wanted...but now? I don't know. Outside of all this, are we still us? Can I fit into Daisy's life? What the hell am I going to do with myself? How do I answer *any* of these questions?

The bed dips and I feel Daisy working her way up my body. Her weight is like a comfort blanket. Her face hovers above mine and she's looking at me with such intensity, I have to close my eyes.

"Hey, what's wrong?"

"I'm just overthinking," I laugh. Her gaze remains fierce. She knows I'm trying to pass off how I'm feeling by making a joke.

"Cal." That's all she says. Just my name and I know I have to voice my fears.

"What if, after all this, we don't fit? You have a life, Daisy, with friends and a job. I have no idea what I'm going to do with myself. How can we fit?"

Shifting her body so she's straddling my waist, she brings her hands to either side of my face. "My life is with you, Callie. I would give everything up here if that's what needs to happen. I will follow you. Nothing in this world means more to me than you."

A lump the size of Pluto is stuck in my throat.

"Will you kiss me?" I croak out.

Her lips touch mine with such tenderness, I whimper in delight. We kiss until we're breathless. I hold her tight to me, because if I let her go, I think I'll break.

"How are you feeling about everything that's happened?" she asks quietly.

I knew I would need to talk to her sooner rather than later about my mum's resurrection. Letting me have alone time yesterday was appreciated. She gave me what I needed, but I suppose voicing my feelings is equally important.

"I feel numb. I don't think my brain quite knows what to do with it all. Everything feels temporary. I haven't had anything permanent for a long time. Even when I lived with Betty, it never felt *permanent*. I think I'm scared to trust that everything will be okay... That I have a chance to live a normal, settled life."

That's what it comes down to: permanence. Nothing is permanent, I understand that, but most people are lucky enough to spend what time they have on this earth with their partners and family.

As humans, we make connections that stick. I want those connections, but so far, the only one that I've been able to cling to is the one with Daisy. What if I let myself forge a connection with my mum and it's taken away? What if I strengthen the one with Daisy and she leaves? Am I being irrational? Probably, but I'm working with what I know.

Daisy sits back on her haunches. "I say this with love, Callie."

Well, that's ominous.

"What you've experienced, right from when you were a little girl to now, is immense. It's far more than most people will ever experience. You need to talk to someone professional. I will always be here for you, but what you're trying to process is huge."

I nod, because clearly she's right. My life has been a shit show from the start. I'm not capable of sifting through all this by myself, and I certainly don't want to put it on Daisy's shoulders. If I have a prayer of living anything close to a "normal" life, I'll need help.

"I will, I promise."

She kisses me, and that's enough to help settle my mind, for now.

"Let me grab some clothes and we'll head back to Janet's."

"Hey, how are *you* with all this?" I'm not the only one who needs support.

"Oh, I'll be seeing my therapist, for sure," she laughs.

There is a whole lot for us both to deal with, but at least we are doing it together.

It's been a week since we arrived in Scotland. Seven days of awkward and difficult conversations with my mum and Janet. Daisy seems to have thawed a little toward her mentor. I still feel numb.

I've been totally honest with my mum, and she seems to have taken it well. I'm sure she hoped I would see her and fall into her arms, but that's not reality. She understands I need help to work through it all.

Honestly, I don't think I can do anything until this bloke who is supposed to be taking out Betty actually fucking does something.

So far, I've caught up on a shitload of BBC dramas, played video games, and drank Janet out of brandy. I'm super fucking restless and it's pissing me off. We should be doing something. I'm tired of waiting.

Mum, Janet, and Daisy have all told me I need to be patient, but it's easier for them. Okay, that's not fair to say. We've all suffered one way or the other. I get that.

Ugh, I think I'll go scream into a pillow. That sometimes helps.

I'm just about to haul my arse upstairs to complete my daily pillow scream, when mum rushes in. Her face is red and tears are streaking down her cheeks. What the fuck has happened?

"Mum?"

"It's over, Callie."

Is she saying what I think she's saying?

"What do you mean?" I need her to spell it out.

"Betty is in custody, as of this morning. It's done, love."

It's done, over, finished! I can come home?

Daisy is by my side in an instant. I can't speak, so my mum fills her in on the news. She asks about her brother. He's safe and in custody.

"Tell me what happened!" I blurt when I emerge from my shock. I need details.

"Well, they served the arrest warrant this morning and took her in."

Hang about. After all this time, and after the bullshit we went through to get the book, etc...etc. That's it? Some cop turned up at the cottage and slapped some handcuffs on her?

Where was the S.W.A.T. team or the car chase? Or the midnight raid that ended up in a bloody gun battle? I don't know about you, but this is really fucking underwhelming and anti-climactic!

"That's it? They just arrested her? No drama, no fighting?"

"Nope, she came quietly."

That is the furthest thing—ever—I would have imagined happening. Betty Compton is a fighter. There is no chance in hell she just rolls over.

"That doesn't sound right to me," I say, because, shit, there has to be more to it than that.

"She probably has no idea about all the evidence against her. I bet she thinks she'll be able to get herself out of it," Daisy says.

That tracks, but surely she knows that I gave up the black book. She has to have made the connection.

"Stop worrying, love," my mum says.

No, I can't. Something isn't sitting right. I know my nan and she would never surrender this easily.

Over the course of the next few weeks, I'm subjected to countless interviews by the police. I have given numerous statements to anyone that asked. It has been ridiculous. I'm secretly missing my time on the lam. At least then, I was left alone.

Once the story broke about the little old woman from Yorkshire who turned out to be a prolific criminal, I was hounded by the press. Fuck knows how they got my name, but they did. The bright side to it all, was that I got to hide away with Daisy for a few weeks until it all calmed down.

Today marks the start of her trial. It's going to be the first time I have seen her in person since I ran. I'm nervous. I know she can't hurt me, but still, this woman is my version of the bogeyman.

The prosecution is going for life imprisonment. I think they'll get what they want. According to Mum and Janet, the information we collected was an absolute treasure trove. The breakup of Betty's empire is the single biggest thing to have happened in UK criminal history.

Apparently, the accounts and names lead to more arrests and discoveries than the police thought possible. I feel good about that. I hope we've stopped other families from suffering at the hands of those fuckers.

My relationship with my mum has turned a corner. I've been able to start letting her in. It's a slow process, but it's happening. I bawled my eyes out the first time I really let her hug me. It was not a pretty sight.

Sitting in the courtroom, waiting for my nan to enter the box, is a weird feeling. I never thought we would get here. A tiny part of me—a really tiny part—feels sorry for her.

I asked mum how the hell Nan became Queen B, in the first place. It was my great-grandad that started it all. He took my nan under his wing and taught her everything, from a very young age. The life she had was all that she'd ever known.

Apparently, my great-grandad came from a poor family and he did whatever was necessary to claw his way out of poverty. I would admire the man, but he rose in society by hurting others. He then taught his only daughter to do the same.

My breath hitches as Betty is led to the box, where she will remain until the trial is done. She looks so old and frail, nothing like the woman I remember. Fuck, I'm gobsmacked. Her hair is still styled like the late queen, but her dominance and confidence are nowhere to be seen. Her face has so many more lines, and her skin is wrinkled and thin-looking. Her height has diminished, too. She was never tall, but now she looks so tiny.

If you didn't know the details of her crimes, there is no way you would believe this little old lady had led the life she has, or done the terrible things she's done.

The courtroom falls silent, and the lawyers begin. All the evidence is laid out, and it is impressive. Betty remains silent throughout the whole thing. Her face gives nothing away. I thought I would gain some satisfaction from this. After all, the woman ruined my life. But there's nothing.

When the verdict lands a month later, it's no surprise she's found guilty. Betty Compton will never see the outside of a prison cell ever again. Once the judge dismisses the court, Betty is escorted out. Everyone in the room starts to leave. As I stand to leave, Betty's lawyer approaches me.

"Ms. Compton, may I have a word?"

"Sure." This is interesting. We move to the side so no one can overhear. I see Daisy watching us from the door.

"Ms. Compton, your grandmother has requested a visit."

"I beg your pardon?"

"Betty is hoping you would visit with her before she is taken back to her cell. I have squared it with the prosecuting lawyer, and the judge has allowed a five-minute visitation. Betty just wishes to make things right." Is he having a laugh? "Please, Callie."

"Okay, fine." I should refuse, I know I should, but I don't. Fuck, she's still my nan.

I follow the lawyer to the holding cells. My Spidey sense is tingling. The judge can't possibly have allowed this? Doesn't she need to be chained to a table or something? Or is that just a made-up TV thing? Maybe she's not classed as a threat.

I walk into the cell. There is a guard waiting by the door, so that's reassuring. The lawyer leaves, and then it's just us: me and Nan.

"Callie, dear." Her voice is smaller.

"Nan."

"Please sit, love."

Why is she being so nice?

"I'll stay standing, thanks."

"Come on now, I can't stand for too long and I don't want to be craning my neck."

I suppose that makes sense. I sit on the bench a few feet away.

"I am sorry, Callie. I never meant for all this to happen. Please forgive me?" She opens her arms to me. Is she actually crazy? I'm not hugging her, for fuck's sake. "Please, love. Just one last cuddle with your nan. I doubt I'll be seeing you again."

I study her for a little while. Her face seems genuine.

"I'm sorry, Nan, but no. I hate that this has happened, that you dragged us all through the shit. You ruined our lives. My own mother, your daughter, fled to get away. I had to do the same. There is no 'sorry' big enough."

"Okay, dear, I understand."

This feels wrong. Why is she being so passive?

I scan her face one more time before getting up. "Bye, Nan."

That was the right thing to do, I think. I said my piece, and now I can go live my life. I stand and turn to the door.

One step later and I feel burning in my back. Shit, there it is again...and again. Fuck! Pain explodes inside my body.

I fall to the floor. Everything is going black. A weight shifts over me and I feel warm breath on my face.

"Did you really think you could walk away from this, Callie?"

And that's when I realise that Betty has stabbed me—repeatedly. That's when I remember... Betty Compton never loses.

Never.

Epilogue

Daisy

It's five years to the day since Callie Compton died. I still can't wrap my head around everything that happened that day. The mistakes made by the people who were in charge of keeping Betty from hurting anyone ever again are unforgivable in my eyes.

I'm here at her grave, laying flowers down for the anniversary like I do every year. I look over to see Ben, my three-year-old son, running around the graveyard, squealing because Uncle Chris is pretending to be a monster.

Ben doesn't understand why we are here. He doesn't know how to behave in a churchyard. To him, it's another bit of land to make his playground. I'm thankful to Chris for keeping him entertained.

Arms snake round my waist and I feel my wife, Jess, rest her chin on my shoulder. How I wish I could turn back the hands of time and save us all from this reality. I close my eyes and take a deep lungful of air. This is the only time of year I return to Yorkshire. I hate we buried Callie here. It feels like a betrayal to her memory, but I wasn't left a choice.

Jess

I'm just going to jump in here and save you from my wife's dramatic ramblings. Yes, Callie Compton is dead, but guess what... I'm not *physically* gone. Daisy should have mentioned that, straight off the bat.

After Betty's attempt on my life, I was in a bad way. Overall, she'd stabbed me seven times, in the back and side. I think I was clinically dead for a few minutes, but by a miracle, the doctors were able to save me.

The police officers who dealt with the situation agreed, that for my future safety, it would be better if Betty, and anyone associated with her, believed I had died. So Callie Compton kicked the bucket, and Jessica Harlow was born.

I have to say, watching your own funeral is all kinds of weird. Daisy argued with me until we were blue in the face about my burial site. The detective in charge of my disappearance from this earth wanted the grave to be close to home. Daisy did not. She really fucking hates this place! I really couldn't have given a shit, considering they were putting an empty box in the ground. It was all for show.

The police spent the next few months rounding up Betty's contacts and acquaintances. Maybe killing off Callie was rash, but I don't think it will ever be safe to take back my name. There's no guarantee they got everyone, and I really fucked up their lives. Criminals aren't very forgiving.

As well as my name, I changed my appearance. Not like physically; we're not in a Bond film. I changed my hair. Daisy acted like I was having a limb removed when I had it all chopped off and bleached. I think I rock a pixie cut wonderfully. Frankly, I look hot as fuck. And even if Daisy won't admit it out loud, she loves it too.

We moved to the outskirts of Edinburgh. Actually, Janet gave us her massive house. After everything had chilled out and we were out of danger, my mum announced she was retiring from her company to travel with Janet. Their lives had been consumed by Betty for twenty years. They wanted to start living again, and I was delighted for them.

Daisy continued to do whatever the hell it is she does. To this day, I'm still not allowed to know, which I think is stupid.

Daisy

My turn to interrupt before Jess gets on her high horse. She's not allowed to know, and that's the end of it!

As she was saying, we moved to the big house. Jess decided to go to university. I couldn't have been prouder when she graduated with a degree in creative writing. It took a while for her to figure out what she wanted to do, and finally she settled on writing. Let's be honest, she has enough material to last her a lifetime.

We married within six months, and I was pregnant not too long after that. Jess told me about the life she had envisioned for us, and I wanted it all. I wanted to give Jess everything she ever dreamed about.

It still feels strange referring to her as Jess. It took a good few months for me to stop slipping up and calling her Callie.

Ben has never known her as anyone other than Jess. He has no clue about our misadventures across Europe. Or the many women still pining over his mummy. It tickles me to wind her up about it, especially when we go on holiday.

Chris found us a few months after the trial was over. Well, he found me, and was almost apoplectic when he saw that Callie was, in fact, not dead. He's been with us every day. Derek and Meryl are like parents to us now, and definitely grandparents to Ben. We met their son and have become close friends with him.

I suppose you want to know what happened to the old bag? Well, she's still locked up. Her access to the outside world is severely limited, and that's the way it will be until she dies.

My brother and dad are serving twenty years for their participation in Queen B's nefarious dealings. They deserve it. I try not to think of them too much because my life is full and glorious with the woman I've loved since I could remember. We have a son, with another on the way.

The only place Betty, my father, and brother belong, is in the past. We look only forward now, and thank the Universe that we made it.

Thank you!

Thank you for reading The Misadventures of Callie Compton.

Spill the Tea (in a Review)!

If this book gave you butterflies, made you swoon, or kept you up way past your bedtime, I'd love to hear about it! Reviews help indie authors like me reach more readers who are searching for their next sapphic romance obsession. Drop a review on Amazon, Goodreads, or wherever you love to share your bookish thoughts. Even a quick "loved it!" makes a huge difference.

You're the best!

Stay Connected

Don't Miss Out!

Love steamy sapphic romance? Join my newsletter for new release alerts, promotions, book recommendations, and special reader-only perks. Sign up now: https://alysonroot.com/

<u>Become a VIP Member</u>

Want the ultimate insider experience? My VIP membership gives you early access to new books, exclusive bonus content, behind-the-scenes insights, member discounts, and a front-row seat to my creative process. Plus, you'll be part of a community of readers who love these stories as much as I love writing them. Join the VIP club:
VIP MEMBERSHIP

Other Titles By Alyson Root

A Dance Towards Forever

Diving Into Her

Always Emilie

Broken Parts Included

Love & Other Wild Things

Finding Molly Parsons

Keeping Carmen Ruiz

The Wisdom of Bug

Sleigh Bells Ring

Risking Immortality

Waiting for Eternity

Fighting for Infinity

Mob's Seduction

Playing Her Heart

Welcome to Ero-TEA-Ca: We're Open!
Once Upon a Time in December
The Admiral's Daughter

About the author

Alyson was born and raised in the heart of England. She moved to Paris in 2015 when she met her wife. Together they moved to the west of France, where they now live with their two dogs. Alyson spends her time reading sapphic fiction books, writing and Scuba Diving.

Alyson discovered her love of writing in her mid-thirties. Her debut book, *A Dance Towards Forever,* was inspired by her wife and their very own love story. Alyson wrote *Diving Into Her* and award-winning *Always Emilie,* which added with her first book, created The French Connection series.

www.alysonroot.com

a.rootauthor@alysonroot.com

HUMAN
AUTHORED™
THE Authors Guild®

4135472

www.ingramcontent.com/pod-product-compliance
Lightning Source LLC
Chambersburg PA
CBHW050612170726
48283CB00001B/208